To: Heather

TIME AND SPACE

by

Rachel Robinson

Rachel Rxx

COPYRIGHT

I shut my eyes. It fades to black
A wilted flower never coming back
A jaded heart torn in two
A life with him, a life with you
Sorrow stalks on windswept trees
A troubled whisper finds the breeze
A dirty window looking out
Hear me, see me, it's a silent shout
A hint of promise never made true
A life with him, a life with you
-Lainey Rosemont

CHAPTER ONE

Prologue

Cody

If you were to open my mind and look inside you'd find binary code, formulas, and endless lines of script—things that make the average human's brain twitch away in protest. Inside my skull also resides knowledge, practicality, and wisdom. If you were to crack apart any of my two hundred and six bones, you'd find *her*. That's how deeply she's rooted inside. She's hidden away, tucked neatly in a place where not even time can touch her. Dementia and other human ailments are capable of stealing the confines of the mind. Bones? They protect everything. You get to take them with you to your grave.

Lainey Rosemont is the woman who owns my bones. When I met her she had this peculiar way about weaving herself into my life: a life that no one else could penetrate, but still she coiled herself around me all the same. Her wild blue eyes and soft demeanor challenged my good side. My bad side merely wanted to devour her whole just to make her mine forever. I knew from the moment I laid eyes on her that my life would forever be changed—complicated, contented.

I met her during the time in my life when I walked the straight and narrow. I did what I was supposed to do—what was expected of me as an upstanding Naval Officer. I've long since left that life behind. The Navy SEAL ethos is too strong for a decent man to break. Good men are SEALs. I was a good man for a long time—a leader of some of the best men in the world. And then I got out of the Navy because I simply wasn't meant to be good and moral anymore. My talents were merely more desirable elsewhere. I still hunt down high value targets, mind you, and my aim with all firearms is just as lethal, but now I don't answer to anyone. That strong ethos I used to live by had to die a slow death for me to fulfill my new purpose in life. The people who now answer to me are usually seconds away from death.

I'm a gun for hire. A consultant. A contractor. A computer genius. A jack of all trades.

Mostly I'm a hand for hire these days, or a knife for hire, or any other way you can dream up to kill a human. My new ethos is much less demanding. Confirm the evil, kill the evil, and never dwell on a job for too long. I've reached the point in my life where my name carries as much notoriety as my long list of snuffed targets. My physical skills combined with my love and proficiency with technology make for a pretty spectacular, lethal pair. I founded, own, and run the newly established Ridge Contracting, which just so happens to be a very legal business. As long as you have wise, discreet people backing you and helping run operations, everything stays on the up and up. Ridge Contracting is comprised of men with all of the above mentioned characteristics and more, because the men are exactly like me. Most of them are former SEALs, hungry for a life they left behind, yearning for the same rush that comes from no other workplace. I'm happy to offer them the opportunity to taste that familiar adrenaline rush. Although it's fairly new, the success rate of my company is unparalleled. I can work from anywhere. It's a blessing and a curse.

Currently, I'm in my NYC apartment among the clouds and smog of a city too busy to stop and acknowledge it. I prefer NYC over my other residences because I can blend into the background, hidden by the influx of life. Lainey frequents NYC on business, which also makes this apartment one of my favorites. I can stalk her. Well, not crazy, asshole stalk, just keep tabs on her every once in a while—remind myself of what used to be before I worked my life away. With my knowledge of technology, I could do far more than keep tabs on her, so that fact helps me sleep at night. I miss companionship, my old life, but most of all, I miss Lainey.

I keep the TV on. It's always muted, only there to shine light into my dark apartment. It masks my sense of loneliness. All I have to do is glance up and see familiar faces smiling on a popular sitcom, or even the overacted gestures of a reality star to give me a dose of humanity. Not that I can be proud of what society has lumbered to, but that it's what most people find normal. I don't need to hear their voices. Human features are enough for me.

"Don't trust him," I say, smirking at the television. The actress will undoubtedly end up heartbroken with more baggage than any decent man wants. She doesn't realize it. They never do.

I tap on my keyboard while chewing the end of the plastic spout of my water bottle. It dangles from my mouth like a dog with a bone. It's not water. Taking a pull of liquid, I glance at one of the three computer monitors when it pings an alert. "Oh, fun," I growl around the bottle spout. A new job. Saving information to an encrypted hard drive, I formulate a plan. Not all jobs require the same tactics. If Ridge Contracting is hired, then one thing is for sure: secrecy is key and the target is a high profile bastard. I've always killed bad guys. My job isn't much different in that way. Now there's no media backlash or mountains of paperwork. I reply to the message, letting them know I have what

4

they need.

I take a long pull out of the spout hanging from my mouth while looking at the TV again, and whisper, "I told you so." Shaking my head at the obvious conflict. *No one gets happily ever afters anymore*, I think. Not even the bastards on TV. I had mine back when I was a good, upstanding man. Unfortunately, it didn't last forever. And it tasted so sweet while it was mine. All I have now is memories of Lainey Rosemont: her head thrown back in laughter, her straight, white, mischievous smile moments before she takes me into her mouth, the way she worries her lip when she reads her emails, the smell of her hair after she showers, the way her eyes become soulful and clear when she whispers, "I love you, Cody Ridge." I swallow down the lump that forms at that last memory. I can't blame her. No, Lainey is not to be blamed for our ill-fated love story. The blame lies squarely on my own shoulders. Absentmindedly, I reach down and rub the deep, jagged scars on my ankles and wince at the nightmare they force to the forefront of my mind.

"The motherfuckers are hiding over there. I know it," Steve growls, sweat pouring down his face, marring the black face paint swiped on his forehead. The terrain is a huge, hot jungle. Humidity was born here and I think I may fucking die. Intel told us where the fuckers would be. Bad weather, which wasn't anticipated, rained on that fucking parade. Literally.

Now we're off target and I'm scrambling to spiff up plan B. It's no big deal. I have this. Severe and extensive training drilled into me over the years served me well. Everything will be okay because it has to be. Lives depend on my decisions.

"No, they're not. Keep your voice down!" I return as quietly as possible. I glance where he motioned, but immediately decide he's wrong. We've covered that area already. Didn't we? So much fucking green. It all looks the same at this point. I squat down next to some kind of fucking jungle plant that looks like it could kill me if the assholes we're after don't do it first. All I can do as the person in charge of this shit show is to thank God that time isn't of the essence. We have time. I just need to recalculate. I pull out a small tablet and try to decipher where we landed and where our pickup boats are located. We can come back another time. Holding down the button on my headset, I communicate to leadership back at base to tell them the current SITREP—the situation report—might as well be labeled "fucked". "Affirmative," I reply, straining to hear over the pelting rain and foreign animal noises echoing through the humid jungle air. I squint my eyes at the canopy of neon green above me. The rain beats down harder and harder. I motion to Steve and Maverick as they point downrange to the slight wake of the water in the river. Our boats are finally coming, thank fuck. I motion to them to let them know I'm going

to head to higher ground. There is a medium-sized clearing, which should lend to more efficient communication.

Maverick nods, smiles, and raises his gun to cover my position. Steve automatically aims his weapon to cover the opposite direction. Our teammates farther down the river follow suit—all following my silent order. They head to the boats. Making my way to the clearing, I move as silently and swiftly as possible. Heavy gear weighs down my steps in the thick mud. I groan, swat at the huge bug trying to fly down my throat, and start giving details over the radio. After a few minutes of conversation I begin breaking down my antenna and repack my radio. It's time to get the fuck on with this. I'm ready to be out of the rain.

It's these moments of minimal distraction that cost me everything. I feel his hot breath, a sharp prick on my neck, and then absolutely nothing. My body goes numb. I fall sideways to the ground. Fuck! Panic rears, and it's what's supposed to help me do my damn job, but in this moment, the only moment that counts, it doesn't. Through clouded vision I see the boats pull up and my brothers board safely. They're safe. The boats appear far away as they drag my limp body through stinking mud, my gear leaving sharp indents in the muck. From all the fucking gear that is utterly useless to me. It's sick irony. They'll see me. My brothers have to see me. I can't yell. I can't move. I'm over here! *I think, praying they glance this way. Far away from the shore, my only hope for survival vanishes. They'll realize I'm gone when they do headcounts. A guy will come back and look for me, but I won't be here. More guys will come, but it will be too late. I'll pay the ultimate price for a single decision. I'm dragged farther into the neon green, farther away from safety. For the first time I envision this as my end. The ultimate fucking demise with a coup de grâce exit. Will they slit my throat? I probably won't even feel it. Will it be fast? Or will they torture me endlessly? They'll want information. They'll keep me alive. I hear my brothers calling out my name. Their voices seem so far away. My life flashes before my eyes and the prevalent vision is that of Lainey. My beautiful Lainey. I cling to a vision of her laughing, her arms wrapped around my neck, her body pressed against mine so tightly that her perfume invades my oxygen. I can taste her like her mouth is on mine. That's what I ensconce myself in because she's what matters most in my life. My heart beats for her. For however many beats it has left. I focus on those beats: Lai-ney. Lai-ney. Lai-ney.*

As my own name being shouted into the wind vanishes, I'm rewarded with terror. Another prick in the neck. Numbness and blackness this time. Nothingness. I'm gone, but then again so is the terror. Silently, I vow revenge at any cost.

Those are the last moments of my old life. Thinking

back, the line that my limp body caused as they dragged me away might as well have been the literal line in the sand: the line of delineation. Before and after. It was in that moment that I locked Lainey Rosemont in my bones. The thing with that tedious process is that once you lock something there, you can't get rid of it. No matter how hard you try and no matter how much time passes.

I was taken as a prisoner of war, or at least that's what most people think. They held me for three years, six months and four days. The U.S. declared me dead after one year and seven months. I now know Lainey waited three years and two months before accepting a proposal from another man.

CHAPTER TWO

Lainey

The Past

"If I wanted your opinion, I'd ask you for it," I admonish, smiling at Dax while I put the shirt he selected back on the rack. He feigns irritation by rolling his eyes, but winks at me in the end. He's a stalwart shopping companion, actually. Right now he has other things on his mind. It's obvious by the way he's stalling this afternoon. He'll open up and talk when he's ready. It's one of his 'things' I've learned over the years. With the amount of 'things' he deals with from me, this is a small thing. I've got more baggage than a train full of adolescents headed to wizarding school. Dax Redding is not only the world's savior as a Navy SEAL—he's my personal hero. He saved me from my grief of losing the love of my life. It took years of Dax's merciless convincing, but I'm absolutely positive he's the only man I'll ever love. There isn't another way. This is the way it has to be…the way it's supposed to be.

Dax grabs my ass, looking both left and right inconspicuously. "I was merely telling you that you could also wear that shirt as a skirt. A really short one." He lifts a blond brow, his lips quirking to one side. He's edible. Perfectly, handsomely, a big bag of muscles, delicious. I laugh as he pulls me toward the lingerie section, his arm wrapped tightly around my waist. "After you pick out the smallest pair of panties known to man, I was hoping we could go grab a coffee. Do you have time before you have to get to work?"

I mentally tick through this afternoon's schedule and clear it. Interior design consults can wait. Time with Dax is more than necessary to my survival. I made sure that my workload was light for the next couple of weeks. I want to spend as much time as humanly possible with him. I nod. He runs a hand through his shaggy, beachy hair and offers a half smile. It's not the megawatt, panty melting smile he's famous for, that's for sure. He returned home from a six-month deployment a few days ago and he's been off-kilter a touch. I chalked it up to him missing me, but I now realize it's definitely something more. I already agreed to marry him before he left six months ago. What if he made a mistake by asking me? Oh, God. Maybe he's disengaging himself from me. He regrets it. A lump forms in my throat. I rely on Dax. He's solely responsible for my happiness. I'm not proud of the dependency, and I'm almost positive it's not healthy. It is what it is at this point.

I don't want to wait. I grab his arm and lead him to a rack with scraps of black lace, and then I turn to face him. "You're making me concerned, Dax. Should I be worried about something? I mean, you seemed pretty into me when you were spanking my ass while I bounced up and down on your lap last night," I whisper, trying and failing to keep a smile off my face. The corners of his eyes crinkle in delight. He loves dirty. When in doubt, use humor. It makes you appear to have the upper hand. "So, I'm pretty sure this isn't a breakup talk you want to have." I let the smile fall off my face. My stomach churns. My hand roves over the lace beside me, but I don't take my eyes off of his. His Adam's apple bobs as he returns my laser gaze. I widen my eyes, prompting him to spit it out. "Dax?" His name slips from my lips in a whisper.

He leans down and presses his lips against my ear. "I love you, Lainey. Let's grab that coffee now. I'd rather have you naked anyways. We don't need to spend money on panties when your naked body makes my mouth water," he growls, taking my hand and leading me toward our usual coffee haunt. His words cause an immediate reaction. My breath quickens. But it's not just from wanting to have sex—I'm mentally calculating the ways he can destroy me on this brisk five-minute walk. Maybe I would survive a breakup. I've survived worse. It occurs to me that I'm being selfish. It may have nothing to do with me at all. Perhaps he's going through something completely unrelated and he needs me to listen to him…to support him. Noisy talking and copious amounts of human bodies flow around us as we make our way. The New York City cabs honk their usual frenzy as tourists clog sidewalks taking photos. It's so commonplace, so normal when I feel like my brain is on fire with curiosity.

I squeeze Dax's hand. He squeezes it back, grinning at me as he surveys the area. He's always on guard. Especially when he visits me in NYC. This place makes him extremely uneasy, even if he says he enjoys the chaos every once in a while. I know the truth. His training has made him suspicious of ordinary life. He opens the door and I hear his audible sigh of relief when the scent of fresh coffee hits us in a rush. I sit down at our usual table and try not to fidget while I wait for Dax to bring me a caffeine blast with a side of information. I glance at a television in the corner, the top news headlines scrolling across the bottom at a furious pace.

Dax cuts off my view with a brown cup extended my way. "For you. A double shot with extra milk," he explains, sliding into the seat directly in front of me. I take a scorching sip and wait. I take another. And then another. His blue eyes tick over my face and neck,

13

studying me. Six months is a long time to be away from the person you love. If I had it my way I would sit here and stare at him just the same. He takes the first gulp of his drink and sighs.

"Out with it, honey. You are killing me here. Hookers and blow? Is that it? A love child in Japan? Fourteen wives on a private island named after you?"

"Lane. Baby," Dax says, face ashen, but completely alight with love. I'm not entirely positive how that's possible, but I think it's a good sign. "I'm not sure how to tell you this." He pauses, winces a little, and waits for some godforsaken cue from me. "I'm not sure how to tell you this and I have no idea how you'll take it, but I can't keep this from you for much longer and I want to be the one to tell you. You know, before the media gets the details and...well," Dax stutters, looks down at my left hand and twists the beautiful diamond engagement ring he delicately placed there. It sparkles a million different colors in the light, reminding me of a happy time.

I slam my hand down on his. "Tell me," I say. "We're engaged to be married. Whatever it is can't possibly be as bad as what I'm imagining right now."

He raises his eyebrows and breaks eye contact. Shit. *Can it?*

"What details will the media get?" I ask again, trying to piece together what he's having such a hard time saying. I glance back at the television and narrow my eyes at the news anchor with large fake boobs and a microphone that should be in a music video and not on location. I see a headline scroll across the screen. The words SEAL TEAM catch my eye. The next words HOSTAGE RESCUE cause a surge of panic.

"Are the guys okay? Did someone get hurt? Die?" My heart in my throat, I bring my hand up to my neck. The pulse there is hammering Dax's cool fingers are on my cheeks. Gently he turns my face away from the screen to meet his gaze.

"The guys are fine, Lainey. No one is hurt. I guess this is a good jumping off point." The lights flicker in our little corner and it draws his beautiful eyes away from mine. "We had a successful mission, Lane. I…we…rescued a high value hostage. We brought him home. He's safe."

I nod at him. "That's great, honey." I fail at keeping sarcasm out of my tone. "I don't see what the problem is then." Navy SEALs don't fail. When they do, they fail really freaking hard. It's all or nothing. It's a life I've become accustomed to. It's a life I've been enveloped in for so long that I'm not sure how normal individuals succeed on a daily basis. If the guys were successful, then he wouldn't be looking at me with such sadness that I feel it down to my bones. I want to wrap him in my arms and comfort him, and I have no idea why. A shiver runs all the way down my spine.

I take his hand with both of mine. "It's fine. Keep

15

talking," I whisper.

He pulls his bottom lip between his teeth and his ocean eyes glaze over. He's a million miles away from here in this moment. "He's alive," he chokes out. Two words that could mean as little or as much as I want.

"Who is alive?"

"The hostage." Again. Dax did his job. What could possibly make him this upset? A man who is never perturbed or shaken by anything is on the verge of a breakdown in broad daylight in our coffee shop.

He realizes I'm still not following because he takes one deep breath and then another. "Cody Ridge is alive, Lane. He was the hostage I rescued."

The next seconds are a blur of Dax's words bouncing around in my skull. Alive. Cody. Alive. Cody. Alive. Cody. I don't even pause to consider if his words are truth. I know they are. He wouldn't lie to me about something of this magnitude. Cody Ridge, my deceased fiancé. I remember the empty casket I buried. I didn't even get to bury his body. They told me it wasn't recovered. There's a stuffed dog, a letter I wrote to him, a photo of us, some childhood mementos, and a memory stick with code buried six feet under a tombstone that bears his name. The flag that was draped over his casket sits above my fireplace in my home in Virginia Beach. How is this possible? I'm burning, my chest is burning. My heart. It's a burn that sears my soul—a jagged wound ripped open so wide I

16

bet New York City just stopped to rubberneck.

"Breathe, Lainey. Breathe. Breathe. Breathe," Dax says. I hear the worry in his voice. I want to do as he says, but I can't. I can't breathe. Cody Ridge is alive.

"No," I finally manage to say. My coffee soaks through my blouse and my skirt. Dax is pressing napkins against my neck to mop up the spill I didn't even know occurred.

He kisses my forehead. "I didn't believe it either. How could I? It was impossible. He's alive." Images of his funeral flash every time I blink. The pain. The unknown factor. The grief. The years and years of grief and unbearable pain. How can this be?

I shake my head as hot tears spring to my eyes. "No." Now I remember fond memories of Cody and I. The time I made him ride a roller coaster and he actually got sick. Vacations spent in Cabo tan, naked and so in love we couldn't see straight…or walk straight. His laugh. Cody's laugh could cure any ailment. The night he proposed and I couldn't say yes fast enough or loud enough. I yelled it at the top of that mountain, all sweaty from a hike. It was Christmastime, my favorite time of year. I never let myself think of these memories. They're too painful.

My gaze darts back to the television. I suppose I'm waiting for a photo of Cody to flash across the screen. Something. Anything—to signal this impossible truth as a fact. Maybe that would make it real. I have so many questions I want to ask. Words don't come, but tears do. They flow in a cascade down my face as a new wave of unfamiliar grief washes over me. Dax's beautiful, anguished face pierces the piece of my heart that he owns. He knows he can't be my hero right now. No one can save me from this.

Cody Ridge, the love of my life is alive, and I'm sitting in *our* coffee shop falling to fragments because of it.

CHAPTER THREE

Cody

Present Day

"I'm sure. No dates." I laugh. Molly, my administrative assistant, tries to set me up any chance she can get. She's this spunky woman with a penchant for organization and controlling things. She is amazing at her job.

Molly sighs on the other end of the phone. "It's Friday, Cody. Just a coffee date?" She's a good employee. I let her schedule a lot of things for me. Dates aren't one of those things. It doesn't mean she'll give up. First it was dinner and a movie with her friend Laura. Then it was just dinner and now we're at a lowly coffee date. "Aren't you the least bit interested?"

I have to think about her question. Am I interested in other women? How can I be? In my fucked up mind,

I'm still with Lainey. It's as if my life here in the real world was merely paused while I rotted in hell for all those years. Obviously I understand that time passed and everything changed, but it's hard to grasp. It's hard to think about moving on.

I chuckle. "No thanks, Molly. You have a good weekend, though. Tell that boyfriend of yours to behave. He has important shit to do on Monday." He's also one of my employees. A big lumbering man with dark eyes and a shot so lethal even I wouldn't take my chances in a draw. Horse is a man no one fucks with. It amuses me to think of Molly razzing him. Does he own a laugh? Something to ponder over another time.

"I know, boss. I'm the brains behind this operation," Molly drawls. Everyone works from wherever they want. This has to be the best job in the world with regards to freedom. "I'll make sure he's well rested…and uh, well, everything'd before his flight on Monday." He better be. He's hunting down someone important—someone I'd give anything to hunt myself, but I can't chase them all. It's physically impossible. The guys know how important each job is. Whether it's just to gather intel, teach others how to defend themselves, or to do more, we are methodical. I need Horse to glean as much information as possible next week. The man he's after has ties with the men I'm after.

My blood boils. Molly clears her throat. "Did you

hear me?"

"Repeat, please." It's common for me to get lost in thought. She knows this. She is, in fact, the brains behind my operation after all.

She sighs. "I said Dances like the Wind called while you were on a phone call. You should really tell Lainey I can recognize her voice." She called me? My heart stutters. The blood that was boiling starts pumping. I haven't heard from her since the first time I saw her after my rescue. That was when I just returned to life. Before I had my business or anything except old dreams and a big case of what-ifs. I can't help it. A cheesy smile breaks across my face. It feels out of place, big time.

"Dances like the Wind called? Really? When were you planning on telling me this tidbit, Silent Secret Harboring Hobbit?" After the joke leaves my mouth I clamp it shut. What did I say?

Molly laughs. It's a snorting, guffawing noise that helps ease the embarrassment. I play with an external hard drive that sits on my desk, tossing it up and catching it on the opposing end while I wait for her to catch her breath. "You made a funny. Cody Ridge made a funny. I'm writing this down so I can tell Horse later."

"Don't tell Horse anything. I'll fire you."

There's a long pause on the phone line. I know what it means. "I shouldn't have told you. Not that you should take advice from me, but it will be a mistake if you call her back. Mark my words." Of course it will. She's engaged to be married to another man. Another SEAL. A brother. Someone I respect. She waited years to move on. Despite all of these things, I already know curiosity will get the best of me. Why is she calling after all this time?

"Where will you be working from next week?" She glosses right on to the next subject. I think about it. Then I think about it some more. Lainey called me. Is she in NYC? Why is my mind even wandering there? I do have a ton of work I can do from my computer. Hacking into accounts, codes that need to be worked out so I can get my hands on information, programs to debug and overall mischief to be perfected. I can do these things anywhere. I toss and catch the hard drive, the beautifully portable workstation, and decide to leave my week open.

I clear my throat. "I'll get back to you."

"Okay. If I hear from Dances like the Wind and she changes her name to Lying Cheating Scandal I'm sending Laura over to lure you away." Laura? Oh, the friend she's trying to fix me up with.

"Molly, go work. Leave me to my personal life, which obviously isn't personal enough."

I hear her shuffle her phone. She' s probably leaving her home office. "Oh, come on. I get it, Cody. Lainey will always be it for you. You'd be balls deep in her right now if those assholes didn't steal you away from your life. But the fact is you're going to have to move on. You can do it delicately or you can do it all at once. All that matters is to move the heck on. I'd screw your brains out myself, but I don't think—"

I cut her off. "No." Horse's face crosses my mind. Maybe he doesn't laugh at all. Ever. "I don't need any favors."

She huffs. "I was obviously just joking to make a point. You're a catch. Be a catch. Play the field." No words have ever seemed more like a bad idea. Not only am I too tied up in my work, but she's correct—Lainey is it for me. Always. There's no moving on after I've had a taste of perfection. It was the image of coming home to her that kept me alive during my years in captivity. Solely her. For that reason alone I know I will call her back. I make light work of confirming my scheduled telemeetings with Molly and give her answers to several questions she asks, and our nightly catch-up meeting is done.

Swiveling in my desk chair, I pad over to the floor-to-ceiling window that overlooks Manhattan. They don't call it the city that never sleeps for nothing. It's nine at night and it's bustling. Office lights in the skyscrapers are still lit, workers burning the midnight oil, or having torrid affairs with their secretaries after hours. I shake my head, thinking of Molly's ludicrous joke about sleeping with me. I haven't slept with a woman in so long that I'm considering adding Born again Virgin to the end of my name. My bare-chested silhouette gleams back at me in the freshly cleaned glass. A few scars mark my chest, and the full complement of tattoos I got when I returned make me almost unrecognizable as a former Naval Officer. My blond hair is longer, my eyes are a little darker, my soul a little less pure than it was before. Surely Lainey doesn't want to talk to me? This person?

I call her back—her cell phone number is still the same as it was all those years ago. I know it by heart. I always will, even if it becomes someone else's phone number. I'll probably go crazy as an old man and call the number every day in hopes of hearing her say hello. Her phone rings a few times and I'm about to hang up when she finally answers.

"Cody," she says, out of breath and obviously surprised. I smile. My reflection in the glass shocks me. I almost look happy. Quickly, I look away. Her voice reverberates in my soul. It sounds exactly the same, yet completely different.

I sigh. "Fast Lane," I reply, my voice shaky. She takes a few more deep breaths and I reconsider. Maybe she's not out of breath, perhaps she's extremely nervous. That would be a new occurrence. I've never made her nervous before. She trusted me implicitly—with her secrets, with her body, and most importantly, her mind. "Molly gave me the message that you called.

24

Or someone who makes up names just like you do called," I say.

I can hear her face turning red over the phone line. "Yeah, sorry. I opened my mouth and it just popped out. Typical diarrhea mouth. You know?" I grin. The woman is utterly endearing.

"I figured. Molly knew it was you. So," I prompt, running a hand through my hair.

I hear doors closing in the background wherever Lainey is. She's leaving the room. Hiding? From him. "I know it's been forever. I just needed time to sort through everything, you know? It took a long time for me to even believe you were alive. Somehow even seeing you in the hospital bed...after you came home just wasn't...real. I understand if you don't want anything to do with me, but I was hoping you'd meet with me. Cody." She says my name because she wants to hear it, I can tell. I wonder if it tastes differently now that oceans of time and space have drowned our relationship.

It feels as if something large and sticky is lodged in my chest. I can hardly believe the words coming out of her mouth. Unsuccessfully, I clear the emotion from my throat. This isn't part of the plan. I've learned the only thing I can count on is change. One quality a man must have in this world is versatility. "Oh, Lane. Is that a good idea? I don't blame you for the less than stellar welcome home. Years passed. No one is the blame for

25

that." Actually there are people to blame. I just haven't tracked them down quite yet.

"Don't feel guilty, but meeting up now? After all this time? Of course I will if that's what you truly want. If it helps you find closure." The words are all lies. I care a lot. I want to see Lainey with every fiber in my being. My bones, all of them, want her in every possible way. When she glanced at me in the hospital bed for the first time in over three and a half years, but then turned from the room without saying a word, it was worse than torture. "It's what you want?" I ask again, praying to whoever is out there she answers with a yes.

"Yes." Firm. Assured. Lainey has thoroughly thought this through. It shouldn't surprise me, but it does. It's been so long. I assumed she was well on her way to a happily ever after with the new SEAL who stole her heart.

My smile wanes as reality trickles into my awareness. "I don't want to sneak around. Your significant other knows you want to see me? This isn't me jumping to any conclusions, mind you. I know seeing me is just that…seeing me. But will he think the same?"

The phone crackles. "I'll tell him." My chest clenches. She's still with him. Of course she is. Who would let a woman like that go? "It's just an innocent meeting. Dax understands." Maybe for her it will be innocent. His name. Dax. I look up at the ceiling. Turning, I walk away from the window and back toward the kitchen, gripping the cell phone tighter against my ear. "When and where?" I ask. "I'm in Manhattan this weekend, but my schedule is flexible." I'm not sure how much Lainey knows about my life these days. She knows about my home here, and about my work, but I'm not sure what else. The media had a field day after I was rescued. My face was plastered everywhere and then again when I opened Ridge Contracting. I remember the headlines, 'Former SEAL opens contracting company. America's elite scramble for employment.' It depends on how badly she wanted information about me. It's all out there. For multiple reasons.

"I can meet you in Manhattan tomorrow," she replies. "I'm in Virginia Beach right now. I'll just tie up some loose ends with work first."

"I can go there," I reply, barely containing my excitement. "I have to ask one more time, Lane. Why now?" It's a valid question. A stronger man would tell her no—that she lost that chance when she refused to speak to me after years apart.

She sighs. My entire body responds like a match lighting. I can envision her face…her small nose pinched on one side as she contemplates her answer, her bottom lip worrying between her teeth.

Slinging a leg over my barstool, I hang my head in

one hand and close my eyes. "Why now?" I ask again.

"Our relationship was…is… like a shoe with really long shoe strings. No matter how you tie those things you still trip over the laces." Always eloquent. "I wanted you to recover. Dax needed me to be…a different person. I couldn't handle it. It was too much. As my wedding approaches I'm finding the shoelaces longer than ever."

I smile. "I think what you're trying to explain in Lainey-talk is that we are unfinished business." My pulse throbs against my neck as I wait for her next words.

She sighs. "I'm getting married soon, Cody. Married. I just need to see you one more time. So I don't trip on the damn laces. You know?"

I nod and then realize she can't see me. "You would be the one to trip on your way down the aisle, wouldn't you?" I try to make light of the heaviness that just entered the building.

"I know what I'm asking is selfish, and I have no right, but here I am asking anyway. I'll just go ahead and apologize in advance. That's how petulant I feel right now. I'm sorry, Cody."

To tell her I understand would be a blatant lie. I'm on the opposing end of true, blue selfishness and her simple request isn't even on the egocentric radar. She interrupts my thoughts. "I have to go. I'll see you tomorrow. La Grenouille at noon. It's right by the park.

That work?"

"Sure, sounds great. See you then." I look up at the large metal clock in my kitchen. Fourteen hours until I see Lainey Rosemont. I won't sleep a wink tonight. I'm sure of it.

"Bye...Cody," Lainey breathes and then ends the call. I stare at her number on my cell phone before it disappears. The stupid sequence of numbers is all I have of her right now. Tomorrow I'll have more.

And I already know that *more* won't be enough.

I want all.

CHAPTER FOUR

Lainey

That fabric won't do. Marney is going to take one look at it and vomit the paisley puke floral print all over my expensive heels. There is absolutely no way around this trip to Manhattan. It has the only fabric store that suits my client's needs. I'll select a few samples for her drapes, eat lunch with my ex-fiancé and be back to Virginia Beach in a jiffy. That's what I keep telling myself. The truth is that I want to heave bacon, egg, and cheese all over the carpeted floor mat in my car. The drive from Virginia Beach to Manhattan isn't all that bad. Especially if I leave in the wee hours of the morning. The traffic swirling around me has signaled my arrival to NYC. Yellow blurs of cabs honk furiously and the morning rush of people cascade from all directions. I tossed and turned all night because I'm almost positive I'm making a poor decision to see Cody again after all this time. I'm. Going. To. See. Cody. He's here somewhere in this madness, waiting to meet me. The thought makes me wild with anticipation. Oh, and so mother-loving nervous I can barely see straight.

It boils down to something extremely simple: I can't not see him before I get married. Dax argued that it really wouldn't make a difference if I saw him now rather than in a few months after we're married, but I think it will. I need single Lainey eyes to lock on my former love. The same eyes that loved him and lost him need to be present. Sure, a marriage certificate is just a piece of paper—a trivial thing, really—but I'll be changed, my views skewed. So, I'm doing this. I'm meeting with him for lunch to talk. Cody will be different; he has to be after what he's been through. How can someone be held captive for years on end and come out on the other side sane and normal? If I'm being honest, I hope he's not my same old Cody. Speaking to him on the phone did nothing to further that hope. He sounds the same. Like no time has passed at all. It makes my stomach clench and my heart squeeze. "Do not vomit in this car, Lainey. It's just lunch," I say out loud, like a complete lunatic. "Surely you can make it through a lunch with your former fiancé.

"How could Dax let me do this? Is he insane? Doesn't he know that Cody sounds exactly the same as he did when I was head over heels in love with him?

How can he trust me? I don't deserve him. I don't deserve anything." A car swerves into my lane and I have to slam on my brakes. "Get a fucking grip, Lane. The solution isn't to kill yourself first." Maybe this time I'll listen to the sound woman in my head. I'm a grown, professional woman and this is what I've been reduced to. One hot, fine mess. I flick some of my blonde hair out of my face and slowly start back into the flood of traffic. Several agonizing minutes later, I pull into the parking garage and find a spot.

And I thought I was going to be sick before. Flipping down the mirror, I try to determine just how deer-in-the-headlights I look. My eyes look wide, but they're still blue, and most of my makeup has evaporated since the early morning application. I apply a few coats of mascara and pinch my cheeks.

"You've got this. It's like meeting a stranger. He's not your Cody. This is completely innocent." Maybe if I repeat this a million times I'll begin to believe it. Unfortunately, there isn't enough time in the world. When I told Dax my plans he looked at me like I was crazy. That crazy slowly morphed into sadness when he realized I was serious. I've always told him I had no desire to go back in time. Heartache. It's all I feel when I think about Cody Ridge and what could have been. I shocked myself when I came to this conclusion and called Cody last night. Because Dax is a great man, he told me to do what I needed to do. Reasoning with me after I've made my mind up isn't an option. He kissed me a little longer than he usually does when I left this morning. I felt it, then—his hesitance to let me go. That small act only made me even more nervous. If he's hesitant, and he trusts me implicitly, how the hell do I trust myself? Dax is my support system, fully, but right now there's nothing he can say that will make me feel better. I have to fix this for myself.

Grabbing my bag and locking my car door, I head out of the garage into the heat and bustle of Manhattan. With a quick glance left and right to make sure Cody isn't near, I set off for the restaurant. It's an odd thing to be hidden by people. Humans are everywhere, but no one sees past their own egocentric bubble—smartphones in every hand, most texting, some chatting, all ignoring the people next to them.

Then I see him. Cody is looking directly at me, standing shock still in the middle of the sidewalk. People move around him like he's a statue or some mildly inconveniencing construction sign. No one sees me either. The rest of civilization melts away.

We only see each other.

There's no making sense of my feelings. I feel everything—the humid breeze prickling the sweaty skin on the back of my neck, the adrenaline pulsing through my veins so thick that it's almost too much to bear. The sight of him walking toward me is the same view I've had in my dreams. It's always the same.

Except the Cody in my dreams was make-believe…a ghost, and this man approaching now is real. He looks older, wiser. He looks broken in a way I know will never be repairable. He looks the same, yet different—challenged, yet privileged. I know this man in every way.

Cody squints his eyes, almost like it pains him to see me, but I see such emotion pouring from his simple gesture that it literally brings me to my knees, out of breath and panting. Tears trickle down my face, a slow assault on my willpower, and his pace falters. He stops. He's examining me, the new Lainey—the person who was born after his death. The woman he knew is gone. The problem with that is I still have *her* heart. It races along, thumping jaggedly for the man I love. For the man I thought was forever gone; for the man I now have no right to. Cody takes a few more steps until he's at arm's length away. Looking down at me, I look up at him. A smile. That smile breaks across his face as he extends his hand to me.

"Trip on your laces, Fast Lane?" he says. "Let me help you up."

Taking his offered hand makes me realize I didn't feel everything a moment ago. I feel *everything* right now. My hand actually tingles where it's pressed against his. "Cody." Wobbling on my heels, I stand to face him, still basically hyperventilating. His white smile assaults me and I can't help it. I let my eyes

34

wander to the rest of him.

Shaking my head, I say, "You're alive." And he's so handsome I could crumple into myself and weep. He keeps his hair a little longer than he used to. My fingers would have something to clutch. His face looks the same. Perhaps the little lines around his eyes have deepened, but they only add to his overall appeal. I can't see his muscles, as they're covered in a blue button-up linen shirt, but they look like they are all still bulging and textbook perfect. I notice a tattoo peeking from his rolled up sleeves. That's something new.

Ignoring my obvious appraisal, his grin widens. "You're alive!" he counters. Taking my other hand in his, he studies me closer. I want to know what he thinks of me after all this time. Knowing full well I have no right to know and definitely no right to ask.

"You look beautiful, Lainey."

"Are you some kind of mind reader?"

"No. I'm just skilled at reading yours." He drops my hands and his thick, tanned neck works as he swallows. He's just as affected by seeing me. A fact that suddenly makes me feel ill. "And right now I'm thinking we should get into the restaurant. You skinned your knee when you tripped on your shoelaces."

Sure as shit, I have blood trickling down my shin. "Great. I'll probably contract some virulent disease." When I look up at him his eyes are darting around, and I can tell he's trying to solve something.

35

He runs a hand through his hair. "My place is just over there if you want to get cleaned up before lunch?" He nods to a beautiful high-rise building a few blocks over. My eyes widen. There's no way. I selected this restaurant because it's close to my fabric store. I had no idea this is where he lives.

He laughs. "I'm pretty sure you're not surprised I have an apartment in this neighborhood, so I'm going to assume you don't want to be alone in said apartment with me? You have nothing to worry about, Lainey."

My heart bangs against my chest. I'm not sure if it's fear or adrenaline, but I can't concentrate on anything except the rhythm it's beating. Cody is right in front of me right now. "I'm not worried," I bark out, indignant that he can really read my fucking mind.

"I have antibacterial ointment," he says in a singsong voice. Damn it. Something he knows about me. I rub that shit on everything. This cut on my leg needs a whole tube.

I squint my eyes at him. "Fine. Only because even you can agree this needs antibacterial ointment. I must really need it. We're just going to talk. I suppose we can do that anywhere." He laughs, the baritone sounds sending shockwaves to my core. God, I've missed him.

Cody quirks a brow. "Of course we're just going to talk. What else would we do?" Someone bumps into me, rousing me into awareness. In that mere second, a million things I would do with him run through my mind. All things I can't do. Not anymore, at least. None of them require clothing.

I lick my lips. "Right. Right. Of course. Let's go," I agree, even though I see carnal desires reflected in his eyes. We're on the exact same page. Same fucking word. He leads me through the crowds, his large presence forcing people to move without saying a word. We cross the street and I watch every step Cody takes. His gait is the same. The sweet smile he aims my way every few minutes is in the exact form it was before he…died. The doorman smiles and nods his head at Cody. "Mr. Ridge," he says, opening the ornate entry to the building.

Cody ushers me in first. "Mr. Ridge?" I ask, lifting one brow.

He merely shrugs and heads toward the elevator. We stare at each other for the entire ride up to the top. Me trying to dispel every thought I've had about Cody for the past three years and him probably trying to analyze me. Why, after all this time, I want to see him? How to explain that this wasn't something I wanted? I needed to see him in the flesh.

The elevator doors open into a cool, large hallway. His apartment is the one all the way at the end, overlooking the expanse of Central Park. It's gorgeous and large. It's lonely. "I'll go grab your special potion. Make yourself at home," Cody says, disappearing down a dark hallway. Palms sweaty, I fish for my cell phone in my purse. No missed calls or texts. My hands shake as I take off the quilted cross-body bag and hang it on the coat rack by his door. I see his old leather jacket. The one he wore when he rode his motorcycle. How did he get this? I remember slamming my arms into the sleeves of this jacket a million times. The familiar smell that made me melt and feel completely safe at the same time.

"Horse saved it," Cody whispers from behind me. I startle, my hand holding the buttery soft leather falling to my side. "Who knows why. It's not like the beast can wear it." He chuckles softly.

"Why would anyone save anything?" I ask, a little irritated. Of course I would have saved everything if I knew he was still alive. I. Buried. Him.

Cody gestures to the couch and holds up the tube of ointment and a package of anti-bacterial wipes. "You'll have to ask him," he says. "I wouldn't have saved any of your things either. Don't beat yourself up. Rising from the dead is apparently one of my better talents. Most people don't have that one." He winks. I grin uneasily.

Sitting on the edge of the couch, I hold my hand out for the supplies. There is no way he can touch me. After merely holding his hand, I can barely stand the thought of his hands on my body. A shiver runs down my spine and there's no controlling the response. I shake. Cody takes a seat on the ottoman in front of me, a good three feet away. A safe distance. *A safe distance would be Antarctica,* I think.

Cleaning my cut with a wipe and smearing ointment on, I realize it's just a surface scrape. Thank God. I won't die of flesh eating bacteria today. While I'm pondering, Cody doesn't take his eyes off me. I feel his piercing gaze urging me to talk.

Sighing, I look from my gross wound to his beautiful, searching eyes and swallow the thick lump in my throat. Cody's gaze trails down to my neck. "This is a pretty large place for just you," I say, feigning nonchalance to take the edge off. "It's beautiful." It really is. I can tell he decorated it himself, though. If I had my way, it would be much warmer. Cool is a bachelor's pad, which he is.

His blue gaze stays steely, but a corner of his mouth turns up. "I like it. It's more comfortable than my other places." More than one place? I know business is booming for him, but I don't know particulars. A year or so has passed since he was rescued. He's accomplished a lot in that time frame. I've tried to steer clear of anything that reminded me of Cody Ridge. Until now.

I look at the large window. It spans from floor to ceiling and has the most beautiful view. "I guess it would be," I remark.

"Lainey." My name is a question. A praise. It packs so much in two syllables. Only he is capable of making me feel so much with a single word.

I shake my head. "I don't know what I thought would happen. I figured you would be different, Cody. That I would finally be able to look you in the eye and say it's over, but how is that possible? Tell me how is that possible, damn it! He's a good man. A good man," I say, turning my face down to the teak hardwood. Dax. It's the first time I've thought about him since seeing Cody. Just thinking his name makes me ill with guilt. "I waited for so long. You were dead and still I waited. And now it's obvious why I was giving myself ulcers about moving on. Call it woman's intuition, but maybe subconsciously I knew you were alive." I gesture to him and his very alive body. "Dax is a good man," I repeat.

Cody lets out a long breath. "Of course he is. I wouldn't expect anything less if you're in love with him." His statement is so casual, but a quick glance up and I know it's anything but. "I am different. I am changed. Time passed and I lost you because of that. Change is the one thing you can't predict nor control. I can respect change. I think it's obvious you want closure with me before you marry him. It's yours. Take it." He leans over, taking both of my hands in his. Mine are shaking and his are solid and warm. "I'll love you always, Fast Lane. Things are different now. Go be with him. We'll start over. As friends." *Lie. Lie. Lie.* He can't be my friend. I can't be his. We never broke up. Our love never died. "This is the life I wanted for you while I was captive—for you to be happy with someone else." My hands shake even more until I feel the tremors moving up to my arms. In the next moment he's pulling me into him, hugging me so effortlessly that I'm reminded of home. I don't fight it, actually quite the opposite. I lean into his broad chest and press my face against his shirt. He smells like the same cologne he always wore. It's the same cologne I sprayed on my pillowcase for a year after he died. My tears would mix with the scent and it would cling to my face for a full twelve hours. I inhale deeply.

"I missed you," I whisper. His arms fold around me. "I'm sorry."

He ignores my apology. Cody never did do apologies well. "Does this make it easier?" Cody asks, his lips pressed against the top of my head. "Will it be easier for you to move on now?"

I pull back and look at him. He hums with life and everything else that makes him so precious. Running my hand over the side of his face, he closes his eyes. I look back at the huge window and think of Dax: my perfect, trusting fiancé who is my pillar. I can't hurt him. There's no way I'll hurt him. "Yes," I lie.

"This is just what I need." Truth.

CHAPTER FIVE

Cody

A sunflower will always turn its face toward the sun. It's called heliotropism. During my years in captivity I wasn't granted much sunlight in my dank dungeon cell, but you can bet my mind was always turned to one thing. Her. Now that I've had another small taste of Lainey, I can't turn away from my sun. It's an impossibility. Seeing her was a mistake. One I'm glad I made because I knew from the first moment she laid eyes on me that it wasn't over. Quite the opposite. Lainey Rosemont is still fucking in love with me. *She's in love with me.* This is what I think of as I work in this dank, oppressive basement that smells of sixty-year-old rust and stale cigarettes.

I wrench the greaseball's head to the side, exposing his sweaty neck. "I will slit your fucking throat. Tell me," I order, my voice quiet—stern. There's rarely screaming in my job. If there is, I'm not the one doing it. This bastard has information I want. Horse told me so. "Where is V, asshole?" There aren't very many tactful ways to get the information you want these days. Men, especially bad men, only respond to violence and typically they need to be within an inch of losing their lives to come clean. This asshole wants to be within an inch of it. Idiot.

He sputters and whimpers. I release my grip a touch to give him some incentive to speak. "I don't know. They don't tell me," he gasps in broken English. Pressing the tip of my knife harder, I pierce his skin. "I'm nobody. They don't tell me where they travel!" His words are erratic now. I'm getting closer. This may be a truth. The men responsible for holding me hostage were many. The ring leader, V, was never around. Especially at night. He would have the lowly pee-ons guard my cell. Nighttime is when the shit always hits the fan. Always.

I grunt. Thinking about V makes me angry. "Well, if you don't know where he or his counsel is, fine. Maybe you can tell me why you have a basement full of underage children, then?" I press the knife in deeper until a stream of blood trickles down his neck, soiling the collar of his fake Armani dress shirt.

"I don't know!" He shits his pants. Perfect, now he has yellow pit stains and crap on his trousers.

I cock my head to the side and spread my legs wider

so I don't dirty my own pants. "Now, that's a fucking lie." I spoke with an older child. I know the truth. This asshole is up to his eyeballs in trouble. Not only does he have ties to V and the counsel, but he runs one of the largest child trafficking rings in Mexico. He makes me sick. With a gloved hand I insert my pointer finger into the side of his eye socket and press with just the right amount of pressure. He feels it.

"He's not in Africa anymore!" greaseball screams out as another violent shudder alerts me to more shit exiting his filthy body. "That's all I know. He's back in the States. Please, please. Let me go!" Not a chance in fiery hell, you sick prick.

I shudder. The motherfucker is back in the States. He's too close. I shake my head. No, this won't do. He's supposed to stay far, far away. I'm to go to him. This makes V easier to hunt, but it forces the stakes higher. He's in my world now. I loosen my grip on the knife. "Why is he in the States?" I already know the answer. I'm not scared.

"He said he's making good on promises." Greaseball chokes on his own spit and starts shaking violently. Shock is setting in. I'd love nothing more than to slit his throat and watch every ounce of his dirty, tainted blood spill onto the floor. But he deserves a fate worse than that, so I radio for my men to come. He needs to be tried inside the U.S. for his crimes. I'll make sure of it. Child rapists and traffickers don't fare well in prison. I expect he'll pray my blade stole his life instead. I remove my finger from his eye socket.

Horse and Van come down the filthy hallway and scan the surrounding area. I nod toward the back where there is a set of large, rusty metal doors. "Kids are back there. Some look to be American. All ages," I say, closing my eyes to force out the image of what these poor children had to endure. "Get them out of here. Some need clothing. All will need food." Horse glares at greaseball as if he is solely responsible for every crime on earth. He wants to break his neck and pick his teeth with his pinky bone. If there's one thing Horse hates, it's men like greaseball. Offenses against children are always the worst. Unforgivable. Van heads for the double doors and radios for more help. I see him shake his head sadly as he enters and witnesses the atrocity for himself.

I point at my bleeding, shitting companion with my bloody knife. "As for him...transport him back to U.S. soil and hand him over to the authorities. They've wanted his ass for a while," I growl. "And, Horse?" He looks at me with his bright, angry eyes and raises a bushy brow.

"I won't kill him," he replies, smiling. I nod once.

"Alive," I command, just to be sure. And with that simple word, greaseball starts wailing. Horse grabs him by his neck and drags him toward the exit. I smile, sling my hand to my hip, and admire the beauty of this

45

moment. One truly hideous criminal is out of the world, hopefully the kids will be reunited with their families, and I've obtained information about V. Troubling information about V, but at least now I know. I can prepare, be watchful…I can plan. I love my job.

I pull out my untraceable satellite phone and call Molly. She picks up on the first ring. "How'd it go, boss?"

"Well. He did have the children here. I got what I came for. Please alert the FBI that we have him and we're heading to the airport now."

Molly pauses. "How's Horse?" I smile. She knows of his harsh tendencies, too.

I snicker. "Having a blast!" I hear greaseball wailing down the hall. I cover the mouthpiece of the phone. "I said alive!" I bark out.

Horse laughs, the sound maniacal. "I said I won't kill him!" I shrug and take him for his word. I recap the events and the timeline so Molly can take notes in case anyone has questions, which they rarely do, and have her ready arrangements for when we arrive back in Virginia Beach. I have to turn away when Van and a few other guys usher the children from the back room. Their wounded eyes are too much for me to bear. It's easier for me to stare down a serial killer, a felon, a monster than it is to look a child in their eyes knowing that all innocence is gone. Why didn't I find them sooner? Why can't I save them all? Why are fuckers so, so horrible? I'll say it one more time. I love my job.

Molly repeats the information back to me and then adds, "Oh, and Shoots like a Star called. She said she'll be in Virginia Beach this weekend. She wanted to get together." I cringe because I know what face Molly is making right now. Lainey and I have been in contact with each other since our meeting in NYC. Phone conversations have been polite and platonic. It's been new and a distraction from my work. I turn around too soon and see the last of the children exit the room. A little boy who can't be more than two years old turns and meets my eyes. I swallow and it sticks there. His face is dirty and his feet are bare and he clutches a rag like his life depends on it. I smile and wave, but his gaze faces forward as he continues his freedom walk. I want to tell him that I can empathize, that he's safe now, but to him those are just words. I radio for Van to get the kids out of here first and as quickly as humanly possible. I can't look at the little boy again until the vacancy in his eyes is replaced by something...anything else. It's too familiar.

"Thanks, Molly," I mutter, ending the call. I'll need a lot of distraction as soon as possible. Lainey wants to get together. With me. I wipe the blade of my knife on a cloth and head for the exit. I don't smell the sweat, the iron tang of blood, or even the stale cigarettes anymore. I smell her.

****

I hate the beach and seawater. Lainey knows it. The years of having a profession that requires early mornings dunked in cold water blossomed the hatred. She wants to get together at the beach. I know her game. She thinks if she invites me to the beach, I'll be the old miserable, complaining stodge from the past. The thing about having years of your life stolen by captivity is that once you're free, you don't take a millisecond for granted. I live every one of them. Even the ones that coat me with a fine sheen of gritty sand.

Of course I see her before she catches sight of me and, oh my, what a sight she is. Her tight black shorts do everything for her. As does the form-fitted tank top. All her perfect curves are hugged, tight, and exactly where I left them. While I scrutinize every nuance that is Lainey, I can't forget that all of her perfection isn't mine anymore even if every ounce of testosterone in my body says otherwise.

Lainey smiles a cheek-splitting grin when she sees me waiting for her with a hot pink yoga mat tucked under my arm. Oh, yes, this woman knows exactly how to play the game.

She whacks me with her rolled up mat. "Mornin'!" Lainey looks me directly in the eye like she's trying to convey so much more than a greeting.

I take in a deep breath. "Good morning. Man, do I

love the ocean air. It's so…fresh." She narrows her eyes as she very obviously appraises me from head to toe.

"You hate the beach."

"Do I?" I ask, raising one brow. Lifting the bottom of my black T-shirt, I pull it over my head. She ogles. I look away.

I hear her shift uncomfortably next to me. "Thanks for coming. I figured we could both use a little Zen in our lives." Lainey clears her throat. I let my gaze wander to hers. Enough time has passed that I'm sure she's looked her fill.

"How can I possibly tell you no?" I ask. Her clear, blue eyes grow wide. I've said what we both know as truth. I can't, nor will she tell me no, either. "Shall we?" I extend my arm toward the water and the deserted beach.

Walking toward the ocean and the firmer sand, I unroll my mat and look at her. "You lead?" She tucks a wayward strand of her blonde hair behind her ear. She has these graceful fingers, long and feminine. When we were together she never had them polished. Each time I've seen her recently they've been a different shade of pink. After she rights her hair, she moves her hands down her body self-consciously.

Lainey swallows, smiles crookedly, and nods. She's nervous. "Sure, I'll lead," she says.

"We've done yoga together a thousand times. It's

49

no big deal. We're two friends hanging out. Don't worry, I'm going to stay on my hot pink slice of beach and you're going to stay on yours. No hanky panky." I actually do need a good stretching after all the time in the gym I spend lifting weights. Every muscle in my body is stiff. Lainey bends over to adjust the corners of her mat and I realize now *everything* is stiff. Her fucking glorious ass might as well be naked and saluting me. It's an odd sensation, wanting her like I do. It's familiar, but it seems so taboo at the same time.

"Your man didn't want to join? Let me guess. He hates the beach?" I sit down to stretch, reaching for one foot, and wince, and then the other. She looks over at me and the smile fades from her face.

"No," she starts, but then pauses. "I mean, yes, Dax hates the beach, but I didn't invite him. I guess I'm confusing him lately." She lies on her mat, flat on her back, with her arms stretched over her head. Turning just her head, she looks at me. "I guess I'm confusing myself, Cody." The doubt is there and there's no running away from it.

I realize I haven't taken a breath, so I exhale. It's noisy. Even audible over the sound of the waves lapping the shore nearby. Before I can reply, Lainey switches poses and I follow suit, trying to decide what the fuck is going on inside her mind while bumbling with my big muscles. It's a challenge I accept. I let her have this silence, planning to attack her with the

50

question the second we're finished. I can't focus on yoga or releasing my ego or any of the other bullshit that is expected. I can't be in the moment because of her proximity and she's confused and fuck, is this my in? Do I throw caution to the wind and just kiss her senseless right here and really set the record straight? She won't be confused after that; I know it for a fact. I go through the motions, pretending to zone out for the rest of the practice. "Down Dog," Lainey says, her voice a hoarse whisper. Long blonde waves cascade on her mat as she lowers her head.

"How do you know I'm up?" I whisper. I am, because how can I not be when her ass has been in my face for the past twenty minutes. I haven't been this close to her in so long that there's no controlling my reactions.

A puzzled look crosses her face. "Huh?" She didn't hear me. I snicker. She's usually the one with all of the jokes. With a sigh, she falls back against her mat. I stay upright, mostly to be able to see her, and also because I want a good view of our surroundings. You can never be too careful, or too watchful. Paranoia set in the second I found out V is on the prowl. Ever so delicately, she lays her hand off of her mat, palm up in the sand in between us.

I take her hand and she squeezes it. "What do you want?" she asks quietly, her fingers stroking mine. Isn't it obvious?

"What I want is quite simple and quite complicated at the same time. I want what I've always wanted." Lainey sits up, keeping her fingers intertwined with mine.

"This," she says, as she looks down at our hands, "was always an impossibility. I want you, Cody. And there's no way for that to happen unless someone gets hurt." You know that saying that 'all's fair in love and war'? It's just not true because nothing about our situation is fair. It's fucked up. Lainey goes on. "Seeing you just makes me want to see you more and more, and how in the hell is that healthy for my relationship? I mean, Charlie Christmas, I'm getting married and all I can think of is the next time I get to see you and talk to you and you guessed it, *be* with you. This is why I didn't want to see you. Deep down I knew this would happen. I'm so messed up in the head I couldn't even work yesterday."

Every bone in my body is shuddering in protest. I grab her other hand, so I have them both. "We should go, Lane. You should get back to him." Can't hurt him now, can we? I wonder if her parents like him as much as they loved me. Do they take family vacations together? Does she tell him about our time together like it was ancient history? Does he know how easily she could be mine? "I promised no hanky panky and I'm not sure how much longer my dog will stay down."

Tears form in her eyes, but she smiles. "Namaste

right here," she quips. Shaking my head, I laugh. "For right now." We talk for a while like that, hand in hand. She asks me about my aunt and my job, and if she can decorate my apartment, and if I have girlfriends. Lainey rapid fires the questions one after the other and I answer her honestly. She doesn't bring up my years away. I can see when her mind veers there, but she shuts it down immediately. We start commenting on old ladies power walking on the beach and mundane stuff that couples always talk about. It's time.

I ask the question that burns a hole in my mind. "Does he know?" Everyone has secrets. Lainey's are paramount. Briefly, she glances at me and then away, her lips a drawn tight line. I can't stay away from her any longer. Crouching in front of her, I force her down onto her back, my hands on each side of her head. Her breath hitches, and my own heart stammers. In the push-up position over her, I bend my elbows so I can get closer—to smell her, to feel her body heat against mine. Her lips part. She wants me to kiss her. I ask her again, "Did you tell him?"

Without hesitation, she simply says, "No." When her beautiful eyes find mine again, I lean my forehead against hers and breathe her intoxicating scent into my body. It's a moment I'll always remember. Similar to the others that are vividly stored in my memory bank. Our first kiss and what happened directly following the kiss, the marriage proposal, the tearful goodbye before

53

I left for the life-changing deployment. It was like she knew, but how could she? And now this: her reply of *no* means everything. More importantly, it changes everything.

It's the moment I know without a shadow of doubt that, after all this time, she's still mine.

He doesn't know.

CHAPTER SIX

Lainey

I didn't intentionally keep the yoga date from Dax, but I didn't tell him either. Of course I knew he'd be upset. I'm fucking everything up and at the moment I can't find it in me to care as much as I logically know I should. Being with Cody gives me a feeling that I don't get anywhere else. It's strange. It's electric. The absence of it makes me want it that much more. You know how some people have secrets hidden so well that they can convince themselves they don't exist? I'm the owner of one of those. I think all of the small lies that aren't really lies trickle into the blank space where the one we don't speak of resides. Cody is the only one who knows. This just complicates everything now when I'm dealing with Dax.

I repeat myself one more time just to drive the point home. "I'm sorry, Dax. I am." He's shirtless, his tan muscles rippling every time he paces my bedroom. His blond hair is wet from a shower and the grit at the bottom of the shower is why I was caught. Yoga at the beach wasn't enough of an explanation. He then asked with whom, and I would never lie outright. I told him the truth and he damn near blew a gasket.

From my perch at the end of my bed he is an angry mess. He stops in front of me, just far enough away that I can't touch him. "You didn't even plan on telling me. How sneaky is that, Lainey? What am I supposed to think? I'll ask once more. Are you fucking him?" Ouch.

I look down at the floor. Not because I'm lying, but because I wish I was fucking him and I feel like a disgraceful asshole. "No. I would never cheat on you, Dax. Not even with him."

"You say that like he's a goddamn deity. *Not even with him*. I mean, fuck, what am I supposed to do?" he growls, bringing a big hand through his hair and pacing in front of me a few more times. He's making me agitated. I'm not in a position to ask him to stop. He drops to a squatting position, his forearms against his thighs with his head down.

I don't dare make a move to approach him. When he's angry he likes space. Wide open space. "I love you, Dax. He's just a friend. At the very least I owe him my friendship. I owe him." More than Dax can ever know.

"Bullshit. If you thought of him as just a friend we wouldn't be having this conversation right now. A smart man would walk away from this fucked up situation. I'm not wise when it comes to you. I'm merely a lovesick fool with hopes and dreams of a future with you. I've spent every waking moment for years trying to convince you of my feelings and then you of yours just to have them stripped away in a freak of nature occurrence. So just tell me now. Put me out of my fucking misery." He looks up at me. Scooting off the bed, I kneel in front of him. It's safe now. I can see his eyes soften. "You still love him?"

I put two hands on each side of his face. Honesty. This is it. This cut will be the deepest. I take one huge breath and another just for good measure. "I've never stopped loving him. How could you think I would be able to stop? That's not fair. This whole situation isn't fair! I can't reconcile my future when my past morphs into the present. Dax, he was my future," I explain quietly, my eyes imploring him to understand. How can he, though? Cody isn't supposed to be here. I said yes to Dax. A knife blade twists inside my stomach. I said yes. I didn't wait long enough. It's my fault. I should have waited longer. I owed Cody that.

Dax looks away, pulling out of my grasp. "What now then? What do you want now? Let's heap a little more unfairness onto this situation. Where do we go now?" His eyes rove over my body. He thinks he may never see me again. I lay my hand on his forearm. Dax's eyes dart down to my touch as he gently pulls away.

Defeated, I say, "I don't know." It's honest, at least. "There's no manual on how to proceed when the dead love of my life comes back to life to meet the new love of my life."

He arches a brow. I see the wheels spinning. "So, it's a fair playing field?" No.

"You know I love you." Not a lie. A tortured expression passes over Dax's face. He sits back in a more comfortable position. I scoot closer to him, feeling every bit of pain that there is no way I can fix. I put it there. After everything he's done for me, I'm causing him pain.

Quickly he takes my hands in his. "I can't believe I'm going to say this." He looks up at the ceiling and then his blue eyes meet mine again. He's tortured and a jolt of unfamiliar uneasiness hits me. I actually have no idea what he's going to say next. "Figure it out. However you need to do it. I'll wait. It's an even split. Fifty-fifty. What kind of person would I be otherwise? I won't give you ultimatums, Lainey. I can't live without you. Be with him if you want to, but pick me in the end," Dax professes. His eyes shine; his bottom lip trembles the tiniest of fragments and I think that's it. I can't hurt his man any more than I already have. I have to live my life like Cody is still dead. That's what a good woman would do. Me? I'm plain awful—a miserable combination of selfish and mean, nasty bitch.

"You're serious? You would let me…" I can't even say it. Sex. Fuck. Bang. Bump uglies.

Full lips in a firm line, he asks, "Fuck him? That's what you want. First you want to see him and then befriend him. Fucking him is the next logical step. An easy step as you've probably already fucked him a thousand times before." My hands are trembling as his words pierce my heart. Dax knew from the beginning that this is how it would go down and yet he accepted my decision to see Cody without question.

I drop his hands. "Dax, please! I don't want to hurt you. How can you even consider this? More importantly, what does that say about me?"

He shakes his head and looks past me. "The hurting has already commenced. This is just an easy way for you to figure out what you want. I'll be as graceful as my patience and God will allow me to be, but I can't make any promises. Do what you need to do and I'll be here for you." Roughly, Dax grabs my shoulders and pulls me to him. Without stopping to let me respond, he kisses me—his hands in my hair and his heart pounding against my chest. He's here for me. He's always been here for me. His tongue tastes sweet and his face smells like his soap and I'm immediately turned on. It doesn't take long for my mind to fix things, though. My eyes flutter closed and Dax's hands turn into Cody's and the smell of soap is Cody's cologne, and the way Dax kisses isn't the way Cody kisses. Dax doesn't bite my lip or tilt my head just so.

I pull away, breathless. "I'm messed up. I'm so messed up over this."

He doesn't make any moves to continue the kiss. He merely says, "I know."

"I love you, Dax. I'm so sorry."

"Why does that sound more like goodbye? I've taken every ounce of my testosterone and manhood and placed it into your hands. Don't make this more difficult. I love you, too. You need to get your head on straight and unfortunately I think there's only one way to do it. Spend time with him; whatever that means to you." With that, he stands up and heads to the closet and begins riffling around and tossing things onto the bed. After years of being around Dax, I know exactly how upset he is right now just by the manner in which he tosses a T-shirt.

Why can't I tell him to stop? That I want him to stay? That it's him? Why can't I tell him that he's my everything?

Because he's not. Not anymore. "I don't deserve you," I say, wiping tears from my face. "Please don't hate me. You mean so much to me."

"If I could ever hate you I wouldn't be standing here right now, handing you my balls on a silver platter. I can't talk about this anymore. I'm going to stay with Griff. You know the number. Call me when you need me." Need, not want.

Panic wells in my chest. "What about the wedding…all the planning." I'll have to tell my mother. Dread doesn't begin to describe the prospect of that conversation.

He shrugs. "Do nothing or cancel everything. It's up to you. People will understand. This is probably the only circumstance that could possibly happen in which no one can judge your decisions, Lainey," he says matter-of-factly. Dax packs his leather duffel bag and leaves the house, his hair still wet. Standing in my foyer with a T-shirt on and bare feet, I feel like a dirty whore mated with a stubborn teenager instead of an engaged woman watching her fiancé drive away.

My heart hurts. My stomach is in knots, but that doesn't stop me from dialing Cody's number before Dax's taillights even disappear.

This will surely be the most uncomfortable phone call I'll ever have. His cell rings once and then again. Padding over to the kitchen, I look out at the neighbors' empty house. It used to belong to my friend Morganna, a real bitch of an attorney. After she moved to the country for her own happily ever after, it sits empty. No one can afford the mansion in this current market. I draw the shades that peer into her living room.

It rings a fourth time. "You," Cody answers the phone call, his voice traveling from my ear all the way down to my core. He has an immediate effect on my body and mind.

I smile through the sadness. "You," I say back.

"A little late for phone calls, isn't it?"

"You're awake deciphering code or working on something ingenious, I'm sure. I'll let you go if you want."

Cody clears his throat. "Of course you're right, and no, you won't let me go." I take a deep breath. This is why I'm in this situation.

"I'm fucked up over you, Cody. An utter mess. Dax just left me, but not before issuing the world's most noble and insane proposition." Sitting down at the dining table, I put my head down on my arm and click on the speaker phone.

"I'm listening," Cody replies. How do I tell him? "And don't be a mess. You're just getting used to the new normal. You'll straighten it out eventually. You always do."

I scoff. "He wants to share me with you."

His reply is swift. "What?"

Might as well spill it all Lainey verbal diarrhea style. "I told him I can't just get over you now that you're in my life. I told him that unfortunately for him I never stopped loving you. I love Dax, Cody, but I loved you first. I still love you. He told me to figure out what I wanted. I guess the better way to put it is that he said to figure out whom I wanted. Dax will wait for me while I figure it out. He said I could *be* with you."

Cody's breath is heavy on the other side of the line.

He must be enraged at this proposition. An alpha male to the core, how could he possibly think this is acceptable? "You're serious," he says, voice low, scary.

"I know it sounds completely insane. There's no way I can consider it."

He groans. It's a defeated noise. "You want to, though, don't you? It would be the weird Lainey thing to want."

Cody knows me too well. "I want you," I deadpan.

"But you want him, too. Maybe we should have a three-way and you can pick your victor. To the winner will go the spoils!" I can't tell if he's joking. It doesn't matter either way.

"I can't imagine a life without you now that you're back in it. Dax and I have a history. A history you're not a part of. Of course I want that part. See? Mess. "

Cody blows out a breath. "Yes. I accept. Only because it gets me what I want."

Silenced by his reply, I wait for him to say something else.

"He's a brave man."

"What? Why do you say that?" I ask.

"He's freely giving what he should treasure most. One can only assume that he thinks he has the upper hand. Which isn't the case, is it?" Smug. Smug. Smug. He's right.

"Hypothetically, if we do this, and I'm not sure if I'm capable of it, I don't want to rub it in his face. I've already hurt him more than is reasonable." His wounded expression flashes in my mind. I knock my forehead against the table to rid my memory of it. Horrible.

Cody laughs. "What type of man do you think I am? I respect Dax as a brother, but as a man, he's being foolish. You haven't hurt him, Fast Lane. You've scared him. You threw him a curve ball he wasn't ready for. That's life. Sometimes shit things happen and you learn to deal with them or you move on. I suppose this is his way of dealing with it because he doesn't want to move on. I can't blame him. Look at you." I look down at my ratty T-shirt and think of the wet mascara running down my face.

"We can go as fast or as slow as you want. Tell me what you want." Tingles rise on the back of my neck. Two sentences and I'm wet, ready and willing for everything he has to offer. Cody didn't even mean that in a sexual manner. I'm so fucked. Literally and figuratively.

"Where are you?" I ask.

"I'm in V.B. this week, but I have a job next weekend, and then I'll be in California the week after that. Breakfast tomorrow at my house? You know where my new place is?"

"Yes," I reply. I hear static on the other end of the phone.

Cody groans. "I've gotta go. Other line. But,

64

Lainey?" My heart kicked it into fast mode the second I said yes—half out of guilt and the other half with anticipation. Now it pounds at a more frantic pace.

"Yeah?"

"In my mind you're already mine. This isn't something I'll take lightly. I want everything that was once mine. I want everything he stole from me. I won't stop until I get it." He clicks off the line without saying goodbye. *He* stole from me. I shiver.

Well, doesn't that sound ominous with a side of possessive? I want him even more for it. He's probably shirtless right now, in front of his desk. Maybe he has his earphones half on and half off, maybe leaning back in his chair looking like a computer sex god. They do exist, you know?

Pulling the phone back in front of me, I tap my favorites and my finger hovers over Dax's name. It even has a little heart emoticon next to it. I've tapped that button a million times, excited to hear his voice, but right now moving my finger an inch to call him might as well be a thousand miles. I turn off my phone instead. When I know what the hell I'm doing I'll call Dax. *You already know what you're doing,* I say to myself.

I plug my phone in to charge in the kitchen so I'm not tempted to use it and head back to my bedroom. The pillows smell like Dax's soap. My shower is still wet from his shower, and you know what else is there?

Probably the sand from this morning's beach date.

Now is the time to dwell with my quite unusual life choices and feel badly for destroying one man's life.

It's just not the man you think.

CHAPTER SEVEN

Lainey

I tossed and turned in my bed for seven hours. Seven. During that time I compiled a list of pros and cons to Dax's proposition. After a while all the points I came up with could be lumped into the same category, not one or the other. A text from Cody sits on my cell phone. It says one word. Ten.

It's six o-clock in the morning and I decide to wake up my friend Chloe because she is the least judgmental friend I have to my name and because she's permanently single and will have a completely different perspective. She yells at me for a few seconds, unintelligible, sleepy slurs, but I interrupt her with my very real, very terrible predicament spilling into around seven sentences, and that shuts her up real quick.

"How can this be real life? Who are you? I think

you have the wrong number," Chloe growls, her rough voice punctuated by sleep. She has the type of tenor that most porn stars have. I can't copy it even if I try. "I'll be over in ten," she says, ending the call before I can tell her I have somewhere to be at ten. I disarm my security system so she can enter without fuss.

Talking to myself while I make a pot of coffee helps me feel better. Chloe rings the doorbell and I yell for her to come in. She's wearing pajamas and her hair in a top knot so high it's waving to God.

As she approaches me in the kitchen, she says, "You're going to need something a lot stronger than coffee."

I breathe out a deep breath. "I know. Hell, do I know. What am I doing?"

Chloe slings her bag onto a barstool next to her and sits down. She nods to the coffee pot and I pour her a cup and fix it how she likes it. "How much of a whore do you want to be?" she asks after I hand her the mug. "On a scale from prostitute to slutty, cheating bitch, where are you at? I need to get a feel of what I'm dealing with right now," she rasps, eyeing me over the rim of her cup. Her eyebrows are perfect.

I shrug. "I'm not even on the scale. I don't think I can go through with it. Spend time with Cody, sure. That's it, though. Dax has been so good to me. After all this time, he just loves me. He's there for me. I'm surprised he even brought this up to begin with. I'm not sure why." *Why did he offer this option to me?* Surely it can't be solely for my happiness. Am I missing something? Selfless, sure, but like Cody said...it's foolish.

Chloe digs through her purse and pulls out her oversized cell phone. "Do you love him?" Her finger scrolls wildly across the screen.

I close my eyes. "Yes," I reply. "What type of question is that?"

She stops scrolling and points her laser gaze at me. "Who were you thinking of when you answered that question?"

Him. I was thinking of him. I shake my head. "What would you do?" I counter.

Chloe smiles. "I'd do exactly what you want to do. When the cat's away the mouse will play." This is why I called her. I knew she would give me the answer I wanted to hear. She looks behind her, trailing her gaze over the expanse of my huge house. It's the product of a lot of hard work and a very small social life. I worked hard, earning every client the old-fashioned way: doing a good job and relying on word of mouth. I've lived here alone for many years, so being here by myself doesn't bother me that much. The reason why Dax is gone bothers me the most. "This house sure is big and lonely when Dax isn't here, isn't it?" she asks.

Her eyes grow big and round. "The wedding," she exclaims at the realization that I'm planning a big ole'

69

party of a wedding. Two hundred people are invited and guests have already started buying off the wedding registry. It makes me cringe. As one of my bridesmaids, it makes her cringe as well.

"I know, I know. Don't worry. It's going to be fine," I say, rising from my seat. I'm too restless to stay in one place for long. "Everything is still on. Dax didn't break up with me, Chloe. He just…wants me to be sure." I think that's what he wants. "The wedding is still on." Saying it out loud comforts me. I've been planning for months. The save the dates have gone out. All of the fine details are tuned and my grandma, God bless her soul, even booked a plane ticket. How can I be so sure of something and have that surety turned on its head in a matter of days?

Chloe follows me into my bedroom as I tear open my closet and begin my search for something to wear. The smell of Dax lingers in here. His clothes all hung color coordinated with shirts on the top and pants and jeans on the bottom. My side of the closet is a fucking rainbow of shirts next to skirts next to jeans and multiple items draped on one hanger. "It maximizes space," I say to Chloe when she sees the disaster.

Shaking her head, she leaves me to my pit and walks to look out of the enormous bay window that overlooks the water. Boats come and go all day, but right now the water is still, peaceful. The opposite of how I feel inside. The water makes me feel safe…like I'm on a tiny island that no one can reach unless I decide to allow them. The reality is that one hurricane could wipe out my entire existence in this house. I'll never be truly safe. Chloe prattles on, saying things meant to comfort me or help me make a decision, but she knows I have to follow through with my friendship with Cody and whatever she thinks that means. Merely thinking of the man makes me weak in the knees. I've missed everything about him. I've missed looking at him and hearing his voice, feeling him beside me, on top of me…inside me. There's no denying what I want to do. Now it's just a matter of feelings. Cody's and Dax's.

Chloe interrupts my thoughts by saying, "I need to ask you one thing."

I nod.

"You knew he was alive for a long time and you didn't want to see him. Why?"

I tell her as much as I can. "Because it hurt too much and it was too confusing and odd. Until you stare down a ghost from a former life, you can't expect to understand. I visited his gravesite regularly, Chloe. Remember the video? I watched him die. He was gone. It took some getting used to before I could come to terms with it. Seeing him again messed me up just like I thought it would—even worse, actually. Look at the decision I have to make."

She asks a few more questions to which I give pointed answers and she helps me pick out an outfit.

Her initial question is still fresh in my mind, as is the legitimate answer.

My proximity only puts him in danger. Followed up by another fact: I cannot stay away any longer.

****

If my phone call with Dax is any indication as to how the rest of my day is going to play out, I should have just stayed in bed. Or perhaps locked myself in my home office and scrolled through design websites all day long. Work is always the answer. Dax is upset and rightfully so. Which in turn hurts my heart and causes my mood to plummet so low that it's now in a dirty public toilet. He's upset I didn't call him last night to ask him to come back. Mostly, he's beside himself that I'm here, standing in front of Cody's house about to ring the doorbell. You know how women say one thing, think another, and actually do something entirely different? I feel like that's what Dax pulled. *Go ahead, Lainey. Be with Cody. Figure it out.* When he really meant, *go ahead, Lainey, crush my soul.* When I hung up the call, he was resigned to holding up his end of the bargain that he created, and I felt like a lump of coal.

When Mother called next, I confessed that I was seeing Cody. The other end of her phone was eerily quiet and then she said, "Be careful." Wow. Thanks for being so ominous. That's great advice coming from someone who raised me and always has a million unsolicited words to give. Only two when I truly need advice. She's worried about the wedding and what everyone will think if it goes belly up. Again. *Lainey Rosemont cancels another wedding!* I can see the email subject lines now. My family back in Russia will flip their shit. Again. I can't dwell without having an anxiety attack and running full speed back home, so I knock on his large, mahogany, wooden door instead. It's the kind of door you see in movies. Like maybe a sex dungeon resides on the other side or some sort of portal to another world. Laughing to myself, I agree that it kind of is a portal. One to the past. I get to be whoever I want when I step inside.

Cody opens the door wide. His hair is tousled, his five o'clock shadow must be like a twelve o'clock shadow, his T-shirt hugs every rippling curve, and for the love of all that is holy, he has a dish towel tossed over one shoulder. It triggers so many memories that it causes me to close my eyes and catch my breath. Definitely a portal, I decide.

He leans against the doorjamb and makes no move to wave me in. "Are you hungry?" he asks. I remind myself of the present and all that has transpired since those memories. A lot. Too much. Not enough. Everything. Right now the only thing I can do is place Dax in a box, albeit a comfortable one, in the corner of my mind and focus on the present, which just so happens to also be my past. Go ahead and make sense of that. I take a deep breath and lock that shit tight. I'll leave the key right here on this front porch for later.

Cody eyes me up and down, his gaze flicking to each body part methodically. The way he looks at me is intoxicating. "Straight to the point, I see," I reply. Peeking around his massive body, I glimpse inside his new world. It's a beautiful, spacious home, but it looks as if he's just moved in. The gray walls are bare, the dark polished wooden floors are pristine, unmarred even by footprints, and the furniture looks like it came directly from a European showroom. This house isn't lived in and that's just at first glance.

Cody notices my appraisal. "I prefer my apartment in the city. It's nice to have a place at home, though. Maybe you could help me spruce it up. Use your finer skills, you know?" His smile is predatory. It holds equal parts of love and destruction. I want to taste it. His NYC apartment is just as nice, but he's right. He spends more time there. I immediately wonder why. "Come in," he says, opening the door wider and ushering me inside. Yep, this shit is definitely expensive European. I mentally tally what this sole room alone must have cost to furnish. Walking slowly through his foyer and taking in every detail I can helps to calm my nerves. I let my purse flop down onto a gothic style bench, slide off my ballet flat shoes, and follow him into the kitchen where I smell breakfast cooking.

The kitchen is beautiful. As my gaze flutters from one marble inlaid detail to the next, I realize why I deem it perfect. It is *my* perfect kitchen. The one we started planning when we got engaged; from the brand of the range right down to the length of the large island. This would be my kitchen if he didn't take him from me. Now it's his. There are so many complicated components that have always hovered around our relationship. We do what we've always done. We ignore them completely. When Cody *died*, I thought my secrets would be buried with him. He is the only one to know exactly how and why I came to Virginia Beach all those years ago. My life has morphed into something less sinister since those days, but the secrets I keep, and what I've caused, eat away at my soul. That's another reason I refused to see him when he returned, although I could never admit it to Chloe. Guilt. It's heavy.

I try to make small talk about inconsequential things as Cody busies himself at the range, his wide back facing me. When I mention that I spoke with my mother he wants to know how she's been. When we dated years ago they were close. My mother, Grace, took his death hard. I don't think she's accepted that he never died. Good for her. It's easier that way. I haven't had the gall, opportunity or the right words to ask about the time he spent in captivity. I assume he doesn't want to divulge details about his darkest hours. If we become closer, I know he'll open up to me. Even though I have no right to that information. Cody asks if I told her about him and I try to steer the conversation to anything that won't remind me of my wedding to Dax or the fact that he was a prisoner for too many years to count. One thing is for certain, it didn't seem to affect him outwardly. Sure, he has some new tattoos and a couple scars, but he holds himself well.

"What are you cooking?" I ask in a quick lull. It's my chance to change the subject.

He lets me skirt around Dax without fuss. "I made breakfast—mostly everything you used to like. You'll have to tell me if anything has changed." He's remembered sunny side up with crispy bacon after all this time? My heart thuds faster. This is the old Cody. My Cody: thoughtful to a fault, with a single goal to make me happy. He turns, a plate in his hand, and walks over to the table. "Sit," he orders. What can I say? I sit, taking a chair at the head of a long rectangular table in his empty dining room. If I speak loud enough it will echo in here.

Cody leans over and places the large plate in front of me, his lips next to my cheek. His head dips lower. I raise my chin up and close my eyes. "It's a new perfume," I say, explaining. I know exactly where he's going with this. If I'm being honest, it's why I sprayed this particular scent where I did. It's a game we always played. Mostly it was foreplay. Hot, fucking foreplay that causes my body to instantly respond like it always used to. I shudder and cross my legs underneath the table. I know he knows. Cody always has a way to tell when I'm horny out of my damn mind. It was his gift, now it may be my curse. Warm breath tickles the side of my face, and I breathe him inside me.

I turn to meet his smoldering gaze. I must look like an animal caught in headlights. "What's it smell like?" he asks, quirking one side of his mouth up. I wet my lips and exhale a pent-up breath. I know what happens next. He leans down further, until the hair on the top of his head tickles my chin and his face is mere inches from my chest. His nose is right at the V in my shirt where my cleavage is exposed. I hear my heartbeat in my ears and my breathing is rapid as I push out small controlled breaths through my mouth. Cody inhales deeply, and as he does, I breathe in, forcing my chest out. I feel the stubble on his face brush against me. I hold my breath there, stilling—wanting this contact I crave so badly. Dragging his nose over the swell of my breast, across my chest, and up the side of my neck, he pauses just beneath my ear. I tilt my head back, and he grabs a handful of my hair. "It smells fucking delicious," he whispers. I knew he'd like this one. A shiver runs down my spine and ricochets to every part of my body. Never in my wildest dream did I imagine feeling this again and it scares the shit out of me.

77

I snap out of it. "What are we doing?" I ask. "This isn't me. Oh my God, this isn't me, Cody." I pant, so caught up in everything. My love for Cody and Dax…my freaking wedding. I am a good person. Lainey Rosemont is no cheater, no matter the circumstance. Right? I don't even recognize myself right now. Cody morphs me into the person I was three years ago. The woman I was with him, before any of this happened.

Cody runs a hand through his hair. "I know. I know," he says, averting his eyes. He's a man and even he is having a hard time with this. "What do you want? Tell me."

I can't tell him the truth. That I want to go against every relationship rule and moral I've ever respected. "I have to go," I say, lying to him, myself, and the beautiful walls of this house. I'm an imposter. I get up and walk to the door, doing my best not to make eye contact. I'll falter. I want Cody so badly that every fiber in my being is pulling me in the opposite direction. My purse and shoes are under my arm and I'm outside in thirty seconds flat.

I hear him following. He sighs loudly. "Please don't go. Stay. We can talk," Cody says. "I made breakfast. You have to eat."

"Right. Talk. Eat breakfast. And then I'll leave," I reply, sarcasm dripping from my words. "Just shut the door, please. Shut it." I'm on this front porch with my back facing the door. "Don't talk. Just shut the door. That's what I want." He does. The heavy wood slides closed and I slump to the floor, sitting with my feet out in front of me. *Fuck, fuck, fuckity, fuck.* Cody's still on my skin and controlling my senses. I run my hands down my face and let myself cry. Just a little. And only because I know I can't control this. Cody and I have a love that overrules everything, including my petty morals. He didn't lock the door.

Standing, I turn and put my forehead against the cool wood. "If I do this there is no going back. I'm that woman. That type of person. Can I live with myself?" I ask myself aloud. The answer is a resounding *yes.* I've done worse—lived through things more horrible. I need him. Opening the door, I push my way in, leaving my things on his porch to find Cody waiting for me. His hands are by his sides and his knowing eyes size me up. We stare at each other, able to have a silent conversation. It requires a certain degree of closeness for that to happen. I'm not sure I have that with Dax and I'm supposed to marry him. Can we have a conversation with just a glance? That answer is a no. This is what I have with Cody and Cody alone. A ghost of a smile crosses Cody's face. He knew I wasn't truly leaving—expected that I'd barge back in.

"This," he says, pointing between us. "Doesn't make you a bad person, Lainey. It makes you human. With a pumping heart full of love for a man. Don't read

79

into any more than that. Okay? It's not easy for me either. Dax is a brother. He rescued me, for crying out loud. What we have is more. You can't bottle electricity. It's impossible. So how about we don't think about anything else and we let go? No sex." He closes his eyes and shakes his head. He wants to, but thinks we shouldn't. Noted.

I don't need to be told twice. The decision was made when I walked back into his world. I leap into his waiting arms and lock my lips with his. He carries me back over to the dining room table and sets me down. His gaze is focused, intent, and concerned.

"I want you and this, Cody." His white teeth peek out from behind his wet, pink lips. He's edible. Leaning down, Cody licks under my ear and then kisses my neck, his hot lips imprinting on my skin. I'll feel that kiss, that *real* kiss, on my neck forever. With my hands I reach up and grab his wrists. I have no control over them. I pull myself to stand, and taking that fucking hot dish towel from his shoulder, I wrap it around the back of his neck. With one hand on each end I have full control of his head. I hop up to sit on the table behind me and get on my knees so my gaze is level with his face.

Cody's eyes flare with interest, delight, with desire. "I'd rather have you for breakfast anyways," he says, letting me pull his head toward my own. The kiss on my neck burns with loneliness. I want more. "My turn,"

80

I say, not breaking eye contact. He smiles and that's the only approval I need. Tugging each end of the towel, I bring his neck to my face and watch his pulse flutter. I'm making him nervous. So far he's kept his hands down by his sides. Always the gentleman. Gently I press my lips to the exact spot his pulse hammers. I can feel it against my mouth, throbbing.

He smells like soap and like Cody. I inhale greedily, wanting more. Opening my mouth and placing my hands on the sides of his rough cheeks, I lick up his neck and under his chin and stop when my lips are a breath away from his. Cody opens his eyes and watches me for any clue of what I want to happen next. "You smell fucking delicious, too," I say, making sure my mouth brushes his as I speak. "I miss you, Cody." Once his name leaves my mouth, I lean my forehead against his. He bites his lip to keep from closing the distance between our lips. "I want you." The confession isn't as hard to make as I thought it would be. I said it out loud. I drop the towel and run my hands through his hair. It causes a riot of emotions. I need to be connected to him.

"You still the easy trigger, I see?" he growls, grabbing my hips, which I've worked overtime in the gym for, in his large hands. The grip is firm, sure. It tells me he not only remembers how to fix my breakfast, but also how to fuck me right into oblivion. I sigh at the heat of his fingers that wrap so perfectly around my body.

81

Looking directly into his clear, blue eyes, I confess, "Only for you." This is another forever moment. Like the time I said yes on top of a mountain and the first time he kissed me senseless after a Christmas party at my house, or the time we made love under the stars at an abandoned baseball field at night because we couldn't wait to get home—this is the first time I've felt like I've been home since he died.

He swallows and sucks in a deep breath. "You want me to fuck you right here on this table?"

CHAPTER EIGHT

Cody

I want to fuck her and fuck her and fuck her until my dick falls off and I know she's mine forever. Right now. Right here on this table I paid way too much money for. I will think of it as the 'got lucky' table from this day forth...a treasure to keep in the family for generations to come. Lainey has this incredibly petite body, all toned, tight and ready to rock. Time has treated her well. With my hands on her hips, I can feel her shiver each time I dig my fingers into her pale skin. Her long blonde hair falls in a particular way over her shoulders and down her back. Not quite wavy, not quite curly or straight, either—just perfectly so. Her parted lips are pink and full and glistening wet in invitation. When I first met her I assumed she was one of those women who know exactly how attractive they are. Upon further investigation, I realized she has no clue how her wide blue eyes make men crazy, all doe like and innocent with a razor's edge of sex. Sex. She's looking at me with those black-fringed sex eyes right now, begging for it—wanting *me*. She puts her small hands on the back of my head and runs her fingers through my hair. I groan.

Lainey finally responds to my question about fucking on the table. "Kiss me," she whispers, the sweet air from her mouth invading my space. Yes. A million times yes. I've waited years for this moment—dreamed about it when I was chained to a wall in a dank room with nothing to live for. I lived for her lips, knowing full well I'd probably never feel them again. She takes on a dreamlike quality. If I snap my fingers, will she disappear? Cradling her head in both of my hands, I lean down and bring my lips to hers. She moans into my mouth and responds right away by tilting her neck and sliding her hands down my chest, and down to the top of my jeans. I still, just a second, because I haven't been touched intimately in a long time and my senses are all over the fucking place. This is really happening. I have my Lainey again. She pauses, and I don't want that, so I put more force into the kiss, twining my tongue with hers, letting her know I'm okay. It's a familiar dance we both know well. She responds by leaning into me and pulling the top of my jeans toward her. I bring her back against the table, capturing her lips as she clings to me, pulling my weight on top of her.

Leaning back, I break the kiss and look at her. Stroking a piece of her blonde hair out of her face, I say, "This is real." Earlier she wanted to ask me about V and my time away. I could tell. She didn't. Lainey showing restraint is a bad work of art.

She looks just as mystified and excited. "This is *so* real," she replies, her eyes sparkling. "You should probably move my breakfast," she says quickly, keeping her hands wrapped around my neck. I need to catch my breath, so I take this opportunity to extricate myself and move the plate. The second I release her, she slides her shorts and panties off. I must look like a feral dog that has gone weeks without food as I stare at her. She smiles a knowing smile. "It's okay, I won't bite. We should probably take it slow." Quirking her head to the side, she bites her lip. Quite the opposite of what she just said, she peels her shirt and bra off and tosses them to the opposite end of the long table.

My jeans are already unbuttoned due to her handiwork, so I make light work of pulling my shirt off and approach her slowly—very slowly. I want to see every square inch of her to know if she still looks the same. The freckle by her belly button is still there, the scar on her ankle from ankle surgery is lighter, her tits—her gloriously natural tits—are pert and the perfect size. They fit in my hands like they were made for me. Lainey leans back and gives me this perfect bird's-eye view and then she lets her knees fall apart. My cock is straining against my jeans, and now that her shaved pussy is on full display I'm wasted with desire.

This may seem like an odd time to think about another man, but Dax slips in nonetheless. I can remind myself a million times that Lainey is mine, that she's always been mine, that we would be living happily ever after right now if not for V and his vindictive ways, and I'd still feel a twinge of guilt. She's been his for the stolen years. I called Dax. We spoke of Lainey and how he wants her to know she has options. He wants to win her fair and square. I didn't have the heart to tell him fair and square loses every single time. The option that Lainey is exercising at the moment has my mouth watering and my dick rapt at attention. A stronger man, a man with more integrity, would resist. I was stripped of everything, integrity included. I just want back what is rightfully mine.

"I want to kiss your entire body. You want that?" I ask, rubbing the insides of her thighs with the palms of my hands. Her body excites me. It's familiar and brand new at the same time. Everything washes away when I touch her. I can block my pain receptors with her pleasure. I can *forget*. "Every single square inch of you," I say, folding my hands around her tiny waist.

She nods, her doe eyes challenging me to merely kiss her. Smirking, I lean over her, drag my lips across her tits, down her stomach, and back up her neck to find her mouth. Lainey whimpers as I rest some of my body weight on top of her. My mouth is watering by the time I bring my lips on top of hers. Her scent is all around me, her warm skin is against my chest, and my cock is nestled right where it wants to be. How to tell her how much I've missed her? Or that her fucking gorgeous face is still the center of my universe? She grabs my face and deepens the kiss, her lips claiming me, and I find myself fighting to breathe. Lainey brings up her legs and locks them around my waist, capturing me to her. My jeans and boxers are still on and I'm thanking God I didn't take them off yet. Gently I slide down between her legs. She keeps her hands on the side of my face as I kiss her pussy. I trace the sides with my tongue, tasting her desire.

"Oh my God, Cody. Oh my God." I know the fucking feeling. Well. She leans back on her elbows, her gaze fixated on my mouth and herself.

I kiss her wet center and smile up at her. She bites her lip as her eyes grow large. She wants to know what I'll do next. A quick flick of my tongue and she closes her eyes briefly. I stop. She opens them. Wrapping my arms under her thighs, I scoot her closer to the edge of the table. I want access to all of her. I settle in between her thighs with my mouth, and taking one finger, I slip it into her slick core. Her muscles squeeze around me. My dick throbs in response. She leans her head back and moans as I start my assault, finger-fucking and licking her exactly how I know she loves. It's not long and her hips start rocking against me, forcing more of her sweet pussy into my mouth, and I know she's about to come. I keep up the same pace as she pulls her knees back and wide so she's splayed open, everything wet and turned on and explosive. Arching her back, she comes, her pussy gripping my finger over and over.

I don't stop, no. I keep licking and sucking her clit through her orgasm, because I know she has more for me. Lainey knows she does, too. Instead of guiding me up to kiss her, she holds my head steady. Her muscles still clenched tightly around my finger, I slip another inside and one more into her back door. I want to take out my cock and watch it disappear inside her pussy. My desire is growing by the second. The noises coming out of her mouth force the issue. She's begging me to fuck her. She needs me inside her. I lick her and fuck her senseless with my fingers. Lainey's body stiffens and she screams my name as she lets go one more time. This time she leans back on the table, her breathing audible and labored. She looks well fucked, but my cock begs to differ.

Slowly, I stand up and remove my throbbing dick from its boxer brief prison. She's still wide open, dripping with longing. She lifts her head to look at me...actually to look at my cock. It would be so easy to plunge into her. Not yet, though. Taking my heavy shaft into my hand, I tap it a few times on her wet slit.

So easy to fill her small body with my huge dick, stretch her until she's full of only me.

"Oh, God," Lainey moans. She wants it. After two orgasms, she's ready. We both watch as I take the head of my dick and tease it at her opening. I slip the head in just a touch. Only enough to make it a little wet and I hiss out a breath. It would feel so good. I need to stop right now. "Yes, yes," she exclaims, her gaze fixed on my dick. When she meets my eyes, I smirk, snap my underwear back in place, and take a gigantic step back. She's panting, smiling, flushed and all fucking mine.

I sigh. Self-control is something I'm trained in—an art form, if you will. They torture me for information, and I tell them to eat my asshole and bring me a beer. Things would have gone more smoothly for me in captivity if I had practiced self-control, if I had given them the information they wanted. Of course, information isn't the reason they took me in the first place. V is much smarter and crueler than that.

Lainey leaps off the table and into my arms. I pick her up and she wraps her naked body around me. "Was it just like it used to be?" I ask, breathing in the sharp flowery smell of her shampoo. I want to drown in this scent. I would've given up all the information if they promised me this scent.

"No," she whispers into my neck. Furrowing my brow, I pull back and look at her face.

"No?"

She smiles her megawatt, movie star smile, smoothens the skin in between my eyes, and says, "It's even better. It's just like *now*. We may need to practice a few more things. You know? While I'm figuring everything out."

Lainey hits her knees in front of me and flashes that beautiful grin back up at me. She begins humming the star spangled banner around my cock and I'm certain that no matter what happens next, this is worth it.

It's worth everything.

CHAPTER NINE

Lainey

Vanity is a fundamental of human civilization. There are those who shun it, those who embrace it, and those who drip that shit from every pore on the surface of their bodies. More often than not, the people we're trying to impress do not care. They just don't. That vanity? It's all for ourselves. Like a Christmas gift of undue stress you bought for yourself and can't return. It's funny the way it works. I've come to realize it's vanity that has me in this situation to begin with. The mentality that I can have two amazing men at the same time has fucking vain roots. One day with Cody and I know I need to break up with Dax, call off the wedding and leave him bereft with grief. We didn't even have sex. I mean, we did everything but, and I felt so much all at once. Chloe called it a nostalgia hookup, but it was so much more. That's what makes things between

Dax and I that much more complicated. It's like a Band-Aid I just need to rip off. I just compared my relationship with Dax to a Band-Aid. *What is wrong with me?*

Cradling my cell phone on my shoulder, I type an email to Dax and speak to Marney. "Of course I can have the samples for you when we meet at the textile store. I'll see you there in an hour," I say. Marney tells me about a couch she saw in Cosmo and asks if I can find something similar, to which I agree, knowing there's no way in hell she'll want to pay for it. I jot down a couple notes on my planner and hang up the call. I read over the harmless email I typed to my fiancé and decide I'll call him instead.

It rings twice and he gives me a breathless, "Hello."

"Hey-ya," I say, relieved and sick at the sound of his voice. How did this happen? Why?

"Lane," Dax breathes. "Spare me the details." I glance at my oversized watch and realize I probably interrupted him at the gym. The clank of weights confirms my suspicions. I choose to ignore the fact that he actually thinks I've called to give him the blow by blow about Cody. Literally. "We on for dinner tonight?" It's Friday. It's our date night.

"Sure, yeah." It will be my opportunity to talk to him face to face. My stomach fills with dread.

Dax breathes out loudly. "I talked to him, you know? He called me and wanted to feel me out about the situation going on."

Dread turns to fear. "Oh?"

"I told him the same thing I told you. How am I supposed to marry a woman who has unfinished business? I'm not sure how this is all going to shake out, but I want you to know that despite my misgivings about whatever is going on between the two of you, I'm okay. Don't worry about me, Lainey. Seriously. I've made my choices…probably questionable ones, but I stand by them. I stand by you. He wants to take you away to the Hamptons."

This is news to me. All of it. "He asked permission?"

"No. He's trying to be as honorable as he can given the fact that you have my ring on your finger, Lainey." I glance at the diamond, once a source of great joy, and have to swallow down bile.

"Well, I guess I'm just the town whore. I should stake out a corner in a dark alley and sell my services." I'm half joking. I'm not a damsel in distress by any means. Not by a long shot.

"Don't be melodramatic. I have to go finish up here. Tonight is mine," he says, hanging up the call. Fuck. God dammit. There's no question what I'll be doing tonight. With Dax. Not Cody. I never thought I'd be the one unable to hold up the end of the two-timing relationship deal. I was the lucky one, right? I'll have to talk to Dax before it gets to that. Since my afternoon with Cody I have a profound sense of cheating on him

93

with Dax all this time. It's nonsensical, of course. The laptop pings a new email alert. My heart leaps into my throat. It's a note from Cody. When he was deployed, he would email me every day. Seeing his name in my personal inbox, an address that not many people have, has always been a jolt of happiness and excitement. Nothing has changed. If anything the feeling has intensified. I can't click open quick enough.

From: Cridge@ridgecontract.com

To: LaineyRostov@Memail.com

Subject: The Star Spangled Banner

I suspect your intended has spoken to you about my plans for the Hamptons. I wanted to surprise you like I used to, but the extenuating circumstances we face take the surprise out of it. What do you say? A couple days away? For old times' sake? I've booked airline tickets. You should receive them by email shortly. We'll return home by private aircraft.

I took a break from coding to research the national anthem of fifteen other countries. I'm sure they'd sound divine as a hum.

I miss you.

C

I smile from ear to ear, forcing crow's feet to the corners of my eyes, and I don't even care. I reread the note a few times, trying to pick up on subtle clues. He's able to hide behind his words well. Other than a hint of jealousy over the fact that I'm wearing Dax's ring, there's nothing to be detected. I love the Hamptons: the beach, the parties, the oversized cottages smack-dab on the oceanfront. Of course I want to go and be there with Cody. I compose a new email.

From: LaineyRostov@Memail.com

To: Cridge@ridgecontract.com

Subject: Coveted humming abilities

I really wish you and Dax didn't talk. It makes this weird. Well, it's super weird anyways, but it makes it even more so. Like I'm the child and you're sharing custody of me. I have a meeting in a bit, but can we meet up later? I need to talk to you in person. I'm not sure how much longer I can do this.

I miss you always.

L (Hums-like-an-old-refrigerator)

He doesn't reply by email, he calls. Exiting my office to head for the garage, I answer the call.

"How much longer you can do what?" Cody asks.

I smile because it's his voice, but I sigh because I wanted to see him when I spoke with him. It's the only way I'll truly know how he feels. "I said in person, Cody," I say, my tone mocking. I pick up fabric samples from the table in the back foyer and open the garage.

"Right. You did. I'm driving to your house now."

I glance down at my Patek Philippe watch. "Now?"

"I'm leaving for a few days." That's the only explanation I'll get. I rub my forehead. Marney.

I throw the fabric in the backseat of my overpriced European coupé and slam the door. "I have a meeting with a client right now," I tell him.

I see his large SUV gleam in the distance. He really was driving to my house—a fact that shouldn't surprise me. He must have been emailing on his cell. "I just need to see you. Please. Ten minutes," he says, his black polished vehicle turning into my driveway and winding its way toward where I stand. The gravelly noise his tires make as they crunch their way toward me is exciting. I want to see him. I need to see him. He pulls up as close to my garage as he can get…blocking me in.

"Ten minutes," I whisper into the mouthpiece. He grins at me through his windshield, exposing white teeth. Sunglasses hide his eyes, but I already know exactly how they shine when he smiles this wide.

I walk over to his driver's side door as he hops out. With the cell phone still pressed to his ear, he says, "You're okay?" Odd question.

I hang up my phone and throw it into the bag on my shoulder. "I'm fine. Why wouldn't I be okay?" I slit my eyes, wary of his response. Even wary, I can't help but drink him in like a tall glass of water. His proximity will never get old. It reminds me why I need to talk to him.

He plays it cool, all shrugging his shoulders and sliding from his seat with the grace of a panther. Cody folds his arms around me and pulls me so close that every inch of the front of my body is pressing against his. I see him glancing around my house from my peripheral vision, and I know something's off. Burying my face in his neck, I inhale. "I'm more than okay now." I raise his glasses. "Something you want to tell me?"

He shakes his head. "Nah. I just worry about you. That's all." A funny thing happens. I can't really tell what he's thinking. Not the way I used to, anyways. "You said you weren't sure how long you could do this. I need details." He takes his glasses from me and folds them into the collar of his shirt. I let my hands wander down from his shoulders to his biceps. He flexes them briefly and smiles.

"What do you want, Cody?" Pain flashes in his eyes, but the mask goes up directly following. "After...everything," I stutter. "It would be presumptuous of me to assume anything about your feelings for me. I need to know where we stand. What do you want?" I ask again.

He grabs my waist. "I want you. How could you not understand that already?"

My hands wander down to his forearms. "You want me now today or forever? Or maybe a time in between those two?"

"Always. Always, Fast Lane. I want you forever. This is hard for me, too. Sharing isn't a word in my repertoire." It shouldn't be in mine either. His gaze darts to the water on the side of my house. My island doesn't feel as safe as it did five minutes ago.

Focusing on the task at hand, I lean my head against his chest. "I need to break up with Dax." I don't need to explain. I owe it to Dax to keep the explanations for him. I feel Cody's hand in my hair and his kiss on the top of my head.

"I'm sorry for this." His voice is low and coiled with control. "I'd deal with it if I could. I'd make the pain go away if there was a way."

I shake my head. "It's my fault. I never stopped loving you, Cody. I should have. My God, I should have." I look up to meet his gaze, ice blue, so much like Dax's. "He saved me, but you own me."

With the hands that are still in my hair, he brings my face up to meet with his, our lips touching in the barest flutter of a kiss. Not enough to taste him, but enough to know he's mine right back. "Be mine again. All mine." There's that word again. I think of Dax.

"That's the problem," I say, my lips touching his as I speak. "I've never not been yours, Cody." He kisses me madly, profoundly, passionately. Cody takes my hips and pulls me against his erection. It throbs into my stomach, causing my core to clench with desire. Every nerve ending in my body catches fire. I feel tingly. I feel warm. I feel *him*. He goes willingly as I back him against his truck, pinning his hands by his shoulders with my own.

"Hey, now. You said ten minutes," Cody says against my mouth. I touch the sides of his face to feel his stubble and let my tongue fall into rhythm with his. He brings one hand between my legs and presses it against my clit through my jeans. "We can make it ten hours if you want." He moves his fingers and presses a little harder. No, ten hours won't be enough. The rest of my life won't be enough.

"I need to go," I pant. My body is telling him I want everything except to leave his presence. He snakes his glorious fingers back and breaks the kiss, leaving my mouth and pussy wet, and my lips raw from the onslaught of his teeth and lips. Cody does everything violently perfect and with intention. Anyone would appreciate his affections.

Cody's eyes are heavy—turned on. He bites his own red, bottom lip. "So, go," he says, smiling— challenging. I swallow, brush my tangled hair from my face, and take a few deep breaths. Leaning over, I put my hands on my knees and try to take in more oxygen. Cody removes the air from my body. He takes everything from me and strips me bare down to my bones. "The Hamptons, then?" he says, pushing away from his SUV with one arm. I take a measured step back. He's making a promise to finish what we've started.

I nod. "Yes. The Hamptons." I'm ready. It's hard to keep things PG-13 when we've dipped into the triple X zone a million times in the past. Sex is off the table now only because of Dax. Neither of us has voiced it, nor have we spoken about him at all actually, but he takes up a lot of real estate in our relationship. Taking another step back, I put more space between us. "I'll talk to him before we leave."

"Don't feel too bad, Fast Lane. He's a smart guy," Cody says. He pulls on the tips of his hair. The sleeves of his shirt bunch up, exposing muscle and tattoo. I have to close my eyes to clear my head.

Clearing my throat, I ask, "Of course he's smart, but how is that supposed to help me feel less guilty?" Mustering strength, I make a go for it and walk into my garage.

Cody follows and opens my car door for me. "He knew this would be the outcome. There's no way he figured this would end any differently, Lane. He knows you. He knows me. He knew us."

Sitting down behind the steering wheel, I look up at him. "I feel so bad. So guilty." I can't stand myself. I fold my arms and let my head fall on the steering wheel.

He clears his voice and takes a deep breath. "Sometimes you have to be recklessly heartless in order to realize you own a heart," Cody says. I feel his lips on my hair and smell his cologne, and then he shuts the door and leaves me with his words ricocheting around my world.

I jump out of my car and catch him as he's pulling himself into his own vehicle. "I do have a heart," I explain. I feel the need to defend myself against what he's said even though I know it's true. I know he didn't say it maliciously.

Cody smiles. "I don't want your heart, Fast lane. You already have mine. Forever. For a man like me, that's enough." *What does that mean?*

I don't have time to ask. He shuts his door and backs out of my driveway and out of my fucking vain world.

CHAPTER TEN

Cody

She had the courage to do it. Lainey broke it off with her fiancé. He's standing here in my home office in Virginia Beach right now, flaming mad and with intent. It's six a.m. He's losing Lainey. Blaming him is the last thing I'll do. Dax Redding was merely a pawn, or perhaps a knight, in our twisted love game. The comfort, love, and support he provided Lainey was integral to her healing. I know her well enough to know she may be a piranha in many ways, but emotionally she can be manipulated and destroyed. She wouldn't be the same woman if it weren't for him. I'm grateful to him. I also fucking *hate* him.

I'm shirtless, sitting at my desk, feet propped up. When he started banging on my door before the sun rose I was sure it was V and his men. Dax was a pleasant surprise. It's too early for gun fights and bloody hardwood. Although, I'm still not sure it's not going to happen. "Lainey can make her own decisions, man. Nothing was said to influence her to do anything. She does exactly as she pleases. You must know that," I explain. He paces the hardwood—his boots making a clipping sound with every step he takes.

"Bullshit. You couldn't send her away, start new with someone else when you saw she was happy with me? You're a fucking con artist!" he yells.

Swinging my legs to the floor, I stand and adjust the waist of my pajama bottoms. Dax glares at me, eyeing my tattoos with an eagle eye. None of them will mean anything to him. I'm sure he's looking for anything related to Lainey. I purposefully avoided that type of tattoo because it would have been unsafe. I walk to the window on the side of the rectangular room and look out as he continues his pacing. What can I tell him to get him the fuck out of here? I wonder if Lainey is okay. I miss her.

"She came to me. She came to me," I say, my tone low. The condescension sticks to my words like glue. "What is it you want to hear me say? What do you want, Dax?"

He stops around eight feet behind me. I mentally calculate how he may attack. There are several ways and I'm ready for all of them. He clears his throat. He must want a fight. It's the only thing a man like him, in his situation, is capable of. "I'm well aware she came to you. I came here to give you something in exchange for something else." My brows rise on their own accord. I wasn't expecting this.

I spin on my bare foot to face him. "Talk." The energy in the room has shifted. A smile stretches across his face and I see something I've never seen before. A sinister cunning. Somehow I know that whatever he says next will be a game changer. He's not a sad man torn up about losing the love of his life. This is something different altogether. "Go on. Talk," I encourage, raising my chin.

He steps toward me. We're eye to eye, heart to heart. "Admit that I'm the better choice for Lainey."

That's easy. "You're the better choice for her. But your choice doesn't fucking matter. It's her choice and she's made it. Why not respect that?" Anger vibrates my bones.

He shakes his pointer finger back and forth like some poindexter on steroids. Lainey has a type. That's for sure. "She's confused. Lainey is confused by her feelings for you. She'd be easily convinced that I'm the man for her with a small nudge in the right direction. I love her, Cody. I fucking love her more than anything. A man like you can understand desperation. This is me crawling from desperation. I want you to break up with her. Tell her I'm the man she needs. The man she wants. Tell her so she believes you." He's lost his goddamn mind. Narrowing my eyes, I look at him closely. Is he feeling ill? Perhaps he's taken drugs.

When I realize he's serious, I scoff, laughing. "I get it. But what can possibly make you think I would agree to this? You're utterly mad. Why would I hurt the woman I love, as well?"

There's no hesitation in his response. He's giddy to tell me. "I have something you want more." There's nothing I want more than her.

Shaking my head, I laugh. It's boisterous and calculating. "No." No need to spend any more breath on a drawn out response. I pick up my cell phone and text Molly. I need to make sure everything is running on schedule, perhaps even early as now I have an entire morning free. I glance up when I hear the silence.

Dax licks his lips. "We have intel you want, Cody. I know where *he* is. We've got a tracker on him." The smile falls from my face and appears on his.

"Where is he?" I can't help it. I ask even knowing what the cost will be. The SEALs surely have intel I don't quite have yet. He's not lying and that makes every fiber in my being squeeze with anticipation. No more hunting. I could be done with V forever. We've had leads during the past weeks and then we lost him. There's no telling where he's at. I'm worried for Lainey. "Tell me."

Dax's smile grows. "You already know what I want in exchange."

I roll my eyes to the ceiling. "Blackmail? Really?

And with Lainey? Even I couldn't convince her that you're the right man for her. Because you aren't." Harsh truths never killed anyone. I have, though, and so has Dax.

Dax starts pacing again. This time it's not as calculated, he's erratic. He was right about the level of his desperation. He could lose his job over this, possibly even face prison time if it's spun the right way. Christ, he could lose his life. I have to respect that. I remember being an upstanding man. How difficult and demanding walking the straight and narrow was. He's cracking. For love. For Lainey.

"You tell me where V is and you get Lainey? That's the deal then?" I confirm, walking up behind him to stop his irritating walk. My floors are new. He's fucking them up.

A bead of sweat slides down his temple. The wall clock ticks away seconds that sound like hours. The blood in my body whooshes with desire to kill. Retribution will be mine. Can I make this sacrifice? My happiness forever gone in exchange for V's life snuffed? There's no choice, really.

"She has to believe that you don't want her, that I'm better for her. That's the deal," Dax says, voice rising. That will be easier said than done. She's keen. Sharp. Lainey knows me well. I close my eyes, wincing at the image of her when I tell her bold faced lies that she will take at face value because of her emotional

106

vulnerability. My hands on my hips I glance at my desk and the stupid plastic dancing flower she gave me. I walk over and swipe it off my desk and into the wall. I swear under my breath and lean over my desk, placing my palms down.

Hanging my head, I say, "Give me The Hamptons first." It's not a question.

Dax's silence lets me know he's considering. "Fine. I'll send over the information as soon as you return. And, Cody? She can never know." My heart is pumping so hard I can barely breathe.

"Yeah," I agree. If she found out about this she would kill him and be crushed by my decision. Just as she can't know about our deal, neither of them can know why I'm accepting it. He's clueless.

"Get the fuck out of my house," I whisper.

Dax, standing a few inches shorter than me, approaches. "Is that any way to treat the person who saved your life?" Dax smiles meanly. I don't owe him anything. "Nice doing business with you. Maybe the next time I kiss my fiancée she won't taste like revenge."

I can't help it. I really can't. I break his pretty fucking nose with my fist.

"She won't. But her lips will taste like my dick," I say, walking out of my office and closing the door. I'll give him the courtesy of privacy while he pulls his shit together and then proceeds to be wrapped up in my girl's arms. The acrid tasting vomit rises from my stomach and I barely make it to the bathroom in time.

It doesn't take three years for things and people to change. Sometimes all it takes is one second—a second in which everything shifts.

Including hearts.

****

If I had three words to describe my years in captivity they would be pain, darkness, and blood—heavy on the pain, and not just the physical kind. Psychologically it messed with every neuron in my fucking brain. I'm not sure how much time passed before I accepted that it was my new life. I contemplated offing myself, but V and his men rarely gave me the means or the opportunity, watching me like a hawk and draining me of all excess energy. Sure, there were days when I was released from my cell, but those days didn't come until the end, when they were sure I was fucked up in the head enough to not want to run, or fight. Then there was the fake video that I helped make showing my death. They sent it to the U.S. media as proof that I was a goner. I made sure that video was perfect. It was a tech job similar to what I used to do for a living. Its perfection is what ensured that everyone would stop looking for me. Figuring that would be the best outcome for all involved, I worked tirelessly. When V was happy with it and was sure there were no sneaky concealed messages within, he sent it to Lainey first. It was relief and heartache at the same time. When SEALs came to rescue me, I wasn't expecting it. It was surreal and attached was a dreamlike quality.

I wonder how quickly I can do three thousand push-ups. Six million sit-ups? How many drips would pass? The drip of water in the corner of my room is steady. It falls from a cracked, black stone in the ceiling. It's lulling like a clock ticking or a fan blowing. The first six months the sounds of the tiny splashes of water made me murderous. It comforts me now. It's time passing, bringing me closer to death and whatever comes after that. They brought someone else in last night. He's wailing down the hall and I really wish he would shut the fuck up. It's making me lose count. I've been able to calculate a formula for figuring out how many days pass by the drips and the guard schedule.

"Dinner, X?" my current guard asks, interrupting my count. They've distanced me from my real name in an attempt to convert me to their beliefs. V knows that will never happen, but still insists that I respond to the one lettered moniker. From my small bed in the corner I reply that I am indeed hungry. Hopefully he'll bring me the good food—what the guards eat, not the slop they give the rest of us. He saunters off to the above ground kitchen and I hear him strike the wailing asshole down the hall on his way by. At least I get preferential treatment after all these years. It could

always be worse, Cody. *My name sounds foreign in my own mind. At this point it's a romantic notion, really.*

Three hundred and sixty-two drips before my guard gets back with the good meal. I open the door to my cell when I hear footsteps approaching. They don't lock me in anymore. Where would I go? When I peer down the stone-walled corridor, it's not the guard I see, it's red sight dots glowing and black figures shifting toward me. Fear escalates into something larger as my stomach drops. Familiarity washes over me, but I still can't connect the dots. I'm too damaged, lost.

One of the gun wielding men yells, "Get down!" I hit my knees. This is it. Someone will finally put me out of this misery, *I think. Death is mine. It's mine. Mine. How many more drips will it take? How accurate can my count be? The shackles around my ankles and wrists prevent me from surrendering fully, but I'm compliant as they approach the screaming asshole first and then me. I recognize a voice—it's one from my old life.*

"Cody. Cody, is that really you? Cody?" Steve says, his voice muffled. These men aren't here to kill me. They're here to save me. These are my brothers. The motherfucking SEALs have finally arrived. How did they know? Thirty-two more drips. I can't respond.

"There's no fucking way. No way," another SEAL says, his gear weighing him down. "How is this possible?" I'm wondering the same thing. Being

110

rescued from this dank dungeon was never a possibility I considered. Why should I? I died when that video released to the world. The SEAL I don't recognize comes and kneels in front of me, squinting his eyes as he examines me. A bead of sweat rolls down his face and drips onto his radio. I count that one, too.

Another man I recognize. "It's him, Dax," Maverick Hart, SEAL extraordinaire, says to the man in front of me. "We need to get him the fuck out of here quick. That little shit rat upstairs said other guards would be here soon." Gunfire lights the air, screams and shouts litter my cold, dark air, and I lose my fucking count. Logically I know what will happen next, they are going by the textbook, but I can't move. The one they call Dax snaps the shackles off. He keeps looking at me oddly.

My first word. "V," I whisper. He hears me over the commotion.

Dax nods. "We'll get him." My heart sinks. He's alive. I'll never be truly free until he's a rotting piece of flesh and broken bones. He shakes his head as he helps me to my feet. "How?" he says, placing his hands on my dirty shoulders. I flinch. "No," he mutters sadly. "No." He hands me a jacket from his pack and a pair of boots…things I haven't had since I was stolen from my life.

I shrug, not knowing what he wants or what he's asking. He guides me out of my prison and into the light

111

and safety of a waiting chopper and then a secure base. The men overwhelm me with a bunch of questions I'm unsure how to answer. Confusion and disbelief war with hope. I only have one question for them before they leave me to myself for the night.

"Lainey?" I ask Maverick.

He smiles, but it fades quickly. He glances behind him and meets Dax's laser gaze, but turns back to me. "She's great, Cody. Lainey is well. Get some rest, dude. Tomorrow will be a long day."

That's enough for now. I curl up on the bed in medical and my head is met with a soft pillow. For the first time since V fucked up my world, I let myself plan a future. The drips that fall into my IV line hydrating my body help me think clearly. It only takes six hundred drips for me to know exactly what my purpose in life will be.

Drip.

Drip.

Drip.

Revenge.

CHAPTER ELEVEN

Lainey

Waiting for my trip away with Cody is torture. When I spoke with Dax regarding how I was feeling about our relationship and the wedding, he freaked the fuck out. I expected that. Then he went to Cody's house at six in the goddamned morning for reasons I'll never know. I didn't expect that. The outcome? I know every gory detail. Dax texted me a photo of his broken, bloody nose while I was in a morning meeting with a client. We happened to be selecting high-end living room furniture when I glanced at my phone. I felt horrible for him. Then I got angry because he was obviously using it for sympathy and to show me how 'bad' Cody is. Something Cody knows and Dax doesn't is that I can read between the lines better than anyone I know. Don't ever play mind games with a woman like me. It's the first time Dax has shown me such an unflattering side to his personality. In my defense, I tried to break it off fully right then and there. Our relationship, our wedding—cut ties completely. I owe him that even if he is game playing. He refused. Dax said I was confused and that I needed more time to sort through my feelings.

More time to fall more deeply in love with Cody? That's what Dax is giving me. How do I explain that without sounding like a jerk, though? Cody's work schedule was hectic leading up to our trip, so I was surprised when I got home from a work coffee meeting mid-morning to find a gift on the table in my entryway. Chloe stopped by to help me pack for the weekend and I said my dreary goodbyes to Dax last night.

"Shiny package," Chloe rasps, grabbing the black box off the marble surface. "What's inside?" She fakes that she's going to open it, but tosses it to me instead. I catch the small package easily. My first guess is jewelry. It's not from a store I recognize. "Your vagina must be made of solid gold. Or maybe diamonds. Not sharp ones, though. I've never seen men act like this over one woman before. Can I see it? Show me the goods. Your pussy, not the bauble. That's got me curious like whoa."

I sigh, shaking my head at my friend. "It's too early for that. My vagina is staying in my panties...for now. Dax and Cody aren't acting any weird way. The circumstances are, well...they're different for us. I tried to do the honorable thing. Dax prefers scandal. Obviously. I just don't see how breaking up with him later as opposed to sooner isn't in everyone's best interest. I'm not sure where his mind is at." I contemplate things from his perspective for a few moments as I toss the package from one hand to the other. It makes little sense. My feelings for Cody are so evident that it makes me sick thinking I'm engaged to be married to a different man. "Go start finding me stuff to wear. I'll order lunch in," I say. "If you're a good girl, I'll let you catch a glimpse of Katrina before I jump in the shower." She laughs. I laugh and Chloe saunters off, shaking her head. It's hard to find a best friend who gets your disgusting humor without flinching.

The tiny gray card reads, "Wear this so I'll know..." *Know what?* I slide my finger under the fold of black wrapping paper and open the velvet box that hides inside. It's a bracelet—delicate in form, shiny, with larger teardrop diamonds hanging every few inches. It's rose gold and utterly stunning. I forget about the ominous message on the card as I fasten it around my left wrist. Cody's tastes are exquisite. My engagement ring, riding high only a couple inches above the bracelet, won't do. I slide it off and head to my room to secure it in my jewelry box. I tell myself it's for safekeeping, not because I never plan on wearing it again. "I tried," I say aloud. I really did. The front door opens and slams. Chloe giggles from her seat in the center of my bed.

"I told Morganna to come over," she says, raising the magazine she's reading directly in front of her face. Our bull-nosed friend has an opinion about everything. I'm sure she'll have a lot to say about my current predicament.

I groan. "You told her, didn't you?" Morganna is an attorney who is married to a SEAL. This is either going to go one of two ways.

I look at the ceiling and pray. Morganna saunters in, a knowing smile on her face. "Well, what do you have to say for yourself?"

Cocking my head, I meet her gaze. "You're not my mother, Morg."

She clucks her tongue. "You're right. I wouldn't accept this behavior from my child. What you're doing to Dax is hideous. The poor man kept my husband out until three a.m. He was crying into his bourbon with a crooked nose." Okay, so it's going *that* way.

Goosebumps prickle my skin. "He wouldn't let me call off the wedding yet. What should I do? Wait, better yet…what would you have done in my predicament?" Morganna lost her first husband, also a SEAL, to a tragic accident during a deployment. She remarried Steve, another SEAL, and now lives happily ever after. "What if Stone came back before you married Steve?" Not many people are brave enough to bring up his name in casual conversation. I'm one of the few who can get away with it.

I watch Morganna swallow. It forces her to raise her chin. Chloe hops off the bed and busies herself in my kitchen, because honestly, who really wants to be in this conversation. I'm sure she didn't know what she was doing when she invited Morg over. Morganna turns her face toward the window facing the ocean. "I don't know what I would have done." Her hundred yard stare grows sad.

"Exactly," I mutter. Lightly I pull on one of the diamonds on my new bracelet. "I loved Cody first. The reminder of his love haunted me when he was gone. What do you think it does now that he's here? In front of me, touching me, holding me, kissing me, loving me? I'm coming apart at the seams, Morganna. Dax's love saved me from being haunted. It's real now. I don't need saving. I know how selfish and awful that sounds, but even Dax wouldn't accept that as a reason to call off the wedding. He's being odd lately. He knows where my heart and mind are, yet he's holding out failing hope." The diamonds on my wrist catch the sun and cause a rainbow to shine against the wall.

She sees the colors and follows them back to my wrist with her gaze. "Of course," Morganna says, voice clipped. "You're in a position most can only dream of. Difficult, yes, but lucky still the same." She traces my wrist with her fingertip. I wince when I think of what

Morganna went through when Stone died. It's hard not to dwell on the awful. She has a beautiful, full life now, but she carries her losses well. Interrupting my thoughts, she asks, "It's pretty. New?"

"Yes. He'll be here any moment to pick me up for a few days. Chloe was supposed to help me pack and give me an illustrated sex talk, I'm sure." Morganna laughs and goes through a stack of blouses I have on the bed, unfolding and refolding a different way.

"You don't need clothes. I think that's the obvious answer. Pack a toothbrush and your stamina," she says, grinning from ear to ear. Her demeanor changes completely now. "He hasn't gotten laid in a while," Morganna explains. I laugh, but the joke causes my stomach to flutter. Am I truly the last person he's made love to? "When you get home from your trip you really need to deal with Dax, though."

I promise to give it my best effort and we talk a little more about her son and Steve, her horses, and how busy she is with a toddler and her law career. I tell her about several of my design clients and how my mother is going to have a fit over the cancelled wedding. She laments, tells me she'll help me get deposits back if I really want, and then tells me a funny story about her and our friend Windsor. Morganna walked in on her getting her bikini line waxed on a dining room table the night she planned on doing the deed. I obviously reject Morganna's offer to do the same for me. I took care of that a few days ago, like you're supposed to, not the day of. We make our way into the living area to find Chloe waiting patiently for us with a teakettle whistling in the kitchen.

Morganna leans back into the sofa and takes the tea Chloe offers. I make myself a cup and begin pacing. Do I want my friends here when Cody arrives? Will that be awkward because they've been used to seeing me with Dax? I know Morganna's torn about what I'm doing with both of these men.

"Oh, by the way," Morganna says over her shoulder. "I finally sold the house next door. An investment group bought it. Hopefully tenants from hell don't move in and throw eggs at your expensive front door." We all laugh and then Chloe starts chattering away about Morganna's shoes. Hm. That's news. Pulling my gauzy curtains aside, I peek out to catch a glimpse of Morganna's old mansion. She's taken care of it, so it looks the same as it did before she moved out. It's a touch larger than my own house, with floor-to-ceiling windows that peer out in all directions. If someone were standing in the upstairs living area, they'd see me right now. I shiver.

The doorbell rings and my pulse skitters, hammering in my temples and stomach. Morganna snickers. Chloe rises ostensibly to get the door, but I beat her to it, pulling it open and stepping back. Cody, dressed in jeans and a T-shirt, wearing a half grin and messy hair, puts up one large palm to wave. "You," he says, as he lets his hand drop. He wants to pull me close. I sense it in the way his hands move. They reach up for me ever so subtly.

I sigh. "You," I return our unconventional hello. "Come in. Morganna and Chloe were just leaving. Let me grab my bag." Morganna laughs. She knows how little is actually in my bag. Cody saunters into the living area with more confidence than he has any right to have and grins at the women.

"Ladies. Ladies. How is your week going?" Rolling my eyes, I take the last swig of tea from my cup, slam it on the counter, and head for my bedroom.

Morganna and Chloe make small talk. I hear Chloe cackle in her raspy, flirty accent. Then Cody asks about the new owners. Morganna explains that she hasn't had much to do with the sale and thinks they're nice people. Or serial killers. She's not quite sure. I shake my head at her dry humor, so unlike my own. Cody's voice grows closer. I know he's behind me without even looking. I can sense his presence from a mile away. "You haven't changed the house much," he says. Yeah, but everything else has changed. "I like what you've done in the hallway."

I turn on my heel to face him. "Thanks, yeah, it needed a pop of color. I have some design catalogs we can go through to help spruce up your house if you want to take a look with me." His blue eyes narrow and a ghost of a smile appears on his lips. Other ideas, ones that don't involve going through catalogs, are running through his mind. Playing it cool, I nod. "Okay. I'll leave them at home."

He nods, crosses the distance between us, and pulls me into his arms. "I've needed you this close since the second you opened the front door," he whispers, his lips at my ear. Sighing, I lean into his chest further and breathe him in.

"We need to get out of here as soon as possible, Cody." I have visions of Dax strolling in the front yard with a head wrap and an Uzi, opening fire on anything that moves. Not really, but he's acting strange and with strange comes volatile. "I'm sure you know Dax is still in the picture," I say. One would think I'd be upset or heartbroken, but honestly, I'm just pissed and confused.

Cody pushes me away gently and takes a large step back. He looks out the window to the left, avoiding eye contact completely. He's about to lie. It's a tell. I sigh. You know that feeling when the bagboy calls you ma'am? A little confused, a little glad their mama taught them manners, but a whole lot of "shit, they won't be checking out my ass when I leave the store"? That's the strange feeling I'm comparing this to. "No fault of my own. You must know how twisted up about this he is seeing as you granted him a broken nose." I'm half joking, but Cody winces. "He can be persistent," I say, trying again.

He coughs and covers his mouth with his fist. "Lainey, right now I don't give a flying fuck about him. I'm sorry I broke his nose. He was being an ass and it was early in the morning, and the list could go on, but I won't make any excuses." Good, I wouldn't believe any of them, anyways. Cody fixes me with his beautiful gaze. "We do need to get out of here as soon as possible, but not for any other reason except I want to get you out of here so I can fuck you. And then fuck you some more. And when you think I'm done, make love to you so goddamned thoroughly, that neither of us remembers we live on planet Earth." Maybe he will be checking out my ass when I leave, then.

My neck works as I swallow. I can only formulate three words. "Good. Let's go."

So we do.

****

The Hamptons are just how I remembered them. Sunny, beachy, a little bit Cape Cod on steroids. I haven't been here for years and years. Since I went with Cody. It's another place his death marred that I can now have back. I thought Dax would give me a new lease on life. Now I realize it wouldn't have been the life I craved. It would have been his version of perfect, not mine. I sense Cody glancing at me as I stare out the window, smiling when we pass something nostalgic as we drive.

A car met us at the airport and I'm officially curious about Cody's financial status. I make very good money with my interior design business, but the bulk of my financial success is due to good ole' Uncle Rostov and my bottomless trust fund. I'm an only niece to a Russian man with no children. This isn't information I'd ante up for just anyone. There's a handful of people who truly know the extent of my wealth and that's only because they were smart enough to dig around. Cody's always lived on a Navy SEALs salary, which is more than the average sailor, but still, it's government work. Now that he's a contractor, and serious into his coding, doing heaven knows what for money, I wonder what he makes.

His hand, warm and big, engulfs the skin just above my knee. "What's on your mind?" he asks.

The past. The beach. Your paycheck. Your dick. "Nothing. I haven't been here in a while. Which house did you rent?" We had a few houses in rotation when we would frequent here back in the day—all of them large and on the beach, with the weathered brown shingles that deem it vacation time. I glance at him and my heart skips a beat. I'll never get used to seeing him. I bite my lip and his gaze darts down to the movement. He bites his lip in return. I smile.

"It's one we haven't been to before. It's new, actually. It's called Dances like the Wind." Playfully I swat the hand on my knee.

I roll my eyes. "Ha-Ha."

He raises his brows. "Scout's honor. That's the name." He only says that when he's being dead serious. It's an oxymoron of the best kind. My skin breaks out into a sheen of sweat and I feel my pulse kick into high drive. "I like New York for more than one reason, Fast Lane."

"You bought a house here?" My voice squeaks. Taking my chin into his hand, he turns my face toward him. "And you named it a stupid name!" I exclaim. He laughs, the baritone sound filling the car like a shot of testosterone.

He brushes a strand of hair out of my eye. "I acquired it a while ago. I just named it recently," he explains. I suck in a deep breath. Okay. I can't deal with this. I should be happy. I have too many loose ends to be happy. Or do I? These days spent with him can be happy. I'll do my best to forget that I have to go back to a reality world that is complicated as fuck.

"How much do you get paid for popping people?" I ask. It comes out of my mouth like a nosey teenager.

He laughs. "Pop people? I gather intel about bad people. You'd be surprised how much people would pay for good information." He looks away. "Most people would pay far more than money for what I give them."

"Oh?" I ask.

Blindly, he grabs my hand on the seat next to him

and squeezes it. "Sometimes we catch the assholes and make them pay for what they've done. It's quite lucrative. But you're wondering about how I can afford my new lifestyle," he says matter-of-factly.

I squeeze his hand back. "I mean, I'm sure you could have crowd funded a new life. You were dead, after all. Strangers would have made you a very rich man. Donated their life savings. Your face was all over the news for weeks." I laugh, trying to make light of my ignorant question. I can't hide the fact that I'm curious, though. He'd read through the lines anyways.

He nods. "You forget where my true talents lie." It's not supposed to, but his words send a shockwave of wetness directly to my core. I want his talent so deep inside me it can't find the way back out. I clench my muscles and draw in a breath, crossing my legs. Cody notices everything. He drags a finger across the top of my thigh and back down toward my knee. The car slows, but I can't tear my gaze from his finger. "Tech, of course," Cody growls. "I sold code, Lainey."

"Oh." Is all I can manage to squeak out. "Of course. Code. That makes sense." He pulls his hand away.

"We're here." Well, smack me silly are we ever and it is beautiful. That's saying something because typically houses here are large and charming, or rustic and elegant. Not this one. No. This monstrosity is a gorgeous peaked, gray brick that reminds me of a modern European castle. The town car pulls up the driveway laid with pavers and stops in front of one of the four garages.

"What. The. Fuck. James. Bond." I'm familiar with nice houses and cars and the finer things that life has to offer, yet this estate is impressive by anyone's standards. My poor uncle, God rest his soul, would have wanted this as his own.

Cody grins, hops out, and comes around to open the door for me before our driver can. "Come. Meet your namesake."

I scoff. "This house cannot dance like the wind, Cody. If shaken it can probably destroy a small country. What exactly did you sell again?" Cody ignores me and takes both of our small bags from the trunk and waves off the car. I watch it disappear down the drive and behind the electric gate and then turn to face him. We're finally alone—so alone and far away from any distractions or real life. He sifts through his pocket for keys and leads me to the front door. I'm left reeling with so many emotions. All of them positive.

He holds out his hand for me. It's like he's reading my mind. "Let's go inside. See if maybe we can make this house dance?" He smiles with his eyes like a tiny child excited for a new toy. The wrinkles around his eyes crinkle. I'm smitten, falling in love with him all over again. This time it's harder and deeper and the connection that was at first a live wire is now a fucking explosion. I never doubted our relationship; perhaps I

126

thought things may be different. I didn't anticipate that our emotions would be exactly the same multiplied by infinity.

"Dance?" I ask. "Let's make the bricks fall to the ground." I tackle him through the front door, wrapping myself around him, causing our bags to spill on the marble foyer. Not before I see at least fifteen security cameras outside and remember that our driver never spoke a single word. I did recognize his eyes in the rearview mirror...an employee of Ridge Contracting. Cody either wants to keep someone out, or keep someone in. I'll figure it out. I always do.

For the moment, I get lost in him. "I love you, Cody."

He pauses my onslaught of wet lips and frisky hands by stilling his movements. "Say that again."

"I love you," I breathe into his mouth.

He shakes his head against my mouth. "Never thought I'd hear that again."

"I'll say it a thousand more times, but I know something better I could be doing with my mouth."

Cody grins. "The Pledge of Allegiance? You're such a patriot, beautiful girl."

CHAPTER TWELVE

Cody

Relief. I got her to my impenetrable fortress by the sea. The only thing penetrating will be me—deep inside Lainey. I saw her eyes when she looked at the estate, calculating, surmising, fitting the pieces together. Good for her. Luckily for me, her lust won out and now we've made it to a fine Italian sofa in a sitting area. You know the kind of room that never gets used because the furniture is too expensive and the decorations too priceless? Yeah, we're about to defile this room fifteen ways till Sunday. I haven't even looked around to make sure everything is how it's supposed to be. I had Molly and a couple of my men come over here to make sure we had everything that makes a house livable and comfortable, and also to ensure the security of the house was top notch. I would've done it myself, but I didn't want to stray far from Lainey.

Which totally fucked up a job I needed to do. Horse went instead, and I came to the realization that my men are fully capable of running Ridge without me. Sure, I'm the brains behind the operation, but their skills make them just as capable and lethal and intelligent as I am. It relieves me further. Fuck if I know how deep down the rabbit hole V is going to have me go. He's playing games now. He's sending Ridge jobs, with his lowly men as the target, knowing I will torture them for information. Each rat gives me a small tidbit of information. I've garnered enough to know he has eyes everywhere. After my time here with Lainey I'll have the final puzzle piece. Dax will tell me and I'll be able to finish this forever. Speaking of finished forever, Lainey won't be mine anymore. My stomach sinks. I told myself I wouldn't let that fact interfere with this weekend or sway my intentions. V has to die. Just like Lainey has to marry Dax. My job is to be okay with that.

Right now, Lainey is all mine. She's stripping off her clothing one small piece at a time. I'm standing on one side of the living area and she's standing on the other, a feral look in her sparkling, blue eyes. A piano that cost as much as my house in Virginia Beach stands between us. She uncovered the ivory keys as she walked away from me, wanting a game of cat and mouse. Always the minx, always the fucking sex goddess that leaves me weak in my goddamned knees.

I see her naked backside reflected in the huge glass window behind her that overlooks the ocean. The sight is comforting and arousing at the same time.

"This is nice," Lainey says, stroking the keys low to high, causing a bad melody to echo off the sky-high ceiling. "Play me something?" Lainey asks. I don't play. That's not what she wants, though. Reaching behind my neck, I lift the collar of my shirt over my head and toss it aside. I've hit the gym extra hard this week. I make quick work of my jeans, sans boxer briefs, and take a step toward her, completely naked. Her hooded gaze studies me from top to bottom and back up again. Her pink lip is caught between her white teeth and my dick hardens further.

I bring my hand down and grasp my cock and stroke it a couple times, never taking my eyes off her slim, fucking perfect body. Lainey reaches down and spreads her pussy with two fingers, showing me exactly where I want my dick to be. With her fingers on her other hand she works her clit in small circles. I smile. She smiles. It's lazy, turned on—erotic. "Play the piano, huh?" I ask, taking another step forward.

She moans a little, her pink pussy getting wetter with each flick of her fingers. "Mmmm, hmmm," she mumbles, too caught up in her handiwork to form a sentence. The floor is cold beneath my feet, but the rest of my body is on fire, aching with the heat of desire. I hit a piano key as I walk past it and then grab Lainey's arm. She pauses.

Leaning down, I kiss her neck and breathe her in. Perfume and sex. Lethal. My dick pulses up now that I'm this close to her. It wants in. I want it in. "Fucking you on the piano would be cliché," I rasp in her ear in between kisses. I see the corners of her lips pull into a smile. "Tell me where you want it, Lainey." I use her name and she shivers, responding to my words just as she used to. I have complete control over her and that's exactly how she likes it.

Lainey spits into her palm, not daintily, never taking her eyes off mine, and grabs my cock. I groan when she starts working me, moving her hand all the way down and then back to the tip. Several more strokes and I'm breathing heavily, eyes closed in fucking ecstasy. Grabbing her arm, I still her. I won't last long once I get inside her if she keeps it up. She smiles a knowing smile. "Let's see the bedroom, then." I inhale sharply and nod.

I pull her back against my front and reach around to touch her wet pussy. She relaxes back against me. "Walk," I tell her. Tentatively she takes a step forward while I rub her clit and dip my middle finger inside her as far as I can manage. She moans, tilts her head back on my chest, and looks up at me. The sight is so fucking beautiful that I want to plunge inside her right here. Her lips are parted and those eyes are begging for me. I grin. "Keep going straight," I command.

She smiles. "Fine. You keep going," she returns. She takes a step and I follow without disconnecting our bodies all the way down the cool hallway into the large master suite. By the time we make it to the bed in the center of the expansive room, she's panting and clutching my arm about to explode. "I want to come around your dick," she pants, spinning around in my arms.

I kiss her lips. They're dry and sweet. Moving my hands up her sides, I cup her perfect tits and pinch her rose-colored nipples. Lainey grabs my biceps and with as much force as she can muster she pushes me back onto the enormous bed. I make a show of landing harder than I should and her eyes widen. "You're so strong." I smirk. Next, she's crawling toward me, straddling my legs and then walking, ever so carefully on her knees up toward my cock. "You're so beautiful, Lane. So fucking perfect." She is. Right now my vision of her is absolutely perfect. "Fuck me," I say, lifting my chin and folding my arms behind my head. "I can't take much more of looking at you like this and not being inside you." My dick is coated in pre-cum and it could cut cold steel with ease.

She's hovering over my dick now, and I can feel the heat radiating from her core. I jut my hips up seeking, hoping to slide home, but she doesn't let me. Not yet. She wants to tease herself by rubbing the tip of my cock on her clit. She works herself with me and I can only watch. I alternate between her face, with her eyes closed in sheer pleasure and my dick, which is almost inside her. Almost.

I'm not a man who begs for anything in life and I hear the words coming out of my mouth like a prayer, begging her to let me in. I'd make deals with the devil to sheath myself inside her right this second. "Please, Lainey," I say again. She moans and then blessedly she sits down slowly, my dick inching its way into her tight, clenching pussy. Yes. Yes. Yes. Grabbing her hips because I can't stand another second of teasing, I pull her all the way down onto me. She cries out in pleasure as I fill her completely, hitting the back. She rises again, rocks her hips back, and slams herself down again. I keep one hand on her hip and with the other I work her clit quickly. She's so wet. "I'm coming," she says, now grinding on me quicker. The pace is one I know I won't be able to stand long.

"I am, too," I rasp. "Come with me," I say. She meets my eyes and I'm blinded by fucking love. I feel her legs shake. Her eyes close and then she explodes around me, and finally, I let myself go, allowing myself to spill inside of her in quick, hot bursts of pure fucking bliss. Lainey leans over and plants her mouth on my neck. She kisses me and licks me, and keeps my cock inside her while she circles her hips, keeping our connection.

"I love you, Cody Ridge. I never stopped. I never

will. I missed this so, so much," Lainey whispers. Love mixes with relief and is quickly replaced by horror.

I swallow down the lump in my throat. "I love you, too, beautiful girl. Forever and always. Remember that." She moves her mouth to mine and kisses me with force and passion I can't ignore. When I'm here with her, inside of her, I can't fathom what would ever lead me to believe I could give her away.

Lainey breaks the kiss and stares in my eyes like she's reading her favorite book. "I won't have to remember because you'll be with me always. Right?" It's like she suspects something is up. Does she? I give her a lot of credit, but how could she possibly know this?

"Right," I lie. "You have to see the shower. It's exactly like the one we designed for our house." Distract her with home interiors. Real fucking smart, Cody. Doh.

She narrows her eyes. Shit. "You mean it has a steam room, too?" Phew. Bait and switch.

I nod. "Yeah. And long, deep benches." I raise one brow. She smiles. When she finally rises enough to remove my dick from her body I feel cold. It's not a good feeling. Maybe if I keep reminding myself that if V is dead she'll be safe, the sensation will go away. She won't be mine, but she'll be safe. That has to count for something. More than that prick asshole she'll marry leveraging information to snag her forever. It's not fair,

134

yet it's completely fair. Lainey smiles and talks animatedly about something, I'm not sure what, because my thoughts have run away from me. The only thing standing between happily ever after and fate is revenge. And even I can't change that. I zone back in when I hear the word *wedding*.

Lainey swings her naturally white blond hair from one shoulder to the other. "When I cancel the wedding, I may need you as a bodyguard," she says, dragging a manicured nail over my chest, tracing a tattoo. When I swallow it's thick and takes entirely too long to go down my throat. I wish there were a switch to control my emotions. How easy life would be.

I laugh. "Surely no one will fault you for making a decision. Women change their minds all the time." Vagueness is key here. Lie, but don't lie. Growing up with my aunt, I saw her do it countless times. It was artful, so well handled that my uncle never saw through it. She never lied about anything significant, per se— an unplanned shopping trip here or there was her M.O. She was vague about which store she visited and my uncle always assumed it was of the grocery variety.

Lainey is too keen to play it any other way. I have to be vague. I rub the skin on her waist. It's warm and so fucking smooth. Goosebumps rise where my fingers stroked. "Right?" I ask. "A woman's prerogative, and all that?"

"They're a fucking angry lynch mob, Cody. You

135

know that. I bet Aunt Velma will send a hit man to my house to either kill me or find the wedding gift she sent three months too early." Grinning, because I know Aunt Velma, I shake my head. "I guess it's just embarrassing, too. When you...left, our wedding plans were cancelled. Surely they forgave me that go round even if I did inconvenience them. This time, they'll string me up by my toes. Grandma already bought a plane ticket." Lainey talks more about her family, but the way she's looking at me, so tenderly, with so much love, I know she's not really upset about calling off her wedding to Dax.

I take a deep breath. "You've thought it through, then? I couldn't fault you if you wanted to marry him, Fast Lane." Her eyes widen and flicker with anger. Shit.

"Your cock is mere inches from my vagina right now and you're telling me it's okay if I want to marry another man? Are you okay?" She feels my forehead with the back of her hand. "There wasn't even a question since the first time we met in the street. He wouldn't let me break it off." She looks away, probably thinking about that blackmailing asshole.

"Hey," I say. She turns her face toward me again. "I'm sorry. Okay?" Saying anything further will cross into lying territory. "I love you." Lainey smiles that glorious smile that lights her whole face. She leads me to the stream room and starts talking about the interior design of the estate. It was all for her, after all. When she marries Dax and has two point five children and a white picket fence, all I'll have left of my Lainey is this house. Which means I need to have her in every single fucking room. Memories I can keep forever. Could I find V on my own without Dax's information? Probably. Would it take longer, putting more people in danger? Yes. I look at Lainey in the full-length mirror in the expansive bathroom. Her creamy tan skin, unmarred by any imperfection except red marks where my hands have just been is reason enough. My cum is running down the inside of her leg. Mine. Not his. My claim. She meets my gaze in the mirror. The corner of her mouth quirks up in a devil-may-care grin. She waggles her pointer finger at me, summoning me over. *She'll always pick me, no matter what*, I think. She has to. This is a risk I'm going to take. I stalk up to her, hit the button to turn on the steam, and pick her up with ease. She wraps her legs around my waist and locks her arms around my neck. I nuzzle my nose into her neck. "You didn't mention the security cameras. What do you think?" I ask.

"Too much," she coos against the side of my face. "Too much seems to be how you operate these days, though."

I press my lips to the side of her face. "Too much of this?" I ask, sliding her down my body onto my dick.

Lainey shakes her head, her eyes closed. "Never too much of that." I walk her into the steam room and fuck

137

her so hard I can't see straight.

We don't even use the bench.

****

"I. Can't. Keep. Up," Lainey says, breathing heavy. We decided to go for a jog on the beach. The morning air is cool and dewy and the silence is peaceful at this time of morning. Well, you know, the silence before Lainey started whining. I laugh. We started about five minutes ago.

"The marathon sex last night didn't help your endurance much, did it?" Sex. With Lainey. It was so fucking hot. Thinking about it makes me want more of it. The tight black workout shorts she's wearing make me want more right now. After a long as hell dry spell her pussy wrapped around my cock feels like nirvana.

She grabs my arm to slow me to a walk. "It's because my endurance is all used up. Plus, my vagina is baboon style. Totally Animal Planet stuff going on. All red and wet and overused. I can't take the D six times in one night and be expected to cardio the next day." Or maybe we should take a break from sex for a short period of time.

I cough, laugh and then shake my head. "Your eloquence knows no bounds. Do you need a doctor? Baboon isn't the best way to describe that part of your anatomy. And cardio was your idea, remember? I wanted to use the gym at the house." It's safer and so we can have sex without worrying about prying eyes. Although if she wanted to right here, I wouldn't turn her down.

"There's a mansion on the beach named after my alter ego. Forgive me for wanting to check out some of the beach that belongs to it. I'm sure the cameras you've installed have zoom. We're being monitored right now, aren't we?" Yes.

"I'm not sure of the reach on the ones in the back." She nods, acknowledging my half lie. We walk in companionable silence for a few minutes. She looks out at the ocean, back up at the estate, and then at me.

"I want to live here," she deadpans.

"Vacation houses lose their charm when you live year-round in them," I explain. "I'm glad you love it, though. It's my biggest purchase since I've been back in the real world."

Lainey stops, halting in her tracks. "How are you perfectly okay?" she finally asks. I know it's not the real question she wants an answer to. I don't talk about the time I spent locked underground, living in destitution counting drips. It's not particularly painful to think about, but because I've tried to push past it, it's like a distant memory I'm no longer attached to. Don't get me wrong, I know exactly who is to blame and what I need to do about it to make things right. V was smart, crafty, a genius in his plans to steal me and keep me away. In my current profession I can appreciate perfect execution. With some distance from the situation, I realize the only flaw in his plan was not killing me. That's not his way, though. Suffering is his thing and I plan on taking his thing and serving him extra helpings. The dinner bell is about to ring, motherfucker.

I realize I haven't responded to Lainey yet. "Who said I'm perfectly okay?" I tease, laying a hand on her waist. A piece of her wavy hair floats across her face and gets caught between her lips. She crosses her arms, obviously not amused by my response. Releasing her, I run a hand through my own hair. I don't want to get into this. "It was bad, Lainey. Forgive me for wanting to spare you the gory details."

She shakes her head, eyes closed. "I'm not asking for details."

"You are. Just not in so many words."

She pulls that wayward piece of hair out of her mouth and tucks it behind her ear. "I guess it's hard for me to fathom coming back after something so awful...and for so long." Valid point. The first few months living among respectable humans almost felt like I was an actor in a Blockbuster hit. I believe my acting days are over, but I can't be sure.

I turn her chin to face me. "I'm the same person. A little beaten down, a little inked up, with some external scars, but inside," I say, bringing her hand to rest on the left side of my chest, "I'm the same. Getting another

140

chance with you was, at best, my wildest dream during my darkest days." And I'm about to throw it away.

She smiles now and hugs me, her small arms cutting me like vices as she tightens her grip. The curves of her body press against me and the wind blows her unruly hair into my face. "My baboon level is about four. We should start heading back to the house now. For the record, I'm glad you're okay. And being with you now is also my wildest dream come true. I never thought I'd be able to think of you without being sad and now I get to have you. And this happiness makes me want to explode."

I hang on to her a little tighter. Breathe her in a little deeper. "Never give up on the good guy, yeah?" I say.

Lainey pulls back and looks at me with bright, laughing eyes. "You remembered."

"Of course. How could I forget?" Good guys finish last, or so the saying goes. When we first began dating she told me that when she found a good guy she was never going to give up on him. "Remember that, okay?"

She looks off into the ocean. Is she thinking of Dax and her wedding? Wondering if there's some hidden meaning behind my words? I don't have precious time to waste wondering. I only have two more days with her in this false, safe paradise.

My phone rings from the holster on my arm. It's Molly. Wrapping my arm around Lainey, we begin our walk back while I listen to Molly panic about threatening messages she's received from anonymous callers. Everything is coming to a head, and I need all my best-laid plans to be meticulous. Lainey smiles up at me, and I force a grin back and kiss the top of her head.

Never give up on the good guy.

CHAPTER THIRTEEN

Lainey

Cody's on the phone again. He's in the library on the second floor of this palatial mansion. A quick mental calculation has it in the mid millions. I'm pretty sure I saw it on an episode of *Cribs* when I was seventeen years old. In between sex sessions and eating and more sex, I check out the different areas of the house. One could easily get lost in here. That fact creeps me the fuck out. He hates the beach, which is how I'm certain this truly is all for me. Obviously it's a grand gesture I could have done without. There's a locked door at the end of a long hallway that reminds me of the movie *The Shining.* I don't hang around long enough to see if I can pick the lock. It's not like I have anything to help me anyways. Thankfully, I threw a light cotton robe in my bag, because Morganna was right. Clothing is optional.

As I approach the library I hear Cody's voice

pouring from the large doorway. He's angry. I make my steps lighter, my bare feet a whisper against the cool floor. My chest rises and falls a little more rapidly. Some women would turn the other way. Others would make their presence known with a cough or a fake sneeze. Not me. This is part of who I am. Cody should know better. I press my back against the door and listen to him speak.

Whatever Cody is currently laughing at isn't of the funny variety. "I don't need you. I have my ways. She's not safe," he growls and then pauses. "Of course that is what's important. Don't start this shit again. I keep my word." I realize I haven't taken a breath in too long and open my mouth to gobble up air. I'm the she. "You better follow through. I have a lot riding on this. More than you realize." Suddenly, I don't want to know what will come next—my nosey nature aside, I want to stay oblivious for a little while longer.

"Yes, dead. And by my own hand," Cody says. I swallow and look at the beautiful ceiling. He has always killed people. Why would it bother me now? Because he is talking about me in the same breath as killing.

"It's for her safety," he growls.

I show myself in the doorway, unable to keep out of view any longer. "Why are you worried about my safety?" I ask, making sure my voice is loud enough to carry the expanse of the wide room. "And who the fuck are you killing now?"

Cody's eyes widen. He covers the mouthpiece of his phone. "What did you hear?" No pleasantries now.

I lie. "All of it." My heart hammers because I think I know exactly why he'd be worried about my safety.

"I have to go," Cody says into the phone. He hangs up before the other person has time to respond. Shirtless, wearing only a pair of blue checked pajama pants slung low on his hips, he walks toward me. I shake away the sex brain and put on my professional panties. He can't woo me now. At least not easily.

I hold up my hand. "Don't play games. Honesty. I need honesty, Cody."

His worried gaze looks me up and down and finally settles on my eyes. "Being with me puts a target on you," he explains.

I scoff. "You sure it isn't the other way around?"

He takes a deep breath and shakes his head. We're in uncharted territory. The place we don't speak of. "People are angry with me so by default anything and anyone close to me is a target. You," he says, waving his left hand in front of him at me, "might as well have neon lights attached to your head that flash the word Cody." He looks away. "You're safe here, with me."

"So you don't want me to leave here? I thought vacation houses lose their charm? You were angry, Cody," I say, my lips pursed. "Also, I can guess who you want dead." I did tell him I wanted to live here.

145

Cody sighs, defeated. "I want a lot of people dead. I'm angry when it comes to your safety. How could I not be? I lost you once, Lane. I know what it feels like. While I enjoy our time here, I know I can't hold you hostage." He smiles at his own cruel joke.

"Stop lying by omitting. I invented that shit. You can't talk circles around me. And when it comes to losing people I'm the motherfucking queen at that. Or don't you remember?" Cody grabs me by my shoulders. It's meant to comfort me, but I feel the rage bubbling inside. Loss makes you feel things that aren't rational. By remembering the loss, it's forcing anger to the surface. "Are you keeping something from me? I'll only ask once." He knows I'm serious because he releases my shoulders and takes a step away from me. Cody knows I need space when I get spun up.

He runs a hand through his blond hair. "There is. I'm keeping something from you. It's for your own safety. I won't tell you."

My jaw might as well be super glued to the floor. "What?"

"You asked if I'm keeping something from you. Yes, I am. There's your honesty." He shakes his finger at me when I open my mouth to speak. "There are worse places to be other than in the dark, Fast Lane. Trust me."

I swallow and nod. Can I accept this? I have to. "You know I'll figure it out eventually."

146

"I'm counting on it," he replies.

I take several deep breaths and watch him. He watches me, tapping one finger on his leg by his side. A nervous habit I'm sure he's done all he can to break. "If I don't?"

"It won't matter if you don't. Listen, I have a serious job to deal with when we get back. I'm not sure how much I'll be able to see you…for a while."

My anger is dissipating. "You're not an equal opportunist? Aren't they all serious jobs?"

He laughs. "You could say this one is more important than most. I can't send Horse or Van. Something I need to handle myself." A pit forms in my stomach.

"Vadim." I say his name like a curse word for pussies. Cody's eyes flare.

"Lainey. Please," he says. Blue pleading eyes meet my own.

I scream several curse words that aren't of the pussy variety and Cody watches me without saying a word. I have a million questions to ask. Pacing the room, I try to think of the last time I heard of his whereabouts. The mere mention of his name and I can't think clearly.

When I reach the end of the room I turn around. Cody's on the opposite end, hands on his hips, waiting. "So this really is about me?" I say.

He shakes his head. "No. It's about me."

"Bullshit! How can you say that? I thought he was

already six feet under." That would have been too easy—too perfect to be true. I grab the ends of my robe ties self-consciously and pull it tighter, until the belt is cinching my skin. I squat down and put my head in my hands. My new bracelet slides from my forearm and tickles the side of my cheek. Fuck. I feel sick. Cody kneels in front of me.

A tear slides down my cheek when I look up at him. Cody brushes it away with his thumb. "You're safe. He'll never find you." With us it's never that simple.

I hold up my wrist to show him the bracelet I thought was a gift from him. Cody takes one of the diamonds in between his fingers and narrows his eyes at my piece of expensive jewelry. He pulls me against his warm chest and kisses my hair. I'm slacking. My A-game is officially F-game. The words on the notecard come to mind. *Wear this so I'll know...*

"He already knows," I whisper, ripping the motherfucking bracelet off.

****

We decided that staying in The Hamptons wasn't the best idea anymore. A few calls and a light, albeit tense lunch and we were on our way to the airport. Molly deserves the world's best assistant award. She wears many hats, but I'm sure finding information on how to dispose of and destroy a tracker placed in jewelry should garner her a pay raise. I told Cody so. He didn't laugh. In fact, he hasn't cracked a smile since I showed him the bracelet. I'm not nervous or scared anymore. That was a fleeting emotion caused by shock. I'm enlightened. The knowledge of Vadim's presence in my life is something I can deal with. I can avoid him, be cautious, thoughtful, manipulative. I can be Lainey from my old, more sinister life. Everything will turn out fine in the end. Bad men don't live very long in this world. Now, Cody took to this information a little more irrationally. Cold and distant are two words I'd use when I think about how he's been looking at me.

We're taking a private flight to Virginia Beach this time. I snap my fingers in front of his face. He's sitting in a plush leather seat across from me. "Earth to killer. Earth to killer. You do realize everything will be okay? I can take care of myself. We're finally together again. Nothing can stop us now."

He looks from me back out the window next to him. Nothing but a small grin lets me know that he heard me. "Have you spoken to your mom recently?" he asks, tapping the side of his leg.

"Ew. Why are you asking about my mom right now? Did you hear what I said?"

He leans forward and grabs my hands in his. "I just think we should try to act like business as usual. You're right. You can handle yourself. Vadim will be out of the picture and life can go on...more peacefully." It

149

works. Cody distracts me. First with a story Molly told him about Horse and then he pulls me onto his lap and kisses me senseless.

His hands are in my hair and his hard cock is nestled against my pussy. As I was hopeful to make myself a member of the mile high club, I wore a skirt and no panties. Something he's currently figuring out.

"You always this naughty when you fly?" Cody asks. I remind him of the time we tried to have sex in the bathroom stall of a commercial airliner on our way to Paris, and he finally laughs. I had on impossibly tight jeans and that poor planning always haunts me. "I guess this needs to make up for that then," he says. Distraction complete.

"Indeed," I rasp.

"Sex won't fix this fucking mess, Lainey," he says.

I press my lips against his open mouth. He watches me warily through semi-closed eyes. I make a big show of sitting up and looking around the empty plane. We're alone. I unbuckle his pants and pull out his hard cock. It's warm in my hand and he flinches. Why are airplanes always so damn cold? Even private ones, for God's sake.

I let my hair hang down and brush his face. It always tickles him. "It's only a mess if you don't fix it. Wouldn't you agree that we're both highly adequate mess fixers?"

Cody sighs, finally relaxing underneath me.

"Whatever you say. Anyone tell you how fucking beautiful you are? You've basically dulled my desire to kill and fly into a murderous rage and morphed me into a horny teenager boy. Skill, darling. You have some serious skill."

He slides my skirt up over my hips and touches me between my legs gently. I guide his dick to my core and lower myself down until his head is inside me, coating him with my wetness. "Has anyone ever told you how unavoidably attractive you are?" I moan in his ear. Cody's cell phone rings, vibrating the table next to his seat. Surprisingly, he ignores it, fumbling with one hand to send it to voicemail.

"No more talking," he says, taking me by the hips and lifting me up. Leaning up, he lays me down on the seat where he just was and positions himself between my legs. I fall back, letting my arms rest beside my head. He kisses me on the chin then looks at me—really looks at me. I want to talk, but instead I pretend to zip my lips and lock the side and hand him the pretend air key. Mockingly he bites the key out of my fingers…and then sucks them before smiling. He enters me slowly, closing his eyes as he eases his thick girth in inch by inch.

"Yes," I say, grabbing his face and guiding his lips to mine.

His kiss tastes sweet, and with the sensation of being filled and rubbed just the right way, I can say this is my favorite place in the world to be. With him. Always with him. Always surrounded by his love. "I love you, Lainey," Cody whispers against my mouth as he thrusts his hips slowly.

I open my eyes and see his glassy, glacier blue eyes searching for something in mine. I'm not sure what. I've already given him everything—all of me. He has to sense that this is it for me. Dax won't even have an opportunity to keep me around. I lost the woman Dax loves the second Cody came full throttle back into my life.

"I love you," I counter. He presses his forehead against mine as he picks up his pace. The friction presses me just the right way, his dick sliding against me at the perfect angle. That paired with the fact that Cody Ridge is making utterly, unforgettable, movie worthy love to me makes me want to lose my mind right now.

"Come," he orders, seeing my eyes go cross-eyed with desire. Pulling him deeper with my hands on his ass, I wrap my legs around him and I explode around him in shock waves of pure pleasure. I scream out. Not his name, and not anything recognized in the English language because this orgasm hits me hard. Tingles from the tip of my head to the tip of my toes relax me. Cody picks up the pace, driving his cock into my wet pussy furiously several more times before he pulls out, scoots up toward my face, and strokes it until his hot cum leaks into my waiting mouth. It tastes salty and creamy. The way he watches me as he comes makes me think this, what's happening right now, is what his dreams are made of. He groans, closes his eyes while he finishes, and then watches me intently.

I swallow every last drop and then wrap my mouth around him and lick it clean.

His breathing is heavy and we're both sticky with sweat and sex. "Way better than Paris would have been," I say. I get goosebumps thinking about all of the times we've had sex. How much he turns me on. How little control I have over my body or my actions when his hands are on me and his dick is inside me.

"Way better," he confirms.

"We'll get through whatever comes our way. Forever. Please know that. Look at what we've already overcome." I kiss his lips and then leaning up I kiss his neck.

"I hope so," Cody replies. I can't see his face, but it legitimately sounds like he's hoping. Cody doesn't hope, he makes things happen. Nothing will separate us again. Not if I can help it.

We clean up, and Cody excuses himself to another area of the plane to make a phone call. Taking my cell phone, I scroll through, searching for a number I haven't used in a very long time. It's a number that reminds me of my old life—something I never thought I'd revisit again. There are some secrets that women should always keep secret. Disgusting habits, how many sex partners they've had, and most importantly the fact that they're skilled in espionage. Lainey Rostov, Russian surveillance spy, trained at gathering information about Navy SEALs and reporting back intelligence is coming out to play. It wasn't easy moving to Virginia Beach with the goal of finding, dating, and then extracting information from a Navy SEAL. Actually it was quite a bit more difficult than that—I had to weave myself into the community, befriend SEAL girlfriends and wives, I had to blend in. You'd be surprised the amount of details men are willing to give out while drinking at a bar and better yet, in between the sheets. I'd fathom a guess that I'm a million times better at espionage than my male counterparts. I have more parts to use to my benefit. Does Cody know? Of course he knows. He called me out right at the get-go. I think that's why I fell so hard for him. Intelligence looks divine on that man with such brawn. I glance over at him with his freshly fucked hair and mussed clothing and smile. He winks at me while he continues his phone conversation. He's just as deranged as I was...am. A match made in fucked up heaven. What happens when a spy falls in love with her target? My fucking life. This is what happens. And Vadim wants to screw with me again. I don't think so. *I don't think so.* I wink back, lick my lips, and calculate just how dangerous this territory will be.

Desperate times call for desperate measures. No matter what the cost.

No one is taking him from me again.

Chapter Fourteen

Cody

The streets of Mexico are fucking horrible. No one obeys traffic laws, stop signs and red lights are optional, and speed limits don't exist. I suggest hiring a driver or taking a Xanax if you have to drive here. I'm chasing some asshole that Van missed last night. He's driving a white beat-up pickup truck down a busy street like a goddamned NASCAR driver on cocaine. He probably is on some kind of drug, but I doubt he'd make one lap in a racecar.

Dax is stalling with my fucking information. I'm sure it has something to do with Lainey's persistence in breaking up with him. I've tried to stay away from her. She comes to me. Once in the middle of the night wearing nothing but a raincoat, another time she made it into my apartment in NYC before I got home. She was waiting for me naked, spread-eagle, in front of one of my computer screens. Like porn, except I actually fucked her and then ate her out and then made love to her slowly on the floor, and then fucked her bent over my kitchen counter. You see the dilemma. She isn't giving Dax the time of day, and I'm basically biding my time until Dax realizes I can't do anything about the way she feels. It makes me puff out my chest a little when I think about it. It also makes me crazy as fuck because I know he has information I need and he's being a childish prick. How the hell can I help it? My mouth waters when I think of Lainey. I'm like a klepto. I need my fix to get through the day. Stealing her love is harder than stealing overpriced electronics. For Dax.

"Come on, motherfucker!" I yell at the dirty white truck in front of me. He runs the red light and I hit a damn pothole at the same time. It slows me down. The Jeep I'm driving was built for off-road, but I don't think the manufacturers had Mexico in mind when they designed the shock system on this thing. I check my rearview mirror and see Horse struggling in his own vehicle and smile. I radio him and make a quick joke, but he doesn't grin. He hits his steering wheel with one Horse sized fist. I tell him to be easy on the rentals and I hit the gas and slide a little to one side. The road is made out of some sort of orange clay that's designed to help bad guys escape. The Federales appear on the left hand side, but you don't stop when you see the Mexican Police. You go faster. They're shadier than a palm tree in Florida. I don't want to get into a gunfight in broad daylight with them. I have other things to worry about.

My tires skid around a corner and I see the white truck disappear down a small alleyway. Fuck. I give orders to the men behind me. Horse turns around to try to corner him on the opposite side and I keep on his tail. A bead of sweat rolls down my face. I crank up the A/C without taking my eyes off the road. The defensive driving courses the Navy forced me to participate in help me during times such as this. They were fun, but I never found them to be practical. Ironic.

A shrill sound ricochets the cab of the truck—my Bluetooth ringing. My satellite phone is only used for work, so Molly is the only person who has that number. Fumbling with the steering wheel, I hit the 'accept' button.

"What?" I roar.

Molly roars back, "She's more persistent than a yeast infection. That's what!"

I pause. *Get to the point, Molly*, I think. Sometimes women are impossible to deal with. With a man you get to the meat of the story in two seconds flat. I can appreciate feminine wiles and the fact they're more detail-oriented, but Molly knows I'm busy right now. Yanking the wheel a sharp turn to the right, I head down the alley. One of my side mirrors scrapes on the dirty cement wall. It doesn't make me mad because I'll end up buying these damn vehicles anyways. It enrages me that I didn't have the foresight to rent smaller trucks. Ones that fit down devil alleyways with room to spare. Several men jump back and press themselves against the dirty buildings as I speed after my target.

"I'm going to patch Lainey through. She won't leave me alone." I should be irritated with Molly for not following protocol, but the sadistic part of me wants to talk to Lainey no matter the circumstances. Will she be in a playful mood? A happy one? Will she be distraught because she's dealing with Dax again? Anticipation of any kind is my favorite.

I hit a huge pothole filled with black water and it splashes the side of my truck, leaving a grimy film on my window. "Fine! I don't need you to do your job anyways," I growl, more irritated at the dirty window than with Molly.

"Fire me then," she says, static marring her cunning words.

I groan. I'd never fire her. "Patch her through already."

She laughs. "You're so predictable."

"Like a tiger," I reply. More sweat rolls down my face. Is the A/C even working in this fucking tank? The white truck is getting closer. He's being pinned. I see Horse in the distance blocking the only exit.

A few annoying beeps sound through the Bluetooth speakers and then I hear her. "You! If you just gave me this fucking number, I wouldn't have to annoy your assistant!" And then I'd never get any work finished properly.

"Hi, you," I mumble. "I'm in the middle of a job. She's only supposed to call me in emergencies. Which limb are you missing?"

Swerving left and then right helps me avoid a mangy dog with a death wish. "Your dick!" Lainey quips. I shake my head, but wouldn't you know I'm grinning like a mad man? "When are you getting home? I miss you." She's acting like I'm at my nine to five job and she wants to know what time I'll be home for dinner. It's refreshing because I don't have to lie to her about what I do. It's also extremely fucked up because who would accept this life and not bat an eye?

"My dick is missing you too, baby girl. I miss you more, though. I'll be back in NYC soon. You have business there next week?" I have to slow down. Too many people are in front of me, flooding out from rusty steel doors on both sides of the alley. My heart rate accelerates. I'm not sure if it's because I'm thinking about my dick and Lainey or if it's my fight of flight kicking in. That's how twisted I am. Van is behind me in his Jeep. I radio him to let him know of the situation up ahead in case he needs to blast a few motherfuckers. The men have guns hanging on their hips like unskilled mobsters in movies. Their white shirts are stained yellow with sweat and dust. Their bandanas tell me I

160

was close when I thought mobsters. Someone fires a gun. I grab mine off the seat next to me. Keeping one hand on the wheel, I put a magazine in my mouth and aim the gun at the window with my right hand resting on my left arm. I'll put the window down when I need to. I can steer and shoot. I remember why we're using these Jeeps. Bulletproof glass and armored metal.

Lainey huffs exaggeratingly loud. "I ordered furniture for several of the rooms in your Virginia beach house. It will arrive in two weeks. Don't worry, though. I'll be there when it's delivered and make sure they don't wear shoes in your house. Or scuff the floors or touch any of your shit. I can always have work in NYC," she says. I'm sure she's smirking. The crowd of men swarm my vehicle and I've slowed so much that Van is now right on my ass. I meet his eyes in the rearview and he nods. "What are you doing right now? Lunch break or something?" Lainey asks.

I laugh. "No lunch breaks in these parts. Thanks for ordering the furniture. Was that it? All you needed to talk to me about, I mean?" My palms grow sweaty. I can see tan, angry faces. That's how close they are. Van and Horse radio call me at the same time. "I have to go, Fast Lane. Be good."

Lainey scoffs. "I'm rarely good."

"I know. It's why I love you." Another shot fired in the air by my evil company. She hears that one.

"My God. What are you doing?" she asks, her tone

horrified.

"Being good," I reply.

"Go. Go. Bye!" Lainey says, ending the call.

Shaking my head, I call Van and Horse at the same time. Horse answers first. "I have the target on this side. He's not going anywhere." Perfect.

Then Van. "Looks like we're not going anywhere either."

"I'm going to hit the gas. They'll move if they value their lives. Stay right behind me. Keep your front on my back. Don't worry about damage, we'll have to buy these outright after driving on these fucking streets." Someone knocks on the side of my car. I lay on the horn, blasting it in short bursts. A few men jump out of the way, but mostly they stay put with malevolent smiles on their faces. Not smart. They want to rob me. I smile back with equal parts evil and scary.

"Rog," Van says. "Do it."

I stomp on the gas and hit someone. Not all the way, probably just his foot or leg, but he's down and people jump out of the way. I piss off others and they charge, but I get the speedometer up to ten and hold fast, not braking even when people jump in front of me. More go down. I cringe when I 'bump' over something that wasn't a pothole. I want to get the fuck out of here. The thrill isn't here anymore. I want to get back home to Lainey and pick out furniture and...what am I saying?

A man wearing a filthy wife beater jumps on the

162

hood of my car like a damn idiot. I speed up again, trying to juke him off. He pulls out a gun from the waistband of his sweatpants and fires it at my windshield. The glass splinters like a cobweb, but it doesn't crack.

I aim my own gun at him so he can see it as I continue my bumpy pursuit and watch as his eyes widen. It's like a light switch being turned when he realizes I'm not a damn tourist. Quite the opposite actually. I roll down my window because we're moving fast enough that I know I'm not in harm's way. These assholes couldn't hit a moving target if they tried. Their balls and the size of their guns are what they care about, not how to properly use either, unfortunately. I stick the gun out of the window and bend my elbow so it's pointing right at the yahoo on my hood. I pull the trigger once and it grazes his arm. He fires again, like a real college graduate, at my bulletproof windshield. Leaning out of the window a little farther to get better aim, I pull the trigger one more time and hit him in the leg. Finally he rolls off my hood and lands on the left-hand side in a deep puddle. That required way more effort than I anticipated.

"Nice one, boss," Van says over the radio. Replying isn't an option because I can finally speed up. Horse is within shouting range and the cascade of gangsters is heading his way. Fuck. There's too many of them. Once we reach Horse we hop out, wielding more guns than a real gangster and help Horse finagle the jerk from the white truck into the back of Horse's Jeep. We put a pair of zip ties on his wrists and ankles and attach them behind his back. It will hold him until we get to our second location away from this fiasco. We have seconds to spare before the group descends on our vehicles again. They're trying to take hubcaps, fucking with the door handles and doing everything in their power to stop us.

"Drive to the hangar, guys. I'll question him when I get there," I say. They confirm, and we are out of the alleyway, back onto the roads, heading toward safety. I take a deep breath and realize how close of a call that was. To be outnumbered was a large concern when I was a Navy SEAL, and it's just as much of a concern with my work now. Molly calls again. "I know you're taking a breather. Horse just called in, so I'm patching you through to another call," Molly says, out of breath. She's probably working from her treadmill desk.

"Go ahead," I say.

The call is transferred to my phone. I try to speak before she does. "So you're missing my dick and what else?"

"Classy," Dax says. "A true fucking professional." I'm going to kill Molly.

"What do you need, man?" I ask. "How's that nose doing? Still just crooked enough to throw off your facial symmetry, marring you unattractive to the general population?"

"I wouldn't be an ass if I were you. I'm calling to tell you that the deal stands. Do what you need to do and I'll meet you tomorrow."

I laugh. "She's not going to go for it. I can lie to her until I'm blue in the face and she'll never believe me. She knows me better than that. If you knew her at all you'd know Lainey gets what she wants."

"I have an exact location that will be valid for the next forty-eight hours. Better practice your acting skills," Dax says. "How bad you want V?"

I swallow hard. I want him badly—more than anything else. I thought, but now I want Lainey more. "You don't deserve her. You know that, right?" I reply.

"And you do? You're even more fucked up than I am. I can give her a good, *honest* life. What will you give her? She already has money and mansions. The only things you bring to the table are a hobby for homicide and an absentee ballot." I grip the steering wheel tighter. He doesn't know her like I do.

But he's right. "Fine. I'll talk to her tonight. I'm out of pocket, so I'm going to have to email or call her. Two things that make it even less believable, but it'll be done tonight. You better have good intel, asshole. I'll add you to my hobby list. Remove you from the equation completely." I hear him breathing heavy on the other end of the phone. "I'm joking, Dax."

"Who the hell knows with you! You're a loose

cannon."

I roll my eyes. "And you are a manipulative, secretive man. I just hope you know what you're doing. Messing with others' happiness will bring you bad karma. Not that I believe in that shit, but even I have to admit what you're doing is pretty low. You could give me the information I need and walk off a cliff. Happily ever afters for all involved."

"She was happy, you asshole. Lainey was perfectly content with me."

"Wow. Content. Everything she dreamed of being when she was a little girl. 'I want a content marriage to a man who reminds me of my one true love.' Yeah, I'd say she was content with you," I say, forcing a mock girl voice. "You don't know her like I do."

Dax scoffs. "Content and safe. Both of those things. Now, tell me if you think that's something she deserves. I'll take care of her. I know her just as well as you do." Now he's trying to piss me off by reminding me he's been inside her. It makes my stomach roil. I'm hungry, and he's making me sick.

"You don't know her as well as I do." Spilling Lainey's secrets isn't an option. I found her out. She had to come clean. Ole' broken nose obviously hasn't done the same. I'd fathom a guess that he wouldn't have the same feelings for her if he did know. Then again, how honorable of a man can he be if he's sinking to blackmail to get what he wants? "It doesn't matter."

166

I cut off that train of thought before he can say any more. "I said I'd talk to her tonight. I'll take a red eye to Virginia Beach instead. Meet me at my place. I'll have Molly coordinate a time that works for both of us." I don't say goodbye or let him object. I press the button that sends him back to my assistant.

I'm really doing this. It's not as selfish as one might think. But I'm going to have to be a real dick to make this work. A monumental prick. A man Lainey Rosemont has never seen before. I'll pull out all the stops. Make the most important lie of my life believable.

No more Mr. Nice Guy. This time it's important that I finish last.

CHAPTER FIFTEEN

Lainey

He crawls into my bed in the early morning hours. He smells of booze, perfume, and sweat. All three of these things separately aren't offensive, but together they paint a picture of something atrocious. I roll over and face him, unable to see any features—just darkness.

"You," he whispers. My skin crawls. He wraps his arms around my waist and pulls me close. He texted that he was coming to see me, so I left him a key to the side door in a spot only he knows of and went back to bed. After ignoring my phone calls for a full twelve hours, to say I'm pissed with him is an understatement. Now he says he wants to talk.

"What's the deal, Cody?" I ask, warily. As my eyes adjust, I can see the whites of his eyes in the dark. A second later I see his white, smiling teeth, too. "What did you want to talk about that couldn't wait until morning? Molly is sick of hearing my voice, but you couldn't be bothered to call me back. What's up?"

Dax is acting weird too. Leaving me to my requested distance without so much as a text saying 'hello.' Maybe I'm the one going crazy. It's a plausible possibility. I've been slipping back into my old ways, making contact with people from my old life. Surveillance equipment and weapons don't materialize via thin air. After all these years of distancing myself from the life, I was surprised how easily I eased back into it. My old friends were still in the business and more than happy to help me out. Still, it gives me a sick feeling in the pit of my stomach that never leaves. It's why I was relieved when Cody finally asked me if I was a spy all those years ago. I came clean. The rush was surreal and much needed.

I found no need to share my past life with Dax. Not only would that have deterred him from befriending and ultimately falling in love with me, but it was my new life free of all of the chains from my past. Cody was dead. My old life was gone. Vadim was dead. I could reinvent myself in any fashion I wanted. There was a point before I got engaged to Dax that I truly forgot about my past. Sure, that was a relief, but I've always felt like an imposter. Everything has changed. Nothing is as it seems. No one is dead and my shackles are very real.

Cody sighs, blowing whiskey breath into my face,

so strong I'm pretty sure I got drunk from air. "I need to talk to you about something important and I'm not sure how to say it." His speech is slurred.

"How about you just say it?" I remove his arm from me. It's too tight. Scooting to the side of the bed, I click on my bedside lamp and see him for the first time. He's a tousled hot mess. "Did you just crawl out of a dirty bar? Seriously?" Still, my heart hammers at his mere proximity, craving his touch, as dirty as it may be.

His eyes linger on my mouth. I make a point of shutting it. His gaze flicks to my scantily clad body. He sits up, rubs a hand down his face, and sighs. Without looking up, he says, "I think we need to cool off." What. The. Fuck?

Narrowing my eyes, I say, "How much have you had to drink tonight...today? I'm not a fucking refrigerator. In case you're so blitzed you can't tell."

He shakes his head. "Not that much. I've been thinking and we're no good, Lane. This isn't going to work out between the two of us."

A deer caught in headlights looks less mollified than I do. "Are you friend zoning me right now? It sounds like you are fucking friend zoning me, bro." My tone is caustic, but still light. He can't be serious, right? After everything we've been through, he *has* to be joking.

Still avoiding eye contact, Cody lies back on my pillow and folds both arms over his face. His jeans are sitting low on his waist and his shirt pulls up to expose his abs. "I'm no good for you. It's not safe anymore."

I grab his arm. "I'm taking care of it. Don't worry about my safety. Don't you dare," I rasp. He glances at me, but shuts his eyes as if the sight of me pains him. "Stop it right now."

He rolls to his side. "I'm going to try to say this the best I can. He...Dax is the better choice for you. I had no business stealing you away from him. In my absence he made right by you. He's proved his worth, Lainey. He's a good man. He still wants you after this," he says, waving his hand in between us. "He's got to be broken and yet he has so much confidence in your relationship that he's still here. That counts for something. It counts for everything." My breathing accelerates. So much so that I'm now sucking air in through my nose and pushing it out of my mouth like I'm running a damn marathon. I feel faint—palms clammy, eyes sparking a million different colors. God, he's doing this. He's breaking my heart again. I shake my head. Cody's blue eyes are pleading with me. His lips so perfectly kissable are saying goodbye. He continues, "Marry him, Lainey. Marry him, goddammit. If not because I'm telling you he's the better man—because I can't give you what he can, because he is man enough to let you do what you want. What more can I say? He deserves you."

"Enough!" I yell, throwing out a hand like maybe that will stop the verbal wounds he's throwing out left and right. "Lies. Nothing but lies, Cody Ridge!"

He sits up straight and covers his face with his large, strong hands. "They aren't lies, beautiful girl. They're truths. That's why you feel so strongly."

"What about you, then? What do you deserve?"

He looks at me. "Not you. That's for damn sure."

"I get to make the decisions about the ring I wear on this finger," I say, pointing to the ring finger on my left hand. "I also get to make the decisions on who gets this finger." I flip him off with both middle fingers and hop off the bed. "Fuck you," I say, walking to the huge window in my bedroom. I hit the remote on the wall and raise the blackout shades. The blue of the night shines on my face.

"I'm sorry," he says. Tears threaten, but I can't be weak. Not in front of him. Not yet. I need to think. Why is he doing this self-sacrificing bullshit?

I lean my head against the cool glass to ground myself. A panic attack threatens and I don't want anything to do with that mess right now. I touch the glass with my fingertips. "Why are you doing this to me?"

His footsteps are heavy as he approaches from behind. "I'm doing this *for* you," he says, laying one warm hand on my shoulder. I spin in one quick motion, my blonde hair a tangled mess in my face. He looks longingly at my mouth once again, takes a strand of hair between his fingers, and then tucks it behind my ear.

"I don't want you, Lainey."

This is the moment that I hear my heart break. It shatters into tiny, cold pieces. "What?" I ask. A traitorous tear sneaks down my cheek.

"He does," Cody says. His words don't match his exterior. I look at him closer and see lipstick at the bottom hem of his T-shirt. I swallow down a mouthful of spit and bite my lower lip. I notice more lipstick at his collar. He sees me appraising him—knows exactly what I'm seeing.

"Fuck you, Cody. Don't do me any favors." I wipe at my face with the back of my hand. "You're a weak bastard. You can't be a man and stand up for what you want. For what's always been yours. If this is really how you feel, that Dax is the better man for me, then you aren't the person I thought you were. I don't want you either." Cody closes his eyes, hanging his head. "You've said what you needed to say?" I ask.

The silence in the room is big and loud. I sniffle noisily, and his breaths are heavy—the exchange of oxygen and carbon dioxide. Except this isn't okay. It's everything but okay. I feel the sutures in my heart unraveling—the place Dax fixed, that Cody lives, is collapsing into rubble.

He finally says, "This has been a mistake from the beginning. I'm sorry I even agreed to see you. I should have followed your lead when you left me in a hospital room without opening your mouth." I lunge forward and slap his beautiful, cruel face. The force turns his head in the opposite direction. It leaves a remarkably large, red welt and I'm satisfied for the moment. The hurt comes back quickly and I want to do more than slap him. I want to kill him. For making me fall in love all over again and snatching it away, but mostly for calling our love a mistake. How can a love like ours be a mistake?

I throw out my hand. "Don't say anything else. You've made your point."

Because he's trying to not just break up with me, but destroy me too, he keeps on. He turns his back to me. "It's your fault, Lainey. I've been a fool to even entertain the idea of loving you again. I'll say it one more time. Marry Dax. He's a nice guy."

"Get out," I order, my tone angry and low. I try and fail to keep the tears in check. Numbness replaces all emotion, but I can't stop the crying.

Walking toward my bedroom door, he pauses at the threshold, turns and says, "It's okay to give up on the bad guy, Fast Lane." With that, he leaves. I hear the side door close and lock. My shaking hands fail as I try to grab my cell phone from the table in my bedroom where it charges. It slips out of my grip a second time and I give up. Who would I call at this hour anyway? Cody's words are on repeat. His boozy breath and lipstick stained clothing tell me he gave up on us before

I knew we were finished. Hopes, dreams, and plans are crushed so small, I know I'll never see them again. I sit on my purple, velvet chaise, pull a furry blanket over my shoulders, and cry harder than I've ever cried in my entire life.

****

Like clockwork, Dax calls in the morning. My voice is hoarse from sobbing for six hours straight. Being the good guy he is, he realizes something is wrong right away and insists on coming over even when I tell him not to. I'm fresh from a shower, still in a towel when he rings the doorbell. "What a fucking gentleman," I whisper to myself. I throw the door open and without saying anything else I walk back to the bedroom. Dax trails in my wake of anger, sadness, and denial. I guess he expects me to cry on his shoulder about losing Cody. How fucked up is that? When I get to the closet I drop my towel and enter. *Nothing he hasn't seen before*, I think, literally not giving a shit about anything. If I was wrong about Cody, I don't want to be right about anything else. Screw. It. All.

"I have work to get done, Dax. It was nice of you to stop by, but I really am fine. I just had a bad night's sleep. Bad dreams. You know how I get them." I glance behind me to see if he's listening, and he's staring at my bare backside. I decide that maybe I should give a few fucks. "Oops," I say, stooping down to grab my towel. "Sorry."

He's horny as hell. I can see it in his eyes and his bulging pants. "Don't apologize," Dax says. "You're not fine. Tell me about…the bad dreams," he orders, without taking his eyes off me. I realize I may not have Cody, but I have Dax. That's one truth that came spewing out of his mouth last night. This man is head over fucking heels for me. Still. It bothers me more than it enamors me. Cody doesn't deserve me? Well, I don't deserve anyone either—especially not Dax.

I lean against the doorjamb, propping one foot behind the other. My hair drips water onto the cool, wood floor. "Why are you so good to me? I don't deserve it. I don't even want it, and yet here you are trying to make everything okay. Some things aren't okay no matter what. That's where I'm at right now, Dax. Not okay. Won't be okay. Ever. Aren't you exhausted? Stop trying so hard." Maybe he'll get the point. I don't want anyone. I want to be alone to lick my wounds in peace and solitude. Even Dax's kind ways can't bring me back to life after this.

"It's Cody, isn't it?" Dax asks. Just the mentioning of his name gives me goosebumps.

I shake my head, saunter back into the closet, and throw on a long-sleeved maxi dress…no under garments needed. When I come back out I approach Dax. His gaze flicks from my hips to my chest, to my face. "Intuitive, aren't you? I'll be fine. I need time to figure things out."

He throws his arms out. "What is there to figure out? I'm standing right here. What do I have to do to get you to notice me? The person who has been right here the whole time?" He's right. Last night's conversation with Cody takes on the shape of my worst nightmare. Because maybe he's right. Maybe I should marry Dax and try to forget Cody is even alive. I was certain he was just bullshitting last night to easily cut ties with me, but now I'm second-guessing myself. *What if he's right?* my inner voice whispers as I take in Dax.

"Basically Cody told me to fuck off. I'm going to need some time to get over this, Dax. I was ready to drop everything for him—a fact that should bother you, yet it doesn't. There's not much I can't comprehend, but this is one of those times."

Gently, Dax grabs me by my shoulders and pins me with his soulful gaze. "Because that's how much I love you, Lainey. That's how much I'm sure of our future. You are it for me. When we first got together, I knew what I was getting myself into. It's not any different now. Don't think, just feel. I know your love for me is in there somewhere. I know it. I trust you." Just as Cody uses words to cut me, here is Dax trying to heal me with truths.

I'm so, so broken, flailing in the depths of confusion.

177

It's in this moment of Dax's beautiful words, with Cody's mean ones warring, that I give in. How can I not?

"Fine, Dax. Fine," I say, smiling a tiny, broken smile. "Give me some time."

He looks confused. "That easy?" he asks, raising one brow and quirking the side of his mouth.

"That easy," I confirm. "Can I just be alone right now? I'll call you later. I promise."

"The wedding?" he asks. He looks so hopeful and innocent. I have to swallow down the vomit I feel rising up in my chest. The wedding. The one I was hours away from canceling.

I give him my best 'we'll see' and send him packing. I try to be as kind to him as possible, reminding myself that he has nothing to do with Cody and his breakup to go down in history, but it's hard. He's male. The female body's initial response is to hate testosterone during times like this. He asks for details about what Cody said, and that's a huge mistake. I tell him the bare minimum. Enough to let him know he broke up with me and as little as I can because part of me doesn't want Dax to see Cody in this horrible light. Would he consider it a reflection of me? My poor choices? Cody is something I've never had a choice in. I think that's the problem. The one who loves most loses all the power in a relationship. My mother once told me that if one can find beauty in tragedy then you'll always have a soul that is free. There's no beauty or freedom in losing him again. There's only pain and shackles that pin me to the past. What used to be will haunt me and what almost was may very well kill me.

My body is quivering from the shock of everything. Nothing is fixed, Cody is gone, and Dax, my good guy, is trying to save the day yet again. I sit down at my computer and open my personal email. I haven't checked it in a while. The notifications have been off for days. There's one from Cody. I click it open and a pang of razor blades slice my heart when I see his words.

From: Cridge@ridgecontract.com

To: LaineyRostov@Memail.com

Subject: All the things I didn't say

I didn't say I love you because with you, it's more. You're so perfectly beautiful, unique, intelligent, stunning, cunning, I can't stop thinking about you. I want to take you to Dances like the Wind and live there with you forever. We'll never leave. No more jobs, contracting, looking over my shoulder. Unless you're naked over my shoulder, of course, I'll look then. I'm ready to make a forever life with you. The one we should have had before life threw us a nasty curve ball.

Don't believe me? Here's how I know: in a person's lifetime there are so many different types of love. Love that's just a verb, love that's merely content to exist, and then there's our love—a feeling so strong that the word doesn't do it justice. It exists in every space on the planet regardless of the circumstances (I know, I've tested it) and it transcends time, morphing to resemble what we need it to during any given moment. I think that's the kind of love that means the most. It changes when we need it to and stays steadfast at the same time. We have the time and space kind of love, Fast Lane.

P.S. I didn't say it, but I *do* love you.

Always. Time and space.

Cody

And with the conclusion of the most beautifully tragic email in the world, I lose the last shreds of sanity. My arms shake, but I manage to throw my goddamned laptop at the wall so hard that it dents the thick drywall. "How about this time and space, you asshole!" I yell. I fold my arms on my desk, crown them with my head, and cry some more.

What else am I supposed to do? You can't lose the love of your life twice and expect to recover fully intact. Wrap it in bacon if you want to make it more palatable, but you can go ahead and choke on your happily ever after.

No one gets those these days.

CHAPTER SIXTEEN

Cody

One Month Later

The endless lines of code on my computer screens are making my eyes blur. Fifteen hours of coding and I'm finally stopping for a break. I forgot to eat today. Molly called and reminded me. I stretch my arms over my head and crack my neck. I need a workout, too—a long, long workout to drain me of my pent-up energy and sexual frustration. You'd think after a month, I would've at least found a woman to fuck on the regular, but I haven't been able to bring myself to do it. It feels…wrong. My dick, on the other hand, doesn't care and we're looming closer and closer to accepting one of the many dates Molly has made for us. I say 'us' because my dick is the deciding factor. I can't make good decisions, maybe he can. I've let the guys take over RC for the time being. I make more money selling code. It's mostly because it helps me forget everything else. Other than a few check-in calls daily, Horse and Van have taken the reigns. V? He's mine. The guys know it.

I've received the intel from Dax and I've got a tracker on V. We're in the middle of planning the perfect method for capturing him. The scenarios play in front of my eyelids when I close them to sleep at night. Most aren't logical or reasonable scenarios, but fuck, it's my dreams. They all end with the same fate. V dead, lying in front of my boots, and me finally sucking in clean oxygen for the first time since my captivity all those years ago. Not only will I be able to rest easy knowing he's paid for what he's done to me, but his wrath won't be available to anyone else either. I'm doing the world a favor, really.

In contrast to my dreams, my nightmares are always comprised of Lainey's tear-streaked face. How cruel I was to tell her those lies. How impossible it is that she believed me. Though I knew she would, it still stings that she didn't question anything. She took it all at face value without reading into it. Literally days before I broke up with her, I wrote her an email that explained how I felt. It was supposed to insert doubt into my breakup speech. It didn't. My words haunt me. They were the perfect deception. It worked. She's marrying Dax Redding, Navy SEAL, Virginia's best catch. I think the wedding is soon, but I try not to dwell. I got what I wanted out of the unfair trade-off. Dax got more. Some nights I miss her more than is bearable. It's worse this time. Knowing she's in his bed, loving him, kissing him, being his. At least when I was in V's dungeon I could wax poetic about Lainey. Keeping my eye on the prize is the only thing that works to clear my mind.

NYC is bustling at this hour. I peer down at the people and cabs littering my view and blow out a pent-up breath. So many people and yet I'm so lonely. "Soon your loneliness will have purpose," I say out loud, reminding myself why I'm here, torturing myself with code instead of in Lainey's arms. To stop the train of thought I pull on a T-shirt, ball cap, and sneakers to head out into the city and grab a bite to eat. When was the last time I showered? Shaved? It doesn't matter. I slide into a café near my house, the one Molly called my order into, and ask the waitress if it's ready. While she's gone in the back to check, I turn to sit at a booth.

"Cody Ridge. Is that you?" a brunette woman sitting nearby says. I raise my eyebrows in surprise and turn toward her voice. Should I know this woman? While beautiful and unassuming, I have no fucking clue who she is.

She puts a palm on her chest. "It's me. Molly's friend, Rosy. I was with Molly that one time she made a delivery to you." How in the fuck am I supposed to remember this? I smile and nod. I pretend. Then I

183

realize what's really going on right now. When will I learn?

"Molly told you I'd be here?"

She looks confused. "No. Well, yes. She said we had a date. I thought it was weird that I didn't hear from you and just her, but I figured you are a very busy, very important man and she is your assistant." Flattery will get you everywhere. The waitress returns and confirms that there was never an order placed. Rosy tucks her hair behind her ears. It's a nervous habit.

Of course there wasn't an order. This is an elaborate set-up from the mastermind of Molly-fired-in-the-morning. "Join me," I say, nodding to the seat in front of me. Not a very gentlemanly move, but I'm calculating just how Molly will pay for this. Rosy smiles my way, showing me all thirty-two of her perfectly whitened teeth, and scoots into the booth. Up close she's even prettier than I first thought. While her face is waxed and preened with makeup, I can tell she's a beauty without it. She's young. Younger than me, that's for sure. With youth comes naiveté and for a brief moment I envy her and her unmarred soul. I'm assuming, of course, but how simple must her life be— how very completely different from mine. Like a damned light bulb flickering to life, it hits me. *Rosy is exactly what I need.* Simplicity at its finest.

She's telling me about an accident involving a cab and bicycle down a few blocks. Her mouth moves quickly, and her voice isn't offensive. She's a talker and a pleaser. Rosy gets animated when I nod, or smile to encourage her to go on. Maybe Molly will live to see another day as my assistant. She's right. I feel less lonely already.

The waitress comes by and brings menus, which interrupts her current story. "Tell me about you," I say to Rosy, cocking my head to the side inquisitively. "I want to know everything."

Her cheeks flush crimson, and her long lashes float down bashfully. "There's not much to know, really."

"I don't believe that for one second," I reply. She giggles—such a pure, innocent, innocuous noise, but my cock responds immediately. *Yes, we are where we're supposed to be right now, cock, fear not.*

"I graduated Julliard last semester. I'm the assistant to the assistant of the CEO of Silver Enterprises. I know, I know, all that money for a degree that I'm not even using. My mom says I'm throwing my life away, but I'm climbing the ladder, you know? Everyone has to start somewhere. I want to run things one day," Rosy says, finally meeting my gaze. Her eyes are light brown, a liquid amber color. They're the wrong color. I close my eyes when Lainey's face comes to mind. I remind myself that wrong is what I need. It's right.

I rub the stubble on my chin with my thumb and forefinger. I should have shaved. "You're right. Sometimes parents don't know best," I say. My aunt and uncle raised me and it's been far too long since I've seen them. Everyone had a hard time adjusting to my non-death. For me it was easier to throw myself in work than stick around and lament with them about the time when I was a different man. Although it's what they would have preferred, I'm sure. Talking about it makes it real and I've developed the ability to mask it.

Like right now. "I can't believe what you've been through! I followed it on the news for weeks. It's so crazy! Are you okay? I mean, of course you're okay. Look at you. But are you okay, really?" Rosy asks, though she has no fucking right. This would have pissed me off, usually. She's young. She can't help it. Twenty-somethings have the tact of the cast of reality TV stars. Zero. *Humor her, Cody,* my cock whispers.

"It was pretty crazy," I say, trying not to let my sarcasm rear. "I'm okay. Everything worked out. Some say the hard things in life are the ones that build the most character." Also, it depends on what you deem 'okay'. It was indeed crazy, and I'm also a little bit crazy. Insanity is character so it's not a lie. How did she flip this around? She's supposed to be talking about herself.

Our food arrives and we both dig in. She can't possibly know that I haven't eaten in God knows how long, that I've been developing code that will sell for more than most people make in a lifetime. I want to attack my plate, but I hold back.

"Where are you from?" I ask. It's a relevant question for her age and status in life. She probably just moved from there before attending college here in the city.

She blushes a little, swallows her food, and then says, "Virginia Beach, actually. My parents just bought a house by the water. Their dream home. It's so beautiful. I'm happy for them. I met Molly when we crossed paths in Virginia Beach. I guess you could say I've been a fan of yours for quite some time now. A fan of all Navy SEALs, actually." Oh, great. A young frog hog. I wonder if any of the other guys have tapped her yet. Molly despises women who seek out SEALs. The fact that she set me up with one should give me a clue about what she thinks about me at the moment.

I nod my head, pull my cap down a little lower, and take another bite of my food while she continues on about the house. The waitress fills our water glasses and leaves again. "So, you're a fan, huh?" I ask in a lull during her praise and worship for my former career path. "I'm not in the Navy anymore, though. You still wanted a date?" I'm half joking.

She looks mollified. "Of course. I mean, not with just anyone. With you." I'm special. How sweet. My dick agrees. "Molly said you wanted company." Now we're going somewhere.

"Did she? What type of company?" I keep my voice low, discreet.

Rosy looks left and right then says, "A friend? Someone to hang out with? You're lonely in the city. She said you would probably be dirty and depressed from sitting in front of the computer for days on end." Truth. The former Cody Ridge would never fuck a woman after the first date. Probably not even after the second. But then again, the former Cody Ridge was always in love with one woman. He still is. It doesn't mean the newer, dirtier, and jaded Cody Ridge can't come out to play for the night. Rosy might even go all fan girl when I pull out my cock. How could I resist that? "So, do you want a friend?" she asks shyly. I do.

Instead of replying I throw my arm out to get the waitress' attention and ask for the check. Rosy hasn't finished her meal, but you should see this chick's eyes light up when she realizes we're leaving together. Can't blame a woman for knowing what she wants. I pay the bill, stand up, and hold out my hand to Rosy. She smiles shyly and takes it without hesitation. "To my place, then? It's right around the corner," I explain.

She giggles. "Yes! This is going to be so much fun." Oh, baby, more fun than you know. No limp dicked college boys for her tonight.

My mind starts racing when I think about what I'm about to do. *You're moving on. She has,* cock says. I can't argue with that logic, but I also have to admit that it feels dirty and underhanded. I'm leading Rosy to the door when in walks the reason for all my hesitation.

Because of course karma, fate, and every other bullshit lie has to crash my pussy party.

Lainey walks in with another woman. She has her laptop and a folder tucked under her arm. She's here on a business meeting. The odds of this fucking happenstance are so ridiculous that I have to laugh. Of course she looks stunning. Blonde hair wrapped up into a bun on top of her head, lips perfect, tits at attention, eyes locked on me and my scruffy face, and unwashed clothing. Then her gaze shifts to Rosy. Ouch. I see the pain flicker across her face. It can't be an ounce of what I feel when I think of her and Dax. She's marrying the guy, for Christ's sake. I can't feel bad for Molly's forethought. No, in fact, I feel good about this.

I swallow down the searing pain and greet her. "Hey," I say.

Her pretty blue eyes turn down in the corner. "Mr. Ridge," she replies.

I smile. "Oh, it's like that, I see." She nods, introduces me to her client, and then directs her to a nearby table. Rosy excuses herself to the ladies' room because I'm sure she senses duress—young, but perhaps not as naïve as I thought.

"I can't talk, Cody. I'm here for business."

"At my house. You're at my house. On business." I miss seeing her. My chest literally aches with longing at the mere sight of her. Will this pain ever go away?

She opens her arms wide. "This café is not your

189

house. It happens to have great salads. I guess you should have mentioned that you got this restaurant in the custody agreement. Oh, that's right, you haven't made any sort of contact for a month. You broke up with me, remember?" Her words ooze with hurt. Clearly she's still upset with me.

I clear my throat. "Didn't want to infringe. I know you're planning a wedding." I glance down at her engagement ring. It sparkles in the low lights. "I'm glad you're happy, Fast Lane."

"Don't you fucking dare Fast Lane me. Never again. You don't get to call me anything except the past and possibly the best fuck of your life. That's it. You're an asshole, Cody Ridge, and I vow to make you pay for what you did to me."

"I'm sorry. I didn't mean to hurt you. You have to believe it's better this way. Right?" I implore her to lie. I'll call her out right here and now. It's unreal that she thinks I meant the things I said. Molly helped me with a tube of her lipstick and a bottle of perfume she had in her purse. She coached me on what to say and then waited in the car for me while I broke up with Lainey. I gave her a bonus check for all her trouble. She did have to put me to bed after that bottle of whisky. I'm also pretty sure I was crying. No one should bear witness to that.

Her blue eyes, rimmed with a soft black makeup, begin to water. "I don't know what I believe anymore,

Cody. I do know you're wasting my time." She brushes past me, causing my skin to burn where her arm touches mine. Electric goosebumps, a touch that is so, so right.

"Lainey, wait," I say. My command is louder than it should be. She only turns her head, not her body. A half committal to whatever I have to say. Her gaze meets mine and for a second I think she understands—she sees how much love I still have for her. It burns like a fucking Olympic torch that will never die. *See it. Please see it.* Rosy and impeccable timing ruin the moment. She bounces up next to me and locks her slim arm around mine. Lainey swallows hard, closes her eyes, and heads to the table where her client waits. I leave with Rosy chattering aloud about everything and nothing. I glance over my shoulder, looking through the windows of the restaurant. Lainey doesn't look my way again. She talks to the woman, but the corners of her eyes are turned down and her smile is false. Broken hearts never truly heal, they mend, beat a little differently, forever after. Lainey and I are the greatest love that ever died.

Fucking Rosy isn't going to help me forget. Not for one second.

It sure is going to be fun trying, cock says.

****

I've tried calling Molly four times this morning. Granted it's before six a.m. and she isn't required to answer her cell before seven, but I want to talk to her. I think it's talk that I want to do. Half of me is angry because of her underhanded date set-up, but the other half is pretty fucking happy with her for it. Rosy left my place late last night. Mostly we talked, and when she tried to initiate more I wasn't game. Because what hot-blooded male turns down sex with a young, intelligent woman who is asking for it? Someone as fucked up as I am, that's who. Her company was nice, and she even pretended to be interested in my coding expeditions. She smiled and asked questions when I told her, in laymen terms, what I was working on. Dare I say her company was a welcome surprise. She got embarrassed when I politely declined a blowjob, assuming she picked up wrong cues throughout the night. I reassured her that the cues were all there, but I was tired and wanted an intimate encounter with a woman such as herself to be perfect. It was a load of horseshit.

I can't stop thinking about how upset Lainey looked last night. She's getting married. She's supposed to be this glowing, happy, radiant bride. Seeing me put her off in a bad way. Did I condemn her to a life of unhappiness with Dax? Surely she knows she has a choice to say 'fuck you, Dax, I'm marrying no one.'

Rosy gave me her phone number and we made plans

192

to meet at the bookstore this weekend. We'll see if she cancels before then. I'm not counting my chickens before they hatch, that's for sure.

I wander from my bedroom to the kitchen. Pouring orange juice straight into my mouth from the container without my lips touching and without spilling a drop is a skill I've perfected over time. I finish off the bottle, order a take-out breakfast, and turn on my computers for the daily grind. I have a meeting with the guys at eleven and a day full of staring at computer monitors again. I click open my email to see if anything has changed overnight. Several emails catch my eye, but one, always the one, starred as V.I.P. gets opened first. It's of the most unexpected sort.

From: LaineyRostov@Memail.com

To: Cridge@ridgecontract.com

Subject: Intimate encounters

I debated for a full six hours whether I should give you another second of my life with this email, but in the end I figured I better. Because assholes stretched as wide as you tend to stink and need to hear the truth sometimes.

1.) I would like custody of the café by your house. I don't care if it's by your house. It's by my favorite fabric store, so I'm there frequently. Good lettuce is hard to find in NYC.

2.) This one is more of a PSA because I feel the need to get it off my chest. The next time you decide to break up with a woman you should do it sober, with clean clothing and maybe drop a few fucking hints before. Definitely don't send confusing emails days before you break her heart.

3.) The real reason I'm emailing after a month of no contact is because Dax is insisting that I invite you to the wedding. The very last thing I want is for you to come and I told him this, but he has some fucked up notions that you being there means you accept the fact that we're married and that you won't change your mind and come groveling back to me one day in the future. I know. He's fucking crazy. Like I would entertain that notion for even a millisecond. After the things you said, I can't fathom you ever choosing to be in my presence again, but just in case you're wondering how I feel. There you go.

In conclusion, running into you was awkward. Let's not let that happen again. Don't be such a heartless asshole. Losing a person twice isn't easy. You should have at least taken me out to dinner before you fucked me over. And you're invited to our wedding. Formal wedding invitation to follow, but you better RSVP 'no'.

P.S. I'm sorry it's late. The delay was out of my hands, but your furniture is being delivered tomorrow. I'll finish the job and make sure it's installed properly. (As long as you're not there.)

P.P.S. I thought blondes were more your thing, cradle robber.

Time (cough, cough) and (give me) Space, Lainey

CHAPTER SEVENTEEN

Lainey

It took far longer to compose the email to Cody than I'm willing to admit. The words started forming the second I saw him with that girl in the café. Jealousy like I've never experienced hit me like a tsunami. It was a horrible feeling that had me seeing green. I think dealing with his death was easier. At least then I thought he was gone for good. Now I know he's living, breathing, and potentially loving someone other than me. I'm marrying another man and I feel like this about Cody. It's the most selfish, horrible predicament that anyone on the face of the earth has ever had to deal with. I'm sure of it. I reassure Dax all the time, because why wouldn't he be leery? I tried to break up with him multiple times while I was with Cody all in the name of true love. Lying to him this time is easy. Cody doesn't want me anymore. He's moved on so thoroughly that he's dating. My stomach flips and I feel faint thinking of him with another woman. Will this feeling ever subside? Will this be my torture for not being right for him? It doesn't seem fair. In fact, it seems like utter, fucking crap. Anger is the next step in the progression to forgetting Cody Ridge, and I remind myself of that daily.

"We don't have to go on our honeymoon directly following the wedding, Dax. I mean, you'll be busy at work and I have a couple of design jobs in limbo." He already vetoed my idea of skipping a honeymoon altogether. He says we need to reconnect on a deeper level somewhere off the map, just the two of us. He's probably right. I'm just going along with the motions at this point because Dax is so sure about everything. It will be enough for me too. It has to. The Rostov clan is coming to town for a big ole' wedding. "I know you think we should go somewhere exotic and different, but what if we stayed close to home?" I think of the house, my house, in the Hamptons and long for another visit. Dax would be severely depressed if he knew where my thoughts are right now.

Dax looks up from a stack of pamphlets, folders, and books scattered in front of him. "Where did you have in mind?" he asks, narrowing his eyes at me.

Picking up my spoon, I dip it back into my coffee and begin stirring it again. "Oh, I don't know. A quick flight. A long weekend somewhere manageable."

Nonchalant enough?

He shrugs. "It's like you don't care, Lainey. I thought we moved past this. You were excited for the wedding before, now you're lukewarm at best. Is it him, still?"

I cough on a hot sip. "Of course not. We've been together for a long time. I'm not the type of person who wants flair and dramatics. I get the desire to get away for a bit, but it doesn't have to be to Bali or Seychelles or some private island off the coast of Australia. Simple is all I'm saying. I'm not lukewarm, Dax. I'm hot," I say, smiling at him over my mug. He smiles back—it's genuine and warm. This is why I'm marrying him.

Standing up, I walk over and perch myself in his lap and clasp my hands around his neck. "You're beyond hot, but I'd fathom a guess you know that already. You're trying to work your wiles at this very moment," Dax says, running his hand over my knee and up my leg.

"My wiles are quite innocent, Mr. Redding," I respond, using my very best Austen English accent.

He laughs. "Innocence isn't something you play well."

That takes me aback a little, but he doesn't mean it the way he should. Because he truly is the innocent one in this coupling. He doesn't realize it. I kiss him on the corner of his mouth, half on his cheek. I feel him smiling under my lips. That's all I feel—the physical response from him. There's no zings, emotions, wanton lust attached to anything these days. Since Cody, I haven't felt much of anything below the waist. I don't crave Dax's touch or dream about bodice ripping sex that melts the bed sheets. Time. I just need more time to forget Cody. I'm not even sure if that's a possibility, but I have hope. He took more than my heart. The casualties were high and far reaching. Hope. He can't have that.

Dax pulls me over his lap so I'm straddling him. His cock is hard and pushing against my core. "What do you think, Lainey? I said we should wait until our wedding night, but maybe we can fuck around a little. I miss you and this would probably be a lot less stressful if we both got our rocks off together." Dax hasn't been staying with me at my house. We've fucked a million times, but now he wants to wait until the wedding. Something about prolonging the longing. I'm not sure how it does anything except frustrate him, but I agreed mainly because I don't care about sex right now. When I do dream about sex, Dax isn't the star of my wet and wild fantasies.

His eyelids are heavy as he strokes the outside of my thighs. "Oh, my, Mr. Redding. You'd have me fuck around before the big walk?" I ask, staying in character. The word fuck doesn't have a ladylike quality with any accent. That's okay. I'm pretty sure it's meant to be dirty in every country around the world.

He leans in and kisses my neck. "I'd fuck you so good you wouldn't be *able* to walk," he responds. What should ignite desire makes me feel uneasy instead. *He's your fucking fiancé, Lainey. Pull your shit together and be a woman.* I'm saved from having to concoct a response when my cell phone rings on the table behind me. It's the morose tone I assign when my mother calls.

I hold my finger to Dax's lips. "Hold that thought, baby," I say, scooting off and into my own chair to answer the call. He'd never have me ignore my mother, being the gentleman he is. Right now, he looks like he may have changed his stance on it, though.

"Mom. How are you?" I say into the smartphone. She greets me, her accent sounding familiar and comforting to my Americanized ears. "Yes, I'm home. Why do you ask?" I haven't spoken to her about Cody. She hasn't asked. It's the unspoken rule that I'm not to fuck up this wedding.

"Your cousins are flying in for your bachelorette party. They can stay at your house, right?" I'd forgotten completely about the party. Chloe has been planning it for months, but we haven't spoken about it recently. Shit.

Chloe invited family from overseas? It's news to me. Unwelcome news. "That's right," I say, pretending to know and pulling my planner open at the same time. I let my finger scroll through the dates and find the Saturday it's planned for. It's not even marked in my fucking calendar. It's this weekend. God help me.

"Sure thing. Of course they can stay with me. Do they need a ride from the airport?"

"No, no. Of course they'll get a driver. Do you need to hire cleaners before they arrive?" Oh, this is where she's going with this conversation.

I scoff. "Mom, my house is always clean." Because I have a cleaner come biweekly. She doesn't need to know that, though.

"It's a large house, Lainey. I want to make sure you're not overwhelmed with anything before the big day. That's enough for you to worry about."

"What do you mean by that?" I ask, my tone sharp. Dax looks up. I see him scrutinizing my face in my peripheral vision. I ignore him the best I can, but I'm not sure where Mom is going, so I stand up and start pacing around the dining room.

She's silent on the other end. I hear her breathing. "I know, sweetheart. I know how you're feeling. Conflicted, to put it mildly. I can't imagine how I'd feel in your situation." Pain sears my chest. Cody. Even my disconnected mother senses my inner turmoil by merely looking at my situation from the outside, knowing no details.

I glance behind me at Dax and give him a little smile before slipping out of a set of French doors that lead to an open deck. "You don't know a lot of things, Mom. Cody made it quite clear that I'm making the right decision by marrying Dax. Don't worry about me. I know how to make good life decisions."

"You're my daughter. I'll always worry for you. Good as the decision may be, it may not be where your heart is. Of course I'll be enraged if you call off another wedding, but I'll get over it if it means you're making a good life decision that also makes your heart happy. I just can't imagine," she says. No one can imagine.

"Cody broke up with me, Mom. The exact words he used were 'I don't want you, Lainey. Marry him.' I can't argue with that. He's a jerk, okay? I don't want to talk about it anymore. Dax is a great man and I'll live a beautiful, loving life with him. When do my cunning cousins arrive?" Maybe a subject change will help ease the tremors in my hands. I suck in a breath away from the phone receiver. Air. I need air. I can't talk about this. My cousins aren't really my cousins. They are the twin daughters of my mother's best friend. I grew up with them teasing me unmercifully. Two against one isn't fun. I'd fathom a guess that I hold the upper hand these days, but the prospect of seeing them, partying with them, and housing them is daunting. At least I'm getting married first.

"Nothing is ever as it seems, sweet girl. You know that. How long did you pretend to be something you weren't? Aren't you doing that now still? Different in some ways, but at the core you're still a master at pretending. You forget I'm your mother. I raised you. I know these things." That small sentimental bone I have in my pinky finger starts aching for my mom. I need to visit her, hug her, let her understand me like no one else can. Still, her words ignite fire because she's right.

"I am myself. I don't know how to be anyone else!" My voice rises and I remind myself to keep my tone down. I have neighbors now. A quick glance in their direction and I see them outside by their pool. It's a middle-aged couple with beautiful hair and a small dog that yaps incessantly. They are the typical resident in this neighborhood. Those that have worked hard for most of their lives and can now afford waterfront property in a gated community. I raise my hand when the man looks my way. He waves back, but turns to go into his house. *Good, take that fucking rat dog with you,* I think.

"If you get cold feet, it may be more than that, honey. That's all I'll say about it for now."

"God, it's like you're on Cody's side or something, Mom. Didn't you hear what I told you? I didn't have a choice! He ended our…affair, relationship, whatever you want to call it."

"Did he really?" she asks.

I growl. "Yes. I'm one hundred percent sure."

"People say things they don't mean every day. You're not the only one who can pretend."

"What's that supposed to mean? You're like a stale fortune cookie today, Jules," I say, sitting down in one of the several iron reclining sun chairs. My sunglasses are sitting on the table next to me, so I pop them on.

She ignores me and begins telling me flight information. They arrive tomorrow. Great. I make a mental checklist of everything I need to get done on top of my never-ending usual list. I hear a door upstairs close and look up. It's the set of French doors that open to the upstairs wrap-around balcony. I wonder how long Dax was listening. This is what it's come to. A month before our wedding and he has to listen in on phone conversations with my mother to garner information. What am I doing?

You're making a life for yourself. A life that would have been perfect if Cody never existed. But he does.

My mom makes plans to come down and spend the day with me when my cousins get here, tells me she loves me and misses me, and then hangs up without another word about her mysterious prophecies about Cody and our non-relationship. Dax didn't hear anything. He couldn't have. I plaster a fake smile on my face, walk into the dining room, and find a note on the counter from Dax.

Went to the store. Call if you need anything. ILY.

I sigh, relieved, yet worried. At least now I have time to make a phone call to the house cleaner and request that she come and tidy up and make up some guest rooms for the girls. Next is Chloe to make sure she doesn't need any help with God knows what she

204

has planned for this weekend. She doesn't. She tells me she has it handled like a large cock in the palm of her hand. Eloquent. I shower, dress in a pair of jeans, and drive to Cody's hopefully empty house to be there for the delivery. Some may think I'm asking for trouble even going to his empty house, but with how he feels about me, trouble isn't even on my radar. Hurt is—pain and bewilderment, too. I'll merely tell the delivery men where to arrange his beautiful pieces and then lock the door behind me and never go back. Never mind that the things I selected were things that I myself loved and thought were perfect. You know, that would go perfectly in the house with my dream kitchen and everything else that was supposed to be mine. Including him. I roll my window down and let my hair air-dry on the drive over to the house.

I'm anticipating this being a sick kind of torture.

****

The trucks are already here waiting when I pull up thirty minutes early. I call Dax to let him know I'm overseeing a delivery and I'll be home for lunch. I also tell him about my cousins crashing the house in the very near future. He sounds happy. Probably because it's the next step to the altar. We're running out of days and activities. He tells me he plans on having a bachelor party this weekend, too. So we'll both be out and distracted. We won't be jealous of each other. I roll my eyes. After what I did to him, I can't imagine being jealous over anything he could possibly get up to. If he wants hookers and blow for his bachelor party, I'll support it. I also know that's not Dax. But I tell him he is welcome to have as much fun as he wants.

I hop out of my car and walk up to the guy holding a clipboard. "Cody Ridge," he asks.

I roll my eyes. "Yeah, that's me. You're early," I say, bending over to untie my tennis shoes. "No shoes in the house, pads underneath the large pieces while moving indoors and please, for the love of all that is holy, be careful with the walls. It has new paint and floors," I explain. "I'll open the garage, the dimensions of the pieces require a larger opening." He nods, looks at me like I'm some kind of freak, and speaks with the other three men off to the side.

"I do this for a living," I say to his thick back. "I know how this operates!"

He turns around, quirks one brow, and says, "Yes ma'am," then turns back around. The nerve of some people.

Huffing out in exasperation, I leave them to their business and unlock the doors with the keys I have from before. I sigh. That realization leaves a lump in my throat. Before. Gross. I push open the heavy door, take off my shoes, and the scent of Cody hits me like a baseball bat to the face—his cologne and the scent that mixes with the flavor of his body wash to create the most mouthwatering concoction of a scent. All of that is in the air taunting me, haunting me, reminding me of what I can no longer have. "It's a man's house. Of course it will smell like a man," I say. Why does it have to remind me of so much? It looks as if he hasn't been here in quite some time. It makes sense, though, he prefers the NYC apartment and it seems that's where his new friend lives as well. I was the reason he was previously here so much. Standing perfectly still, I look around and let my mind wander back. Not just to last month, but back further, when we first fell in love under the stars in the middle of the night. His arms wrapped around me and I'd never felt so safe in my entire life. I felt like every glistening star could fall from the sky, but his skin covering mine would shield me from harm, shield me from everything the world could throw my way. At the time, I didn't know that my love for him could destroy me completely. The innocence and purity of that moment gives me chills. That was the beginning of our love story. This, right here, is the end.

I close my eyes and savor that happy memory. I'll always have our memories, no matter where life takes him—no matter where it takes me, either. These memories can be my new dirty, little secret. My phone buzzes in my purse, shaking me from my reverie. It's my intel man. He's been digging up information for me.

I answer.

He speaks without saying hello first. "No, I'm not in the city. I will be, why?" I say.

His voice is muffled due to the technology he has that makes his calls untraceable. Shady business. "We've been talking and we think it's safer if you head into the city. It's more crowded. If anyone is looking for you, you're a sitting duck in your large house by the water." The movers start unloading furniture into the empty great room. I scrutinize their every single move.

Without taking my eyes off them I say, "Duh. Obviously I'm well aware of the basics of survival and evasion. I know how to disappear. Has something changed?"

I hear papers shuffling in the background. "Well, uh, there was your wedding announcement in the newspaper. That may not have been the best idea, Ms. Rosemont."

Fuck. Dax. He's clueless. I can't get that irritated. I look at my watch. "Of course it wasn't. I didn't do that. I'm headed into the city this weekend for my bachelorette party anyways. I'll stop by in a couple hours to pick up the tracking devices and cameras. Are they ready?"

"Yes, ma'am."

"Good." I hang up the call. Heading toward the direction of the smell of new furniture, I round the corner and smack directly into a broad chest. That's what I get for being distracted.

"Watch it," I mutter. Then I realize it's not one of the ungrateful slobs, it's Cody.

My eyes widen and my heart kicks into gear. My palms are sweaty. This can't be happening. "What are you doing here?" I ask.

"A little incredulous of a question, no? It's my house, Lainey. The last time we spoke I got the impression you wanted to murder me. Setting my house on fire with the new additions might be high on your hit list, too," Cody says, smiling and holding his arm out toward the new, gorgeous table. I admire it because it is fucking beautiful. "I wanted to help move *my* things into *my* house." Rational, yet infuriating.

"Of course. Just making good on promises. I'll let you handle it from here, Mr. Ridge," I say. "If you'd let me know you were handling it, I wouldn't have intruded." If I knew he would be here, I would have dressed up, put on makeup. I would have actually done my hair instead of hanging it out my car window like a Labrador Retriever. There's never anything wrong with showing him exactly what he doesn't want anymore.

Cody shakes his head. "Thank you, Ms. Rosemont. Your services are most appreciated and of the highest caliber. How much do I owe you?"

I scoff. He raises one blond brow. "You were the one handling this with such professionalism. Do you

209

make it a habit of working for free?" he asks.

"Closing this chapter of my life is payment enough, Cody." My damn voice shakes. He's so beautiful. Standing in front of me bronzed, smiling, like in my dreams. "I should go. Dax is waiting for me." Now it's Cody's turn to scowl. "I hope you like everything."

"You're going to see Phillip. You're not going to see Dax. Don't lie to me. I heard you on the phone," Cody replies, folding his arms across his chest. "That's a bad idea, Lainey. What are you up to?"

"You have absolutely no right to know my business. How long were you being an eavesdropping snake?"

"Long enough." He licks his lips. My gaze is immediately drawn to his mouth. "Don't do this again," he orders.

"Why do you even care?" I shout, throwing both of my arms up in the air. I get the grand gesticulations from my Russian side of the family. He catches my wrists and holds them lightly. I hate that his touch heats me everywhere.

He takes a step toward me, continuing to hold my arms. "I care."

I shake my head. "Bullshit. You made it crystal clear that you don't care."

The fingers wrapped around my wrist aren't so gentle anymore. He pulls me close to his body, grabs my waist, leans down, and lightly touches his lips against mine. It's a kiss, but not really. It says I love you, but not really. It's everything and nothing. I melt against him. It's an uncontrollable response that confuses me to no end. I'm his puppet. As quickly as the embrace began, it ends. He steps back and away from me and turns around, facing his back to me.

I hear another voice, one that does not belong here, clearing his throat, and it causes me to jump into the air. My fiancé.

"I knew you'd be here. I read it in your planner when you were on the phone with your mother," Dax says, standing at the edge of the hallway that attaches to the garage. What did he see? Oh, my God, what did he see? Maybe he saw nothing. *Pull your shit together, Lainey.* I give myself a mental pep talk.

I walk to him because that's the proper thing to do if you're not guilty and flash him my megawatt smile. "Yes. I'm just finishing up. Cody showed up unannounced, so he's taking care of everything now." I know he didn't see anything. He's assuming. Relief washes over me. I give Cody a contrived smile when he sees us standing together. "I'm finished with the job, happy with everything that's arrived. I'm sure Cody is as well." Keeping the professionalism alive when I feel like having a panic attack is difficult, but not something I'm incapable of. And Cody said that returning to my espionage roots was a bad idea. Psh.

"Brother," Cody says, approaching both of us. He looks like a goddamned panther stalking prey—real, reassuring jerk. Your mouth wasn't on mine a minute ago. Dax tenses beside me, readying for a fight. I have to shake my head. Sometimes men are so stupid and territorial. Cody and Dax are about the same size, and I've always known they look similar, but seeing them together is odd. Same builds, eye color, hair color, bad ass attitude, and they've both been inside me. This meeting needs to get nipped in the bud, quickly. Cody extends his hand to Dax. "How are you? Lovely furniture your girl picked out, right?" Dax finally looks somewhere other than my face and Cody's body.

"Yeah, it's nice." He takes Cody's hand in his and shakes it firmly. "Looks like your deal is finished then, huh?" Dax asks me, but looks at Cody.

I'm confused. "Uh, yeah. Unless Cody sees something he doesn't like or wants to change."

"Something I want to change, you say? I think I do see something I want to change," Cody mutters, Dax's hand still in his.

"All right. All right. I don't know what type of pissing contest you're both engaged in, but I'm hungry. Let's go get lunch, Dax. I have a million things to do before this weekend, Dax." I say his name twice in hopes that he'll pull himself from whatever testosterone driven hate fest is taking place. "And, Cody, you have my email. Send me a message if there's anything you want to change."

Dax spins to me. "What's that supposed to mean?"

I see Cody over Dax's shoulder. He's smiling like a lunatic. "The undertones are so glaring that they are now overtones. I'm not sure what you guys are talking about, but if Cody sees a table, or a piece of artwork, or perhaps an upholstered chair that he finds to be of bad taste, he may email me and I will exchange the said piece for him," I say slowly. "Does that make sense to you, Dax Redding?"

He nods, looks at Cody, and then returns his gaze to me. "Cody, you'll let me know?"

"Of course. Hey, do you have the time?" Cody replies, cocking his head to the side. His laser gaze is locked on my face. It's so fierce and promising that it makes me uncomfortable in front of Dax. What must he think? We'll need to have a long conversation about this. I'll be reassuring him for the next week. It's not really lying if even I myself don't understand what it means. Cody didn't say anything. He just almost kissed me.

I wrinkle my nose. He's wearing a watch. I look at mine. "Eleven twenty," I deadpan. Dax shifts his weight from foot to foot next to me. He's antsy, wants to get away from here. Can't say I blame him. I do, too. I'm confused and more heartbroken than ever. What does the almost kiss mean? Even if it meant something, does it matter at this point?

One of the employees walks by with a packing blanket. "Do you have the space for the bar on the other side of the dividing wall in the lounge?" Cody asks. The mover shrugs his shoulders and assures Cody that he'll measure. Cody meets my gaze with narrowed, intelligent eyes. Dax storms off after mumbled goodbyes.

No one else picks up on it. Why would they? Time and space.

I swallow hard. I don't know what else to say. "Good luck," I whisper.

"I don't need luck. I'll see you soon," Cody says, smiling.

My stomach does a flip-flop, spinning my morning coffee around in circles, making me feel sick to my stomach. For someone so hell-bent on not wanting me, he sure knows how to make a woman wonder. His words still wrap me tight. *Marry him, Lainey. I don't want you. We're not going to work out.* I can't stop thinking about his lips against mine. And I shouldn't because I hate him. He will pay for being so cruel.

I hate him.

CHAPTER EIGHTEEN

Cody

"Write her a song. Chicks love songs," Maverick says, stretching his bulky arms above his head. Steve is off to the side, testing out my new bar, pouring more whiskey and bourbon into glasses than he has any right at four in the fucking afternoon.

I shake my empty glass with one large ice cube. "Songs only work for you, dude. Maverick Hart is the only man who can seal deals with lyrics. My voice sucks," I reply. Maverick smiles that million-dollar smile and shrugs his shoulders. Smug bastard.

Steve walks by, refills my glass with high-end bourbon, and heads back to the bar. As he heads back he says, "I like your new bar and the new furniture. I'm sure Lainey does, too." He cackles. They have jokes. They're here to hang out because far too much time has passed and because I'm a fucking mess over Lainey and they sense it. Tough guys we may all be, but damn, women really do a number on us.

Mav picks up a throw pillow and tosses it from a chair onto the couch. "She's the one who picked it out, moron. Give him woman advice. That's what he needs. Morganna is like a damned piranha. You have to be able to tell him something about the perils and rapture of keeping a woman. It's been too long for me." I haven't told them why Lainey and I aren't together. I'm sure they can formulate their own ideas and reasons. Neither was too surprised when I told them she was still marrying Dax. They must hang out with him too and not tell me. They are still SEALs and I'm not. I'm the odd man out these days. It's strange. I can't even tell them about V and the intel Dax gave. It would get him in trouble. And as much as I'd love to see him rot in prison friendless and Lainey-less I'm not a rat. I'd never go back on my word. A promise is a fucking promise and all that.

Tossing another throw pillow off my couch and into the same chair, I say, "I don't need advice. Women are a species better left to go wild and unexplored. Let them have their mystery. I just want to hang out with you. My coding takes up so much of my time that I forget to eat, let alone have fucking friendships." I don't count the dozen or so times per day I speak with Molly as friendship. Nor are the guys from RC counted as real friends. They are employees of my privately funded company. By privately funded I mean that my bank account rolls everything at Ridge Contracting. Within the next month or so it will be successfully independent and turning revenue.

I hear Steve stirring a drink and then he smacks his lips after the first sip. Maverick sits in one of my new chairs, tossing a smaller pillow in the air. It's now that I realize there are far too many pillows in this room. They must go. "I need you to teach me how to do that techy shit. Morg would love it if I could stay at home more with her and the kid," Steve says. He tosses his head back and forth as if considering something. "Nah, never mind, I don't have the patience, but maybe you should take some time off from it? Make time for other stuff?"

"Do you have any idea how valuable this is?" I ask, tapping the side of my head with one finger. It's ridiculous how much money you can make if you're code inclined. I can develop software from nothing. I can formulate codes that program computers to diagnose blood tests. I can write apps and improve upon others' mistakes. The skill I possess is invaluable. As long as the world is run by computers, I'll maintain my wealth.

"How's the other job going?" Mav asks. For a second I think he's referring to a particular job. V. Then I remember he has no clue about the peculiar deal Dax and I made. He's just curious about RC.

I sigh, take a sip of the honeyed liquid, and say, "It's great. Taking out bad guys one at a time. You know all about that, though." They both laugh. Steve joins me on my new overpriced sofa and puts his feet up on the coffee table.

"Your life is like a fucking dream, Cody Ridge," Steve says. Is that how other people view me? It's news to me. It's more like a nightmare with dream like sections.

I smile. It's weak. "I don't have everything." I don't have her. I don't have my lost years back. I will have peace soon enough, though. My pulse picks up its pace when I think about his death. The twisted part of my persona loves thinking about it. The average Joe that just wants his girl and a happily ever after cringes. One day I'll be able to reconcile the two. "I miss the teams and you guys."

Steve grabs high on my leg with a big hand. "If you wanted to make out all you had to do was ask. I missed you too, baby," Steve says in a singsong girl's voice. Maverick laughs.

"You know what I mean," I reply, swigging the rest of my drink and putting my cup down on a coaster. Pushing Steve's hand off my leg, I punch his thigh. "You're so busy with Morg and the kid that you have no clue about the outside world. Does she let you take your balls out of the glass jar when you leave the house?" I ask.

Maverick chimes in, "No. She keeps them on the top shelf of their kitchen. I've seen them."

"Fuck you!" Steve says. "She does things with my balls that should be in the record books. My big ass balls are right here between my legs. If they were in the kitchen they'd be covered with chocolate frosting getting tongued."

"Fucking sick, dude," I say, wrinkling my nose. Kitchen play has never been my thing. "I'm sorry I brought it up. What about you?" I say, raising my chin in Maverick's direction. "You have like a million spawn running around. Does Windsor even leave your bedroom?"

Maverick stands up, stretches his hands over his head, and lets them fall by his sides. His face morphs into one of complete and utter happiness. "Windsor," he says. It's a prayer, a name said just because he likes the sound as it rolls off his tongue. "I'll never get enough of that woman. Just two kids, not a million. If I had it my way, though? She'd be barefoot and pregnant for the rest of our lives. Maybe even when we're old and gray."

"Jesus, that's even more repulsive than chocolate frosting. Is this what happens when you get married? You lose your minds and your ability to determine what's hot and what's not? You guys are getting up in the years." I throw a pillow at Mav to wipe the weird ass smirk off it. He tosses it back, laughing.

"Only if you're lucky, bro. Only if you're lucky," Maverick says. His expression softens and his smile vanishes. "Are you going to their wedding?"

I swallow. Steve shifts beside me on the couch. "Question of the hour. Dax is a good guy, yeah?" I ask. Knowing what they'll say, I only say the words to buy myself time. I don't want to talk about her. It makes me upset and with a few drinks in me, I'm half in the mind to call her and tell her exactly why she shouldn't marry the asshole. "He has to be if she's with him," I say, mostly for my own benefit.

"He's a good guy." They both say it at the same time. I wonder how good of a guy they would think he is if they knew what I know. How low he slipped to get what he wants.

I nod, lean my head back on this deliciously comfortable sofa, and close my eyes. "Some things just aren't meant to be. I think she'll be happy. Have a normal life. Our engagement ended on weird fucking terms. Dax is normal and I think that's what she needs to stay out of trouble," I explain. I stop before I say anything further. They have no idea that Lainey came to Virginia Beach in order to spy on Navy SEALs. There are countless women here for that exact reason. The guys are familiar with the tactics, but I don't think they've ever seen one up close and personal. They wouldn't take too kindly if they did know, either. In the beginning, Lainey gathered information about us.

220

When we started work, where we took our training trips, where our private airport was located. All innocuous things that meant a great deal to the person she reported back to. I called her out right away, but I was keen with things like that. The house next door to Morganna? It was planned. Her friendships with the other wives and girlfriends? A scheme to get in good with them to get even more information about us.

She stopped spying when I asked her, straight up, and despite her reservations, she fell in love with me. Not that she had much say in that. When I fall in love, I make sure everyone around me knows it. She knew it and was helpless to repel my charms. By the time my fateful deployment rolled around she was putty in my hands, so in love with me that she agreed to be my wife. Slipping that diamond on her slim finger was one of the most memorable moments of my life. Now, I'm invited to watch another man marry my woman. That man happens to be the only reason why it's not my wedding ring going on her finger. Talk about a fucked up situation.

Steve sighs. "I can't say anything about what the fuck you guys have going on, but Dax is a good guy and Lainey seems hell-bent on marrying him. Are you two still fucking around?" So they know about the fucked up arrangement we had going on for a while. Who told them?

"No. I broke it off a while ago. It was too much

221

trouble. How did you know about that anyways? Doesn't seem like something a man would brag about. Sharing isn't caring in this instance."

"Pussy," Maverick says, coughing to cover his insult. Then he says, "It was mentioned in passing. Trust me, I think Dax was drunk off tequila when it was revealed."

I wrap my hands behind my head and look up at the expansive ceiling. There's a peak in this room and the glass windows at the top make the lighting in here perfection. "I did what was best for her, dude. My life is too dangerous. Like yours, except I don't have to answer to anyone, so shit is even more fucked up. The last thing I want is anyone hurt on my account." They're both nodding when I glance at them. At least they get it. "Imagine if it were Windsor or Morganna at risk," I say, looking at both of them to drive the point home. No one says anything. They're lost in thought, thinking of worst-case scenarios and how to stop them.

Steve speaks first, "Well, I'd say let's hit the strip club and get some drinks, but we don't do that anymore."

My turn. "Pussies." I smirk.

They laugh, but wouldn't you know, those pansy asses don't refute me. They're happily pussies. I want to be the same. One day, maybe. When V is cold in the ground, when I'm finished with working contracts. Maybe I will move to the Hamptons house and settle down eventually. Vacation year-round never hurt anyone.

I tell them about Rosy and how the date went all to hell. They explain what they would do if they were me and I listen. I even pretend I'll take their advice and call her as soon as I'm back in the city. I won't, though. I cancelled the second date and haven't spoken to her since. Try as I might, I can't bring myself to fuck anyone else yet. What if it feels different? Worse, what if I'll compare women to Lainey for the rest of my life? I have nothing but love for Lainey, but now I realize I might hate her, too.

"We have Dax's bachelor party this weekend in the city. Can we stay at your palace by the sea?" Steve asks. He's back at the bar, rummaging through my mixers.

"What? Like together? Have a romantic weekend together?" I ask jokingly. Maverick gets up and checks his phone. His screen saver is a picture of his wife, Windsor, and their kids sitting on her lap. The kids have his smile and Windsor, in all of her brunette glory, is stunning. I can't blame him. If she were mine, I'd want her all the time, too.

Steve punches my arm without spilling his new drink—a Manhattan. "No. We'll bring the families. Of course. Morg will love that place. I saw photos online when you bought it. Wasn't the seller dude a Sheik or something? Did you sell code formulated out of your left nut for it?"

"I think he was part hostage negotiator. He didn't budge on the asking price at all. Happily for him, I wanted it badly enough. So, like go to the bars and then head home to them at the end of the night?" What is this madness?

"Exactly," Maverick says, smiling like a fool. "I like to have my cake and eat it out, too."

"God, you're so fucking witty," Steve mutters. "What do you think?"

I nod. "Sure, sure, of course. You know I don't mind at all. I'll give you the codes and the keys before you leave. I'll let security know you'll be there. I have them patrol every so often to keep it on the up and up."

"So teenaged rat bastards don't throw eggs at your ten-thousand-dollar door?" Steve asks, cackling loudly at his own joke. It's also a joke that his wife, Morganna, made almost verbatim.

My phone buzzes in my pocket. It's Molly. "Exactly," I tell him, lying, before answering the call. I hold my finger up to let them know I'll be quick and head for my office. They're wrapped up in a conversation about pop culture and how kids don't have respect for their elders anymore.

I close the thick wooden door. "What's up, Molly?" This office reminds me of Dax and his bloody nose. Redecorating needs to go on my to-do list. Lainey will have to help me with that. Oh, shucks.

Molly prattles on about how she wants Horse to

have time off so they can go on vacation. It's what she starts her conversation with, so I know she wants me to remember it. I tell her most important first and the rest can come next.

She surprises me, though. "The guys say they're ready when you are for operation cooler shark." I obviously did not give this moniker to the operation that will kill V. I approved it, though. Sounds like the Is are dotted and the Ts are crossed.

"Why didn't you say that first?"

"Because, well, you have enough on your mind and cooler shark needs to be done before I can take a vacation with Horse, anyways. One in the same, really."

"When are they thinking?" Even if they say they're waiting on me I know the timeline is already in place. Professionals are always professionals. Time is precious and the most integral part of a successful mission. A minute the wrong way is enough time to destroy all chances of success. It may even mean your life taken instead of the bad guys'.

"Sunday." My heart skips a beat. It's soon. I'm ready. I've been ready. I hear the drips of stale water in the back of my mind. I don't count them anymore. They're always there waiting, though—background noise that reminds me of what I've become and what I'll never be again.

Molly confirms that everything is scheduled, set up, and ready to go. I won't be able to sleep until this is over and done with. I hang up the phone, but I'm not ready to face the guys again. I stand in the center of my office and contemplate everything that has brought me to this moment. The cost was high. Love. I think about putting my lips against Lainey's, how warm and comforting it was. She leaned into me, pressing her body against mine in a way that told me she still wanted me. She despises me for everything I am, but she still wants my body. Can I use that to my benefit?

Maverick raps on my office door a few times and then saunters in, a water bottle in his hand and one of my small remotes in the other. "Office windows?" he asks, then hits the button that opens the shades automatically. "Yahtzi!" he shouts.

"Good thing I'm not on the phone anymore," I say.

He clears his throat. "I heard you hang up. I wanted to tell you that I know this must be rough for you. Seeing Lainey marry another man. Telling you that means nothing, I know that. I think you're doing the right thing, honestly. Letting her go, that is. So I'm here to give you the best advice I can think of. Well, it's not my advice, it's Stone's. Tighten your towel, Cody. You got this." Maverick slaps me on the shoulder, presses his lips together, and nods his head. I nod. Emotion is so thick in the room right now you can cut it with the side of a dull fork—Maverick, remembering Stone, his dead best friend, and me realizing he's right.

"Put on my big girl panties and all that?" I ask,

smiling, trying to take the edge off.

Maverick runs his hand through his hair. "Something like that, man." He punches me in the arm, takes a sip of water, and disappears from my office. If he knew I was also contemplating a high profile murder alongside my obsession with Lainey, I'm sure he would have chosen different words.

Words. I owe some to Lainey. I email her at her old, personal address because it's safest.

From: Cridge@ridgecontract.com

To: LaineyRostov@Memail.com

Subject: Repaying debts

I'm sorry for things *I did* say. I realize now that I should have gone about breaking things off differently. My words weren't gentle, nor did they hold much truth. They were words I knew would send you away without looking back. I still think that's what you need to do, but I can't stand for another second to pass where you think I don't want you, that you're not the love of my life. I'm changing my words to better represent my heart. Marry him because he's the better choice for you. Marry him because you love him and he loved you when I couldn't. Spend your life making him as happy as you've made me. That's what would have happened if I never returned and that's an honest life. I'm okay with this now, Lainey. I mean, I'll never be truly okay because I can't lie next to you in bed at night, or see you round with my child, or know what your laugh lines look like twenty years from now. These are the privileges Dax has earned in my absence. I'm grateful to him, Fast Lane. You should be too. Surely you know I don't think this message will fix anything. My words were unforgivable. Hopefully they'll help you move on with a sense of pride and love for our years, and not the horrendous lies I asked you to believe. Don't let them mar what we had just as the joy we did share shouldn't overshadow the memories you'll surely make in the future with Dax. Let them exist in the same space if you ever find it in your heart to forgive me.

The café is yours. I'll stay away. Lettuce isn't one of my favorites, so I trust it's hard to find decent lettuce in such a voraciously foodie city. There's another one two blocks down I can frequent instead.

Forgive me. I'm not sure if I can watch you walk down the aisle to marry another man. I'm a lot of things, but a masochist isn't one of them. Also, I'm not sure I'll be able to keep my mouth shut at the 'speak now or forever hold your peace' bit. While I've said multiple times I think you should marry him, my illogical side isn't as keen on the idea. You don't want me there anyways. I'd only be a ghost from your past haunting a happy day.

(Remember that) Time, and (here is your) Space,
Cody

I hit send and return to the guys in the living room. My overall demeanor is morose, so they try to fix it with bourbon and stories from the old days. Maverick even starts singing a song he wrote for Windsor. As if I needed a reminder of how desperately beautiful lasting love is.

I hate that shit.

CHAPTER NINETEEN

Lainey

"The dress is too tight, the heels are too high, and my makeup is too dark," I say, staring at the foreign creature in the mirror in front of me. "And the wig…really?" We're getting ready at Chloe's mom's house. She lives on the outskirts of Manhattan.

Chloe scoffs. "Fuck no, it's not. You look perfect. This is the last hurrah as a single lady. You're doing it right, Lainey." Coming up behind me, she rubs her hands down my sides, smoothing the bandage dress over my hips sinfully. I admit that the dress is hot, the heels are to die for and the forty dollars' worth of makeup on my face does highlight my light eyes and high cheekbones, but it doesn't look a thing like me. Maybe that's the point. Disguise myself. The brunette wig falls in waves down my back like a high-class stripper. I move from one foot to the other, trying to see how steady I can be in these shoes. I roll up a pair of nude flats and stuff them in my small handbag. Emergency shoes seem like a good idea tonight. I come fully prepared for anything.

"Shouldn't I be at least a little comfortable? God knows what you have planned," I reply, wincing when I see her open another bag of penis straws in the reflection of the mirror. "None of this was necessary. This is for twenty-year-olds on their first engagement, who still have the party gene from college. Not for me. This isn't for me." I itch my head where the wig meets my true hairline. "Can't we just grab a couple of drinks and call it a night?" No one can stop Chloe. I'll make my displeasure known on principle.

Chloe rolls her eyes. "You think princess cousins Oksana and Natalya will be okay with that? They flew here for a party. A fucking party is what we'll be having. The party bus is stopping to pick up Windsor and Morganna before heading here. Your cousins are almost ready. This is going down," Chloe explains, reading her itinerary. It's not that I'm not grateful, I'm just…not as happy as I should be. I don't feel like celebrating. After reading another fucking beautiful email from the man I hate, I'm having a hard time grasping what I have to celebrate. Hooray for doing what's best for me and settling for second choice? I sigh. Giving Dax my all has been challenging.

"You're really having a hard time with this, aren't

231

you? You don't want this at all?" Chloe asks, finally realizing I'm not fishing for compliments and attention. I'm *really not* into this.

I bite the inside of my cheek. "I do. I do," I lie. "It's just a lot for something that everyone does. Weddings happen all the time. There's so much pressure to have parties and showers and floral arrangements dripping with diamonds, and cake that tastes like Brad Pitt's dick, that you forget what this whole thing is about to begin with."

Without looking up from her paper, she says, "God, I wonder how heavenly that tastes."

I stomp a heeled foot on the wood floor. "What about the rest of what I said?"

She meets my eyes in the mirror. I turn to face her. "I get it," she says, brushing a strand of hair that isn't mine out of my face. "You'll have fun. I promise. If it's the last thing I do tonight, I'll make sure you have a good time."

"I'm holding you to that, Chloe," I whisper. My cousins, matching in black dresses that look similar to mine, come traipsing into my room, all thick accents and huge, sprayed hair.

It's hard to tell them apart when they're not naked. Oksana has a mole at the bottom of her back, right where her ass starts. I know because of all the years they tried to be sneaky. She'd lift her shirt and show me and then pretend to be Natalya. Little bitch. Time didn't help matters any. They have the same laugh lines. It's creepy. "You. Look. Amazing," one says. I assume it's Natalya because she's always been a touch nicer.

"Thanks. I'm not sure about this wig and everything else. You both look stunning as always," I compliment. They both smile, thank me, and reassure me that Chloe's hard work is top-notch. The twins head to the kitchen to start pre-gaming. That's the one good thing about Russian twins. Those bitches will drink everyone under the table quicker than you can say 'vashe zrodye'. Cheers!

I strap my Chanel purse over my shoulder and join my cousins. Chloe comes up behind us and drops pink penis straws in each of our glasses then says, "They're almost here. Morganna says the bus is luxe. She also said Maverick was having a heart attack as he watched it drive away with Windsor in it." I laugh because I know how protective of her Maverick is. The fact that he's followed her to New York is a testament to that. "They're not staying with us at the hotel, though," Chloe mutters.

Chloe tries to change the subject to music. She has enough nineties rap music loaded onto her phone to bring Tupac back to life. "Why? Where are they staying?"

"They're not staying in the city, Lainey. They have a house in the Hamptons for the weekend. They'll just have a driver take them there after we're done smashing the town flat. Their husbands are staying there too." I already know. I don't have to ask, but I will anyways just to say his name out loud.

"Cody's house."

She nods.

"Of course. It's a beautiful house." It's named after *me*. I'm jealous and it makes me crazy. Will Cody be there, too? Why do I care? Dax. You're marrying Dax. I have to remind myself. I swallow the last of my wine without using the penis straw and hear the bus pull up in front of the house. Chloe's mom has a very nice house in the suburbs. The walkway is manicured and lit beautifully. The twins hobble down the walk before me, and then Chloe, who has two roller suitcases and enough food and supplies for a week. *You can never be too prepared,* is what she says. Morganna bounds out of the bus, her heels higher than mine, and her dress just as short. Windsor is next. Her tanned legs appear as she carefully walks down the steps. Her long brown hair is styled in fifties waves, pinned in an updo, and her rich purple dress is also skintight. They both look flawless.

"Children did your bodies well, ladies. Thank you for coming!" I hug them both one at a time, getting annihilated by their expensive perfumes and hair spray.

"The wig. It's fabulous," Morganna says, nodding as she examines me with her sharp eyes. "I didn't think we were going to get away from the hotel for a second.

234

Her husband, bless him, didn't want to let her leave. Wearing that." Morganna nods behind her.

Windsor blushes and looks down bashfully. "He's an animal. What can I say?" she says.

"The wig is something, huh? I'm channeling Windsor tonight. All brunette bombshell," I say, flicking the long strands over my shoulder. It makes me feel different with darker hair. I kind of like it. Maybe in my new married life I'll dye my white blonde hair dark for prosperity's sake. Most women chop off their hair into the wife bob after the wedding. I'll dye mine brown—transform into a new, here to stay, Lainey Redding.

Chloe bought the fake hair, but if everyone knew why I'm keeping it on, then it would be a different set of compliments coming. Blending in when people are following you is of top priority. "Stop it! You guys ready to go?" Win asks, adjusting her shoe.

I make introductions with my cousins and in no time everyone is sipping champagne and singing along to Chloe's playlist while lounging in the back of this very plush vehicle. She really should get all the credit for music. Everyone knows all the words, embarrassingly enough. By the time we reach the edge of the city we've downed two bottles of champagne and talked about our favorite sexual positions. My cousins, while not married, seem to have all the experience. I guess twins really do everything together. Morganna is curious,

Chloe is intrigued, and I'm a little grossed out.

"One decent guy is hard enough to find during a night out. Imagine trying to find two! We'll share if we have to," Oksana says, giggling when her sister playfully hits her arm.

"Ew," I say. It comes out louder than I intend. "I mean, will you marry the same guy and share him then?"

"Lainey, please," Natalya chides. "We're obviously not serious with these men we date. When it comes to finding husband material we won't do it at bars."

"Yeah, Mother will probably do it for us," Oksana scoffs. Sore subject.

Morganna gets up and dances when a new song plays. She pulls Windsor up to her feet. "Come on, you. I only get you away from him for six hours a year. Let's take wagers. I bet he's following the bus right now, your little munchkins strapped in the back."

Windsor bites her lip. "He'd never put the kids in a cab," she says, her voice growing louder as she contemplates it. "Would he? I mean, you're right. He'll show his face at some point during our night's festivities. Steve will be on babysitting duty. That's the wager I'm placing."

Morg laughs, throwing her head back. "It's good practice for him," she says, looking at me. "Is Dax in town tonight?"

He is having his bachelor party tonight, but I'm not sure where. Dax didn't make a big deal about it and I didn't ask for specific details. It wasn't as big of a deal as Chloe made this, so it will be low-key with his friends.

I shrug. "I think he's in Virginia Beach still. I'm not sure what his plans are." Everyone turns to look at me like I just spoke another language.

"Wow. You're pretty trusting," Natalya says, raising her voice over the music. Chloe catches the hint and turns it down.

Windsor clears her throat. "She's marrying him. Of course she trusts him," she says.

Chloe buts in with our itinerary. "Speaking of trust, everyone listen up!" Chloe shouts. We have bars and clubs that are color coded by our reservation type. VIP is red, which means our stops there will be longer than the yellows, which are just open seating, but a lot of fun. Orange bars are places that are a lot of fun, but will probably be super busy and/or have a line. Between Morganna and Chloe our evening is mapped out perfectly. She's already checked us in to our hotel and arranged transportation for everyone. Shit is about to get crazy. The honking of cabs and the glare from the lights let us know we've arrived in NYC. The bus is high, so it gives a better vantage point to see the bustle of life. I think of Cody. We won't be far from his apartment if we do visit one of the red bars.

Chloe shoves a sash at me. "Put this on. It lets everyone know exactly how loose your morals are

237

tonight. I have a list—don't worry, it's not long—of things you have to do before the night is over. Here," she says, shoving a typed notecard at my face.

I read it aloud while everyone laughs. "One. Seduce a stranger," I say, raising my eyebrows. "Wow. That will be easy wearing a sash that says 'bride'. Most men love that." My sarcasm makes my friends giggle.

Chloe nods furiously. "Men love it, Lainey. You're almost taken. The *almost* part is a huge draw. They'll be all over that shit like white on rice. Trust me. Go on, read the others."

"Take a body shot off someone. Oh, come on, this is juvenile!"

"No, you should definitely do it," Oksana chirps.

I fold my arms across my chest. "Fine. Off you," I say, giving a pointed look at my cousin. She shakes her head.

I continue, "Take a picture with a man. And the last one is don't say 'no' all night long." I pause, look at Chloe, and then say, "Wow, you really set me up good here. I'm sure I won't fail at all." The introverted section of my brain is cringing while the other side is gloating with the ease in which these can be completed.

"Perfect. Game on," Chloe says. The rest of the women finish their drinks, strap their shoes back on, and get ready for our first stop at a red bar. Our driver deposits us in front of the entrance and gives Chloe a business card with his phone number so we can call him when we need a ride to our next stop. The subway isn't safe enough for Maverick's liking and our shoes aren't solid enough for walking any place, really. This was a great idea.

As we step onto the street, I hear a couple whistles and hoots because of this fucking sash. I'm garnering more attention than I'm comfortable with. The bar is loud, but our enormous leather table in the corner shields us from some of the noise. Bottles are waiting for us. The twins take empty glasses and shoot vodka straight. Windsor and I stare wide-eyed at their obvious talent. "Let's go grab a couple of waters," Windsor says. I nod and follow her through the crowd of people. Men ogle her and try to get her attention, but she is skilled at ignoring them.

Working our way to a quiet corner, Windsor stops, turns to me, and says in a rush, "Lainey, are you happy? Wait, I know you're happy, but are you 'I want to get married happy?' What you've been through is tough. You don't have to do the stupid bachelorette stuff or drink out of plastic penises or even pretend you're happy on our account. I want you to know that."

"You get it," I say, leaning into her so she can hear me better. "I'm happy. I love him. I truly do. I want to marry him." Positive affirmations. Say it enough and it will be a fact. The same goes with forgetting something. Don't think about it and that shit never, ever happened.

Windsor nods, accepting my lie. "I know what it

239

feels like to be cheated on, lied to, and torn in two directions. If you don't follow your heart you'll regret it more than anything else in the world," she says, with soulful eyes that belie her age. She's been through a lot.

"What does that say if I'm the liar and the cheater, though?" Cody and I are over. The kiss, though, and his emails lead me to believe something completely different. *Remember his words, Lainey. You hate him,* I remind myself.

She bites her lip. "It says you're human and you're unsure about your life choices. I can't tell you what the right decision is. I do know that when you make it you'll feel peace, calm, and love so strong that you'll feel it can destroy any doubt."

A shot of clear liquid appears in front of my face. "Suck it down, cousin!" Natalya yells. Chloe peeks over her shoulder guiltily. "You're not allowed to say no, remember?" I have to smile at their attempts to be good, fun friends.

I take the shot and raise it above my group of friends. "Here's to not having any doubt!" I toast. Windsor smiles. I smile. Then I pour the vodka down my throat without tasting it.

I mean, what's one more lie to pile on the heap?

CHAPTER TWENTY

Lainey

"Schred or lorange?" someone asks. I have no clue who speaks because that would mean I'm sober. And I'm not that by a long shot. Speaking of shot, I just took one off a male go-go dancer's stomach. I'm pretty sure he was gay, or at least that's what I'm telling myself. He was skinny fit, as opposed to the hulking, muscular fit I'm used to.

We're headed down brick steps into a club pumping music so loud that I can't hear myself think. Maybe that was the champagne we drank in the bus on the way to this club. It could be either. I put on my flats about three bars ago, but my feet still have blisters. Two thousand dollars for shoes that should be torture devices. The sick, sick world we live in.

"What language was that?" I ask over my shoulder without letting go of the railing.

Morganna steadies herself using my back and the side of the wall. "I made it up," Morg says, laughing. "Lorange sounds like it belongs to a romantic language." She sighs.

"Or a drunk language, but who's paying attention? You can do everything else. Why not create your own language?" I ask. "Chloe!" I yell. "Why did you pick this place?" We just came from uptown at a lounge on the top floor of a swanky hotel, now it seems we're headed underground to a sex dungeon of the opposite caliber. It's close to *my* salad café.

"Trust me," she yells back, her heels clacking far too hard. She's going to pay the piper for those four inchers tomorrow morning. "This place is bitching!" she says, making her way next to me. "Have I led you stray yet?" I shake my head. We pass through the entrance and veer toward the VIP area. This place *is so* bitching. Chloe did well. As the drinks go down, the night gets more exhilarating. It's a night out with my girls, plus my cousins, who seem to be on their best behavior. No three-ways are arranged at the moment. My phone vibrates in my purse. It's a text from Dax. More specifically it's a photo of a glittery ass, that I imagine smells like vanilla. Strippers always smell like fake vanilla. It's a historical fact. I smile.

The next text says, "Sorry. Someone got my phone."

So he is most definitely partying tonight. He wasn't sure what the guys had planned when I spoke with him earlier. They must have kidnapped him. I wonder where they are. NYC is six hours from Virginia Beach, so if they drove here, they are just getting started.

What would a response be from a concerned fiancée? I type out, "Glitter is a bitch to clean out of clothing. If you bring it home and get it in between the cracks of our hardwood you might not have hard (wood) for a while. In the city?" I double-check my words for spelling and because I am extremely drunk and hit send. I snap a selfie inside the dark club. It makes me look like a half vampire and send that, too.

His reply is immediate. "Yes. I wish I were with you instead. Maybe later tonight?"

Oksana pulls on my arm, hands me a drink, and says, "You can't say no."

I type back a quick reply. "Not sure what Chloe's plans are. See you soon. Don't bring home the clap."

He texts back a sad face.

"I love you," I tap back quickly.

In return, I get a smiley face. Tossing my phone back in my purse, I clasp it closed and then drink the lethal potion my cousin handed me. I should be mad or upset. I should care that he's potentially cheating on me right now, but I don't. Guess what else? The fact that I don't care doesn't bother me either. The total indifference is what helps me get from day to day. Dax hasn't broken up with me yet, and that's something I never anticipated after I changed into this indifferent creature. I'm his project child that he needs to see through to the end, I think. Of course I love him, because I know he loves me, but I'm not sure at what cost. He wouldn't hear me if I called him anyways. I shrug and start on another drink.

I watch my friends dance around the table in our roped off area. It's nice being away from the crowd by only several feet, but I don't want to be cordoned off anymore. "I'm going in!" I announce loudly. Everyone, just as drunk as I am, smiles, waves, and continues dancing. The twins found a couple of guys to talk to at the adjoining VIP table, and Windsor and Morganna are holding each other up while they sway to a popular song. I double-check that my purse is secure across my chest and make my way into the mob with my arms up, carefree and feeling lighter than I have in months.

I dance with random people as I head toward the center. I don't care when men grab at my waist, I merely turn out of their grasp. The 'bride' sash is a magnet for the wrong kind of guys. Closing my eyes, I turn my face to the low ceiling and dance like no one is watching. I'm lost in the music, drunk on the sensations, and my mind void of anything else, when I feel a pair of large hands fold around my waist. Those same hands pull me back against a wide, hard chest. My breath catches. I let the arms fold completely around my sticky body.

"Can I have this dance?" he whispers, his lips

touching my ear as he asks for permission he doesn't need.

I can't speak. I nod furiously. The crowd melts away and I can't concentrate on anything except for where his skin touches mine. He spins me around, and my head spins a little more wildly than it was doing by itself.

"You," I mouth, looking up into his eyes. His features are dark, venomous, lethally attractive.

His neck works as he swallows. Leaning down to put his face in my neck, he inhales and then whispers, "You."

With him this close I can smell him. The same scent that fills his house with memories is taunting me right now. I glance at my cousins, but they're oblivious to anything except the music and staying upright. Windsor is wrapped around a man—Maverick—and Morganna and Chloe are laughing, probably at the fact that Maverick couldn't stay away. We're hidden by the mass of moving bodies and colored laser lights.

Cody fingers the white sash, then picks up a strand of my fake brown hair. "Last night of freedom, then?" he asks, talking into my ear over the music. The tenor of his voice sends shockwaves to every nerve ending in my body. Between that and the alcohol, I've forgotten why I hate Cody Ridge. He inhales loudly by my ear, causing my skin to prickle with warmth. My fucking traitorous body. "I thought blondes were more my

245

thing?" he asks, tightening his grip on my waist.

Oh, God. What am I doing? Leaning up on my tiptoes, I throw my arms around his neck and press my open mouth against his soft, full lips. I do exactly what I've wanted to do since he gave me an almost kiss in his living room. There's no denying what this kiss means. I let my tongue wander into his mouth and am rewarded when he lets his slide against mine. His hands splay over my ass. He pulls me against his erection, hard and ready right now. This is his way of telling me what he wants and is asking if it's what I want. I'd fuck the man right here in front of everyone if it meant I could be with him one more time—feel this connection to another human being. I could play pretend one more time before I become the wife to a noble, fine man who will never make me feel like this for as long as we live.

"Yes," I say, teeth clicking with his. I repeat myself, "Yes." He smiles against my mouth. More insanely hot teeth clank against mine. He pulls my lip into his mouth and bites down. It almost hurts, but feels so fucking good I actually moan. Sexual desire hits me all at once. Let me tell you, after nothing like this for weeks, the feeling is overwhelming. My stomach is flipping, my pussy is soaking my panties, and my mind focuses on one thing. Cody. The way the top button of his shirt is undone, showing the bottom of his throat, that hot way he has his hair slicked back and to the side, and of course how utterly, tragically in love with him I am.

246

"This way. Come on," he commands, without breaking our kiss. I'm supposed to be angry with him. Mad. Hurt. Upset. Ignoring him should be my favorite sport, but the lure is too strong. Because tonight I can't say no, I follow him, holding his hand as he walks us through the hot bodies swaying to the beat. His steps are quick and precise. He knows exactly where he's going as he leads me down a dark hallway and into a door near the rear stairway exit to the street. He closes the door behind him and slides the lock into place. Our eyes adjust when he flicks on the overhead light. It's dim, but it still feels like sunshine in comparison to the club on the other side of the door. There's a couch, a coffee table and not much else in here. We don't need much.

I take a step back away from him and take the wig off, letting it slide to the floor. With the remaining bobby pins out of place, my blonde waves are down, cascading over my shoulders. Cody doesn't move. He watches me intently, his gaze flicking from one body part to another. His eyes are a mask of indifference, but his chest is rising and falling at a hurried pace. "What's the matter, Cody? Cat got your tongue?"

His nostrils flare, his eyes sparkle. A ghost of a smile crosses one corner of his mouth the second before he grabs my waist, forces me down on the couch, and kisses me like he owns me. With one hand he plays with my hair, and with the other he works up my dress

247

that is tighter than hot sin. "I plan on showing you just how present my tongue is," he growls, tilting my head up by tugging my hair. He drags his nose down my throat, over my chest, and settles between my legs. My body is buzzing with excitement. Every pleasure sensing cell is concentrating on where he's touching me. I can't help the moan when he slides my panties down my legs and parts my legs with his head. The shaved sides of his head tickle the inside of my thighs. Warmth floods my core. "You want that, right?" Cody asks, his lips tickling my pussy as he speaks. I raise my hips toward his mouth. More. I need more of him.

I can't speak—the sensations are too much, so I take his head with both of my hands, grab him by the ears, and guide his face where I want it. He stops when he's so close that I can feel his warm breath on me. "I need to hear you say it. What do you want, Lainey?" I'm frantically panting like a dog. I'm so hot for him. "This is what you want?"

"I want you, Cody," I say, still with my hands on the sides of his stubbly face. "This. I want your mouth on me. I need your dick inside me. I want you. All of you." That about covers it. This isn't an old habit dying hard, this is me falling back down the rabbit hole. A druggie getting her hit of drugs. A woman grasping at the last shreds of a former life.

He smiles with his eyes, pleased with my dirty talk. "You're so fucking wet for me," he says, dipping a finger inside me. I keep my gaze fixated on his hand and sharp angles of his face, shadowed by the dim lighting. Even still, this man is akin to a dream. Or a nightmare. Right now, it's both at the same time.

He settles between my thighs with his tongue licking small circles around my clit. I scream out. Not his name, no. I can't even remember my own name. "Fuck, I've missed this. I want you. I want you so fucking bad that it hurts," I rasp out, pulling his face into me. I melt into the couch when he slides his fingers inside me while continuing his assault with his tongue. He likes the encouragement, so I tell him exactly what I like and he groans in frustration. He wants to be inside me just as much as I want him to.

I arch my hips up to get his fingers as deep inside me as they'll go and because I need more. "I'm about to come," I whisper, gently bringing his face up so I can see his eyes. They're shock blue and full of complete and utter satisfaction and hunger. Thankfully, he keeps his mouth on me and his fingers inside me. I repeat in a breathless whisper, "I'm about to come and I want your cock deep inside me when I do. Can you help me?"

He kisses me one more time on my clit, a long lingering press of his lips, and then says, "I thought you'd never ask. Let's get you out of this dress so I can fuck you senseless."

"Yes. Please. Yes," I say, rolling over so he can

unzip the dress equivalent of a straight jacket. I stand because there's no way it's coming off lying down and Cody slides it down over my hips and pulls it off in a couple of tugs. He runs his hands up my legs, traces a path with his fingertips up the sides of my stomach, and ends with his hands in my hair. My whole body is on fire. He gazes at me with such intensity that I'm not sure what to say. Or think. Or what I'm even supposed to do. "I want you so badly," I say, returning his gaze. Can he feel this connection between us? "Not just tonight, Cody. I want you always." His eyes turn down in the corner. Just like that, sadness replaces the worshipping look of love. "What is it?" I ask.

He kisses me instead of responding and I let him because I don't want to hear the words. I'm playing pretend right now. Gently he backs me into the coffee table and lays me on it. I stumble a bit as the alcohol is still pumping through my veins like crazy. I hear him unbuckle his belt and watch as his slacks hit the floor. Cody's cock is standing straight, thick and ready. "I'd say I want to make love to you, but that wouldn't be appropriate now, would it? So let's fuck for old times' sake. One last time before..." he says, his voice cracking at the last word. *Before what?* Before I marry Dax. My fiancé. The cloud of alcohol lifts for a second and I'm appalled with my actions. This is really it, though. My last time with Cody forever. I can give myself this as a goodbye present.

"Fuck me then. No emotions. Just for old times' sake," I say, gazing at him through lowered lashes. I spread my legs to give him a view, guide his dick into my mouth, and push forward until he's deep in my throat. Cody rolls his head back and looks at the ceiling.

"Yes," he hisses, folding his arms behind his head. "Fuck yes," he says again. I swirl my tongue around the tip and pop him out of my mouth. I spit on his hard, pulsing shaft and smooth the liquid with my hand. Cody's busy unbuttoning his shirt. The dim light highlights every ripple of his abs, every line of muscle in his biceps, and the shadows they create make my mouth water. His chest tattoos look a little more sinister, and I think it's perfect. I want to play with the devil right now.

"You're slick now. Slip it in," I say. Cody kneels in front of the coffee table, pushes me back on the long rectangular surface, and settles between my legs. He trails his lips up my neck as he teases the head of his cock at my entrance. "Inside. Now," I command. Raising my hips to help ease his erection inside me doesn't work. He uses a hand to push me back down.

He takes his time pushing the head in. "You are so tight, Fast Lane. So fucking wet and tight. I want to feel every fucking inch of you," Cody growls, pushing in a little further, then stops. It has been a while since I've had sex.

"It's only you. You were the last person to be inside

me," I say. This brings out the caveman in him, like I knew it would. He pounds into me, filling me solidly. His girth stretches me wide that I'll feel him there in the morning long after he's gone. I grab his face and press my lips against his. He slams his eyes shut and thrusts into me over and over. "Open your eyes," I say. He doesn't.

Instead he takes me by the waist and flips me over so I'm on all fours on the hard table. He enters from behind and starts his assault of punishing strokes. I moan because I love it when he fucks me doggy style. Reaching a hand around, he strokes my clit while he fills me with his dick. This is my favorite and he knows it. The pleasure is strong that it makes my legs weak. I know I'll come soon. He picks up the pace, his skin slapping against my ass in loud thwacks as he hits the back.

"You feel so good," he says, almost incoherently. "So fucking good." I feel him grab my hair and put it over one shoulder. "I'm going to come," Cody growls. Our sex noises are muted by the blasting volume of the music outside. I don't think it would matter even if it were completely quiet. My legs start to shake as my own orgasm builds and builds.

"Keep fucking me," I order. "I need more. More." He plunges into me, his hand firmly on my hip. He uses it to pull me back onto him and I know I'll have bruises there tomorrow—one for every one of his beautiful, punishing fingertips.

I let my head hang down and I come, exploding around his cock in waves so intense that my eyes actually water. He feels me coming because he groans and lets a string of curse words pass his lips. My legs tingle and the warmth of my orgasm floods my whole body in that relaxing, pleasurable way. He removes his fingers from my clit and puts both hands on my hips and pulls me back, hard.

I feel his orgasm inside me. "I'm coming," he says as he quickly pulls his dick out of my pussy and lets a stream of cum land hot on my ass. He spreads my ass cheeks with one hand and I feel the tip of his cock at my back door. "I want my come in every part of your body," he explains, pressing his large member a little further into my ass, letting a hot burst of his juices leak into me.

"That feels so good," I moan, letting my head lie on my arms with my ass high in the air. God, I want more of this. "Fuck me in the ass, Cody. Just a little." It hurts because he's so large, but it also feels so good to be so full. He presses in more and I flinch.

"Does it hurt?" he asks, rubbing my hip with a big, warm hand.

I shake my head, adjust, and tell him I want more. He sinks in further and that's literally all it takes for me to orgasm again. He's not even all the way in and the pleasure is rocketing around me. He takes this opportunity to really go inside of me deeper and starts thrusting.

"Fuck, it feels so good. Your fucking perfect ass is mine. Do you hear me?"

"Yours," I respond. More than my ass is his. He knows it. I know it. And I'm pretty sure everyone else knows it, too. He fucks my ass until he comes in a hot rush again, until I'm sticky and covered with his sweat and semen and sore in every orifice possible. He eats my pussy until I come all over his face for a third time. We only talk about how good this feels and guide each other to our next orgasm. We don't talk about tomorrow, when I'll wake up and go back to my fiancé and never see him again, let alone get to fuck him again. We don't talk about how he tore my heart out with his cruel words.

His lips are still wet with my juices when someone pounds on the door. "Time to go," Cody says. His eyes turn wary, almost as if he expected someone to interrupt us. We dress quickly, clean up as much as we can with the small sink in the corner, and he helps me back into my prison dress. My thighs stick together, and I'm so sore that I could have run a marathon...with my vagina. I tell him how amazing I feel, and he tells me how beautiful I am. He apologizes a million times vaguely. I don't forgive him. Of course not. But it's nice to hear him apologize. For a millisecond I think that if I were to forgive him, would that change everything? Could I break it off with Dax for good and in return get Cody forever? Somehow I don't think it's that simple.

We exit the shady room into the secluded hallway, my wig back in place, and it's like we were never missing. Cody doesn't follow me out of the dark hallway, though. He smiles sadly, leans into my ear, and whispers, "Maybe next time, in a new space." Then he turns to leave up the stairs out of the rear exit. My stomach sinks as the finality sets in. The magnitude of what I've just done. How little it meant. How much it meant. Nothing has changed.

When I return to the table my friends are all just as drunk and none the wiser. I pull out my cell phone and send a text I've been stalling on. It's not to Dax, nor to Cody. It's to get the ball rolling with my destructive plan.

When I sit down, very carefully, I might add, Chloe pats me on the shoulder. "Told you this place is bitching, didn't I?"

Narrowing my eyes, I look at her quizzically. She smiles a knowing smile and tips back a glass of champagne. Half of it runs down her face.

"Yeah. You were right!" I yell over the music.

"Time to go!" Morganna announces from her perch on top of the table. Her red soled heels lift and lower in front of my face as she dances.

Windsor is dancing with Maverick, some dirty ass

255

dancing that should be reserved for the bedroom, but I don't care. I throw back another shot and we head up to the street.

We get outside and the bus is nowhere to be seen. Maverick says he's going to go get our party on wheels, which is sitting a few blocks down the road, and come back for us.

"It's raining, though. We can just call him," Windsor replies, holding his arm in a death grip.

Maverick quirks a brow at her, then looks at the rest of us. "Who told you Navy SEALs can't get wet?" He jogs off, listening to a cacophony of female laughter behind him.

CHAPTER TWENTY-ONE

Cody

It was a mistake. A huge one. I tried to keep my emotions hidden for her benefit, but they blared through like a rainbow flag in Hillcrest, California. It wasn't *just* sex. I approached Dax to ask if I could *see* Lainey one more time before their wedding seeing as I wouldn't be attending. I promised to disappear after. He agreed. The man knew exactly what would happen and he still agreed. I shake my head thinking about it. A testament to how much he wants me out of the picture, I suppose. He didn't have to agree to it either because we made a deal fair and square. I would have told me to fuck off. His face held pity when he told me, "Sure, if she'll see you." Do I feel guilt for what happened in a back room of a night club? I can't. Because it was with her. In my eyes she'll always be mine. Dax is a respectable man who makes questionable decisions. Honestly, Dax didn't even cross my mind. Being with her transports me back to happier times of my past. We were planning our wedding when I left. That's where I'm still at. Granted, I did need a little help from her friend, but she was easy to convince. I told her Lainey should wear a disguise. Not just so she'd blend in more, but because shit is about to hit the fan with V, and her out in the city probably isn't the safest right now. She can take care of herself, for the most part, but she's been out of the espionage game for years. You'd be surprised how lethal she is with a handgun and a bad attitude. When we dated we would go to the shooting range together and make it a game. Whoever could fire the most kill bullets in the shortest amount of time got to select a sexual favor. Sex with that woman would drive a man to do wicked things. Lainey is so far distanced from that side of her personality, I'm not sure what's left of it.

It's the day before her wedding. I haven't heard a word from her or from Dax. The manly beast inside me wants to think he knew right away when he saw her what had transpired in the nightclub break room, but the logical part of me knows that if he found out I would know by now. Why was I hoping she'd tell him? That he'd find out? Am I still that desperately seeking her love that I've hit this new low?

Lainey responded better than I hoped. Her love for

me is stronger than the disdain for my callous actions and words. I apologized because she deserves to know half of the truth before I leave her life. The sex, well, that was a bonus I wasn't expecting and it was fucking mind-bogglingly hot. My dick hardens thinking of it. She let me fuck her so good that I'll never get over that night for the rest of my godforsaken, lonely life. My daydreams used to be about sequences of numbers that I need to remember for coding, now they are flooded with Lainey's pussy. How it tastes, the pink color of her folds as the head of my dick spreads her apart, the feeling of her wetness squeezing my cock as she explodes around it.

Yes, this will haunt me more than anything else. The man I was in captivity is still there. I think of him sometimes, but traumatic incidences in the past are better left in the past.

"How does it feel? Tell me. How does it feel to be so far away from everything you've ever known? That life as you once knew it is moving on without you?" V asks, his lips next to my ear and his vile breath blowing in my face. My hands are tied behind my back with thick zip ties and my feet are bound with an even larger sort. They cut me, dig into my skin, causing blistering pain. We're in a small office not long after they stole me out of the damn swamp. I only know his name because I've heard other men call him that. They respect him, take orders from him. He is the boss around here. I can't

*say how much time has passed because of the drugs
they use to sedate me. V peels the tape off my mouth
without taking his beady, dark gaze off my face.*

*The second it's off I yell, "Fuck you!" V tsks me,
shaking a finger in front of my nose. Mentally, I add it
to the list of all the reasons I want to kill him. The tally
has far surpassed anything I would have previously
thought possible. I've killed for much less. He has a
world of hurt coming to him.*

*"Is that any way to treat me? I have all the power,"
he exclaims, picking up a pair of rusty scissors from a
table. "I can free you from those restraints." If he does,
I'll fucking kill him with my bare hands.* And then
what? *my subconscious asks.* Kill all of the other men
on the other side of the door with your bare hands? Get
out of here alive? Probably not. *Playing it cool is
difficult when you're being held against your will in a
disgusting place without food, water, or any glint of
promise of a future.*

*"What do you want? Information? Money? Power?
What do you want?" I ask through gritted teeth. My
mouth burns from the tape residue and the fact that my
lips are raw from being gagged. The assholes don't like
when I speak. So I yell any chance I get. V wants all of
these things, I'm sure. Why else do you kidnap a
fucking Navy SEAL unless you have a death wish?*

*He shrugs. "Nothing really. You're merely a pawn
for revenge." What does that mean? I'm surprised.*

"They'll look for me. They'll find you," I threaten. My brothers won't give up. They'll come and pop me out of this hellish place at some point. I hope it's soon. V can't have been that thorough. He messed up somewhere along the planning line. My kidnapping was well-thought-out, but the problem isn't how he took me, it's that he took me hostage. Not some average Joe. Not only am I important, I'm lethal. Give me the fucking chance. I'll never stop fighting. For my life. To get back to her, I'll do anything. I can't give up, but I'm tired.

With a closed fist he punches me in the face. The force knocks my head to the side. I feel warm blood trickle from my nose and down my lip. The stinging on my lips worsens. I clamp my jaw shut and add this to the list. "They'll never find you. Give up that dream now, X." The letter irritates me. This man infuriates me. If anything, I'm glad because it dulls the pain.

I spit blood at his feet. I just miss his scuffed up dress boots. "Fuck you, asshole. When they do come, I'll make sure they know exactly who is responsible for fucking up my face," I reply, smiling. Blood sprays out of my mouth as I speak. It drips down my chin.

I've pissed him off more than usual today. His left eye twitches as he takes three measured steps toward me. He's cautious. He knows how dangerous I am. He grabs my chin with one hand and leans his face close, uncaring that my blood is getting on his hand. "There will come a day when you don't even remember your name. I will take the life you once knew and loved and bury it so deep that you'll never even dream of it. You will be one of my men. Your life as you know it is over. The sooner you accept your new fate, the easier your life will be. Do you really not know why you're here?"

I wish I did. Hostages are taken all the time with no good fucking reason. It's usually a power play. Or for intelligence. I cringe thinking of the power this asshole feels knowing he's successfully kidnapped a goddamn Navy SEAL. It makes me fucking sick. The blood is falling at a steady pace out of my nose and down my face. It's broken. "Why would I know?" I ask. The draw for information is strong. Along with my physical strength, he also has this to hold over me. I may be tied and bound, but I won't let him see my curiosity outright.

He grins. His crooked, dirty teeth peek behind cracked lips. "Because it's all her fault."

"Don't play games with me," I growl. "Who do you mean?"

"Why, Elena Rostov, of course. Who else?" My body melts into the wooden chair. A chair many a man have died on, I'm sure. He's said the only name that could illicit a reaction. Lainey. I choke on my own blood and spit a mouthful on the floor beside my chair. Anything to break eye contact from this monster.

"Taking you is her punishment. She loves you, no?" he asks. I can't respond. My breaths are coming too *fast and I want to destroy this atrocious man for letting her name pass from his lips. Lainey is a spy with a history I was never sure of. I knew she gathered basic information about SEALs to pass on to her superiors. This man is her superior. Her life is far more secretive and dangerous than I ever would have dreamed. He hits me with an open fist. "I asked you a question, X. Answer me."*

"Yes," I reply. I answer honestly because I'm too busy piecing the puzzle of Lainey Rosemont together in my mind. I can't make up lies when I'm too busy reeling from the truth.

"That love is the reason she stopped reporting back to me. I need this information; you see? I sell it for a lot of money. Elena has cost me a lot of money. Her love for you, more specifically her disloyalty, makes me angry. She was my best agent. I thought about it for a long time. About what the proper punishment for something so costly should be. Take what she loves most? Yes. That's what I needed to do. Either that or you give me the information I need. You know how I caught you so easily?" He pauses, watching my face. I'll never talk. He knows that.

When I don't say anything he says, "Go ahead. Ask me! Come on, I know you want to know."

"How? How did you catch me so easily?" I humor him. It has to be blind fucking luck. I swallow, anticipating his words. My spit tastes like iron and

stale air. Oh, God, Lainey how deep was she? To be working for a man like this—a man capable of orchestrating a kidnapping successfully and fuck knows what else he's into. Drugs, sex trade—anything that makes a lot of money the illegal way. V is the type of man Navy SEALs hunt down and extinguish. He's surely responsible for mass amounts of lives lost.

He cackles, exposing disgusting teeth again. My empty stomach flips. "With the information she gathered from you in the beginning, before she fell in love with you. Isn't that ironic? She did this to you. I love a good romantic story gone bad." He laughs. It's loud and echoing and pure evil. "She's the reason you'll live in a cell for the rest of your days. I mean, I've debated whether I should send you back into the world after I've dismantled you beyond recognition, but in the end I think it's better if she suffers your death," V explains through laughs. His hands are on his fat stomach as he chuckles. I envision him dead on the ground. His fucking fat stomach is what I will shoot first, just to watch him suffer. Men like him don't deserve a quick death.

My head is spinning. I can't think quickly enough to form coherent questions. Lainey. Oh, God. Is she strong enough to survive this? Knowing she is responsible for this atrocity? "Kill me," I spit out. He shakes his head, a knowing, evil look in his eye.

"Oh, I'm not going to kill you. No." Leaning

against the shitty desk, I watch as he grabs the old scissors and then approaches. Every muscle in my body tenses, readying for pain.

"How did she get messed up with you?" I ask. My voice is a quiet whisper. He hears.

He laughs again. "She never had a choice. She was born into this. That little bitch defied her heritage when she cut contact with us. Think she's crying right now? She'll never suspect it was me because you were on a mission with the rest of the SEALs. I mean, how well planned was this?" I'll admit, he's good. This will look like a normal hostage situation to the rest of the world.

I shake my head. She's an artist. Better at her espionage than any other person I've met. Had I known I could have better protected myself. I could have protected her. "You're going to help me with the rest of the master plan. Faking your death. A true death isn't warranted, I don't think. I enjoy your company after all."

"I'll never crack. I'll never give you any information. Make it a true death." Begging for my death isn't part of my skill set. It's an odd combination of relief and sheer terror.

V rubs his hands together. "I'm thinking of a beheading video. Those have gotten so much play lately, though. You're so good with computers. What are you thinking? How shall we fake your death?" He's so far gone in his reverie that he's basically forgotten I'm

265

here. "We'll send it to Elena first. It needs to have a lot of gore. Lots of macabre."

I swallow down my blood. It makes me wretch next to my chair. Bloody bile spills onto the cement floor. He hasn't forgotten me completely, because when I look up he has the sharp end of the scissors pointed at my chest. My eyes widen in shock. I try to jerk away, but I can't. He carves a fucking V on my pec with the dull blade. He leaves me passed out in the little chair in the little office when he's finished.

I awake listening to my blood drip on the cement floor. It pools in a huge puddle. That's how I want to kill V. I will drown him with my blood—until my life essence takes away his.

Merely remembering V and that little office chills me right to the fucking bone. That is one of the memories from my horrid past that I'll never forget for as long as I live. I think it was the moment I truly found out who Lainey was. And I realized it didn't matter. I love the woman regardless. It didn't matter then, of course. I was prepared to die. Now, though, still in light of everything that has transpired between us, my love for her has only grown. It's because I love her that I'm letting her go. I need to kill V, and she needs to move on with her life.

Molly calls my cell, but I let it go to voicemail. The ceiling in my bedroom is far more enticing right now. I don't ponder things nearly enough. Maybe if I did I wouldn't make such poor decisions. As I send her call to voicemail, I notice I have a new email. The lure to rid my inbox of the red number one is too strong. I click the icon and see her name. My heart starts hammering and my eyes search for her words.

From: LaineyRostov@Memail.com

To: Cridge@ridgecontract.com

Subject: Wedding

This is the last email I'll ever send to you as a Rosemont…or a Rostov. Or to make it less complicated I will just say this is the last email you'll receive from me as a single woman and perhaps the last email ever. I feel bad about the other night. Dax deserves better. Hell, I think he even realizes his mistake now. There's no turning back now, though. I told him everything. Well, not quite every detail, but I couldn't lie because honestly, it left me emotionally wrecked. He was angry, hurt, dismayed. All the things he was before when I was 'figuring things out'. He's been programmed to expect the worst from me and still love me. That's how I know I'm probably making the right decision. Through thick and thin, it's hard. Especially when I'm mostly thin, with a penchant for getting a wild hair up my ass.

That night at the club, I thought it meant more than it did at the time. I waited for you to say, "I'll see you tomorrow, Fast Lane." Or maybe, "Let's take a weekend at Dances like the Wind." I thought it was the turning point, that you finally realized we belonged together. Instead I just got a goodbye. I get it, I do. It's just hard for me to wrap my brain around the fact that the man I've loved for a good portion of my life isn't going to be the man I love for the rest of it. Granted, I can't magic my love for you away even if I wish I could, but I can love Dax in the spaces you left. While you may see me smiling and kissing him (I'm not sure if you're coming to the wedding), know I'm probably still thinking of you. Love takes time to forget—especially a love as thick as ours. I hope you know I'm okay—I'll always be okay. I'm taking care of myself, if you catch my drift. In return I want you to take care of yourself. My world is better knowing you're in it. When I walk down the aisle to him, know it could be you just as easily. You're right, though, it would have never worked out between us. Love isn't enough during this time. Maybe next?

The Space between your Time and his,

Lainey Rosemont (soon to be Redding)

CHAPTER TWENTY-TWO

Lainey

It's ten o'clock at night and my house is abuzz with guests. It's mostly my family from overseas and a few of my close friends. It's like a florist puked in my kitchen, and a dress shop opened up in my formal living room. I have four spare bedrooms and all of them are piled high with bitch stuff. You know the kind, shirts tossed over bed frames, makeup bags and hair tools on dressers, and seventy different kinds of perfume wafting in the hallways at any given moment. I can't be in there with them. They're too happy, too excited for the wedding tomorrow. I'm outside by the pool with a lowball of bourbon. It's the expensive shit Dax left in the bar. I've killed almost half the bottle and I'm still lucid enough to remember what the fuck I'm doing tomorrow. The sane decision of emailing Cody for a final time was made during glass numero uno. I check my email on my cell phone again. Nothing new. This time, the last time, he'll leave me to my life without inserting any more confusion.

I take a sip and relish the burn down my throat as I gaze to my left. My neighbors must already be asleep because all of the lights are off at their house. Their boat bobs in the water off their dock. I wonder why it's not on the lift. It's odd. The husband is usually meticulous about maintaining the expensive boat and he's just left it out here to bang against the dock all night.

The raucous noise coming from behind me signals that someone said the word 'wedding' and has to take a shot of vodka. Oksana is creative like that. Drinking games are her specialty. I tried to tell them to tone it down. My side of the aisle will have the drunken lunatics still hung over from the night before. I shake my head, check my email one more time, and then wander across my plush lawn to the neighbors' back yard. I pull my silk 'bride' robe a little tighter around my waist to cover my pajamas. My feet get wet in the grass because I'm wearing a pair of cheap flip flops to balance out the pain I'll be in tomorrow with the sky high heels. My mom said I should cheat and wear flats under my wedding dress because no one would see them. The last thing I need is to start my marriage off with a lie, even a small one about fucking shoes. I groan. A little because wet feet suck and a little because weddings are stressful. The bourbon hits me tenfold as I consider the fact that sitting down and drinking all night was a bad idea. Standing up after is like a ride on a Ferris wheel you're forced to endure after a bag of cotton candy.

"What are you doing over here?" a male voice asks. I turn toward the sound. Squinting in the dark, I see the outline of a man, my neighbor. I startle. He's standing in his yard in the middle of the damn night.

Forcing a smile, I put up a hand to wave. *Can he even see it?* "Hi. Sorry," I say, and then point toward his dock. "Your boat wasn't put away properly. I wanted to make sure everything was okay." Turning on a small light, he approaches. I get that sinking, chilly, hair prickling feeling that signals something's not right. Fuck. I'm unprepared. Embarrassingly so. I glance behind me at my house, but everyone is still inside. I see figures dancing through the large glass windows. It looks like a movie screen from this angle. My neighbors can see into my house like in a fish tank. Chill bumps rise on my arms and legs. *Why didn't you check out the new neighbors, Lainey?* Dumb move.

I take a step back toward my property line. "I'll just head back home now that I know you're here and will, uh…take care of it, I guess." I take another small step and my foot slips in the wet flip flop. It also squeaks. Irritated, I blow out a small breath.

"Why are you leaving so quickly? You just got here,"

271

a female voice chirps from behind me. I spin and come face to face with a pretty brunette. Her face triggers a memory and I realize she's familiar. She smiles as she watches understanding cross my face. "I, I, know you," I stutter, trying and failing to place her. I don't have long to ponder because my other neighbor, the wife, comes from the side, her gaze focused on me in a scarily intense way. I take another step toward my property. I should scream now. Call for help or fire or tell someone to throw me a fucking gun, but they're too close to me and my house is too far and loud. No one would hear me. My cell phone is sitting next to my glass of bourbon next to my goddamn sunning chair. I make a run for it, but the women catch me almost immediately. These fucking shoes aren't just cheap and ugly, they are dangerous.

"What do you want from me?" I yell. They each have me by the arms and their grips are like vices. You know how in moments of importance you can put on a sober face and feel fine, when you're actually drunk off your ass? This isn't one of those times. My vision is whirring and my head is lighter than a kite in summer. Through the bourbon haze, my mind is flicking through images of women I know. Is this woman a client? Someone met in passing? I don't get the friend vibe when I look at her. I must not like her for one reason or another. The darkness of night doesn't do me any favors either. It's hard to see her true features.

The man speaks to someone on the phone. His voice is low and measured. His conversation is quick and matter-of-fact. He snaps the old school flip phone closed. It's a burn phone. He's going to toss it when his job is done. My stomach sinks as I understand what exactly is happening right now. It's not my fucking crazy neighbors trying to rob me, it's way more sinister than that.

He clears his throat. "It's up to you. Easy or hard." I can fight like a cat in a mesh bag, or I can hope that my pliancy gains me a favor. I pull away from the women and they let me go.

"I'm getting married tomorrow," I say, my voice pleading. Dax. Oh my God. I spent all of our time together trying to keep him from my past and it's going to rear its ugly head and destroy our wedding. What can I do to fix this? How can I buy some more time? "Please," I ask, because it's the only thing I can think of at the moment. Please save me. Please don't hurt Dax. Just please leave me alone.

The girl who I can't place gets right in my face. "I can't believe you're going through with it. Think of this as us doing you a favor." They know too much about me. They've seen too much. How long have they been trailing me before they moved into Morganna's old house? Gaining information? My schedule, my hobbies, my friends and clients. My intel guys said they were around these days, that I should watch my six, but

273

never in my wildest dreams would I have guessed they'd be so permanently around here. The woman snickers. She sounds young.

It hits me all at once staring at her big eyes. "Cody," I whisper. This is the woman…girl, Cody was out on a date with at the café in NYC. The expensive bourbon wants to come back up. I won't let it.

"Name's Rosy," she says. "You're an idiot for not staying with Cody. His dick tastes like candy dipped in cocaine. I'm addicted." I planned to go easy, but then she opened her mouth. I uppercut her so hard that I hear her jaw crack, and her teeth click together. Maybe I even chipped one. Rosy stumbles backward, but doesn't fall. It was my last bit of freedom before I'm met with fifty thousand volts of electricity. Helplessly, I watch as he puts his Taser in the back pocket of his slacks. Shaking his head, he scoops me up like a baby and carries me to his fucking boat that's bobbing against the dock. It's primed and ready for a midnight sail.

I walked right into a trap, unarmed and completely drunk. My only hope is that I broke a bone, even a small one, in that bitch's face. I can see the lights shining from my house like a lighthouse. I'm not headed toward it, I'm motoring away from it into the inky, dark water I used to take solace in.

If I wasn't one hundred percent sure what was going on before, I am the second the man shocks me again and stuffs a gag in my mouth. The strip of duct tape on top of it is the icing on the fucking Vadim cake.

That motherfucker is going to pay.

****

White flowers are everywhere. They hang from trees that obviously do not flower, they drape over arches, on top of chairs, on the grass, in the sky. Wait, no, there are so many that it feels like flowers are falling from the sky. Guests have arrived at the outdoor venue and have parked themselves in the white folding chairs. There's a lot of them and my nerves are causing my entire body to shake with unease. My teeth chatter.

"Calm yourself," Chloe chides, rubbing my bare shoulders. The strapless dress was selected a long time ago. So long ago that I don't tell anyone exactly when I picked it out to marry another man. It's a beautiful dress. It should have its time to shine, that's my thinking. Everything else about this day and wedding is different.

I nod. "It's just a lot. After all that we've been through, I can't believe this is actually happening. It feels so final. Like death," I say, looking out of the window of the large bed and breakfast. A harpist plays a tune that sounds vaguely familiar.

"Did you seriously just say death?" Chloe asks.

I realize my mistake and try to cover it up. "Well,

275

death is the most final thing that can happen to a person. And I'm feeling like this is pretty final," I remark, petting the sides of the expensive beaded silk.

Chloe scoffs. "You're so morose. Come on, everyone is waiting downstairs. You're holding this crazy train up." My mom appears in the doorway wearing her finest old lady suit. She looks like she's supposed to attend brunch with the Queen. That said, she's still beautiful. Her blonde hair that was similar to mine is now almost a silver color. Her complexion is flawless for a woman her age, and her smile is the smile of a mother who is finally giving away her daughter.

I roll my eyes. "Don't get all emotional, please. I have so many of my own emotions right now that I think dealing with yours might set me over the edge," I say in Russian. She laughs, but I see wetness in the corners of her ice blue eyes. I point a finger at her in warning. "I mean it." She tells me that I need to indulge her. I let her hug me and kiss me and tell me a story about how when I was five years old I dressed up in an old sheet and forced the boy next door to marry me. I stuck a daffodil in the pocket of his jean shorts because he didn't have a pocket in his shirt. She told me I was serious about it and expected our parents to attend. He ended up running away with tears streaming down his face because I told him he had to kiss me on the cheek to seal the deal. She tells me this as we walk down to the quaint lobby and then out of the back doors. I hang

276

on to every word, like a sponge requiring water to breathe. I try to envision the scenario from her eyes, looking at myself trying to marry the little boy. It calms me down, makes me feel more at ease.

The wedding march starts and she clings to my arm tightly. I lay my hand over hers and we start down the aisle. I smile at familiar faces and even some faces I don't recognize. We make it halfway down, and I finally look toward the altar at the man I am to marry.

I take a breath so deep that my mother feels it. She squeezes my hand a little and leads me forward as I lag behind. It's him. He's waiting for me.

He's always waiting for me, I think. How long will he wait?

The flowers are everywhere. They cloud my vision. It's a white blur of wedding and confusion. I can't see my husband's face anymore. It blurs like it's a penis on daytime television. I squint and it still doesn't make it any better.

"Who is it?" I ask. My mother doesn't answer. She laughs nervously like I'm crazy. She's the crazy one if she thinks I'm going to marry a man who has a blurry face.

"Who is it?" I yell louder. Gasps from the guests break out, and I hear hushed whispers.

I know I make out a female voice that says, "Bless that girl."

I scoff. "Oh, fucking bless you!" I yell. My mother

lets go of my hand and I freeze. She's what's keeping me grounded. I look beside me, but she's vanished into thin air. All eyes are trained on me. They surround me like vultures. They judge me. I look one more time at the altar but my groom is gone, too. I'm left with family and friends, who look at me like I'm Satan incarnate. I can't speak because something is over my mouth. I scream a muffled, strained sound. My breaths are shallow and quick and I fall to the ground. My white dress pools around me and turns ice cold.

Someone slaps me across the face. It's not clear, but it looks like it's a man with small eyes and cruel lips. Another slap, except harder. "Wake up, bitch!" he yells. My mouth burns as something is torn from my face.

A dream. It was all a dream. I open my eyes and I'm met with a nightmare.

Tears form in my eyes without my permission. "V," I gasp.

CHAPTER TWENTY-THREE

Cody

I raise my shot glass to the sky. "Here's to new beginnings," I say, toasting the air. "And to old endings, too," I slur. I'm more tired than I am drunk and I've been doing too much thinking. I'm at my house in Virginia Beach because I wanted to be away from people. Horse, Van, and Molly are here because they don't count as people. I like them. They've helped me ignore the fact that the love of my life is marrying another man tomorrow. Molly has gone down the entire list of her single friends in an effort to not leave me lonely tonight. She scrolled through her social media page on her cell phone and I vetoed as she pointed them out.

"Wait! What about Rosy? You should call Rosy, boss. She's bugged me for months and months to score a date with you. Give her another chance," Molly says, taking a sip of her drink. Her brown hair is tied back in a taciturn ponytail and her pink lips press to the side in thought. Horse is seated behind her on the outdoor sofa, staring into the flames of the modern fire pit. It's sunken into the center of the cocktail table. He looks as if he wants to sink it further. Molly sits next to him and he pulls her small frame close to his side.

I shake my head. Rosy. She wants more than I'll give her. "How do you know her again?" Months and months seems like a long time to bug a friend to hook you up with her boss. "Where did you meet her?" I glance at Molly as I think about what she's said.

Molly shrugs. "She called me up one day looking for a job. I told her we don't hire people you don't know, but she seemed nice enough, so I met with her for coffee a couple of times to see if she would be beneficial to me at all. She seemed so fucking enamored by you that I let her come with me when I dropped off some dry cleaning to your house. Remember?"

I raise my brows. Vaguely. "You make it a habit of bringing strangers over?"

"Hot ones that have the potential to change your life. Yes," Molly replies. Horse grunts out a laugh. "She wouldn't do me any good, not quick enough, but I figured maybe she could still do some good for you."

"If she wasn't quick enough for you, she damn well won't be quick enough for me," I joke. Van laughs and tells me about a time when Molly successfully matched him up with a one-night stand that he kept around for weeks after. The woman evidently works miracles if that's the sort of hookup you're looking for. She's *Tinder*, but in a cute human form.

The outdoor bar has everything I love stocked to the brim, but I grab a bottle of water instead. If I'm going to contemplate my future in dating I need to be stone cold sober, or completely annihilated. I'm closer to sober, so I pick that. My cell phone lies in front of me on the high bar. It lights up and starts vibrating. Everyone looks from the fire to my phone. Their heads turn as if it's their phone instead of mine. We're all on edge, just waiting for the call that tells us it's go time. By go time I mean time to settle the score with the asshole who ruined my life.

"Who is it?" Molly asks, taking Horse's hand in hers.

I clear my throat. "It's a blocked number," I say, answering the call with a short, "Ridge."

I hear sobbing. "Cody. I need you to come to me. I can't go through with the wedding," Lainey says. My eyes widen, my heart hammers, and my palms grow sweaty with unease. I lift my arm to check the time. It's late as fuck. One a.m. It's technically already her wedding day. I want to ask if she's okay, but she's obviously not. One glance at my friends and it tells me they know who it is and why she's calling. They all go back to their business of chatting and staring into the flames.

"Where are you at?" Her sobbing is uncontrollable. "Are you sure you want me to come over?"

"My friend's house. It's on the other side of the bay. Hang on, let me find the address," she says, slurring the last word. "I need you. Please." If she needs me I'll be there for her no matter the circumstances. She gives me the address in a rush. I have to ask her to repeat it twice. I know the address. If my memory serves me correct the street is literally right across the water from Lainey's house. Who does she know over there?

I sigh. "How much have you had to drink, Fast Lane? Have you called your fiancé?" I can't even use his name. Tonight I was conditioning myself to forget he existed. It's not working out in my advantage.

She wails. "Don't you think I know I should want to call Dax? I fucking want you, Cody. I need to see you. Talk to you. Be with you. Right now."

"And you won't regret it in the morning?" It's a valid question. Especially if she wakes up in a few hours and actually makes it to her wedding on time. Seeing me tonight is as good as putting a nail in the coffin of her marriage.

"I can't regret you. Any part of you—any part of us. I never will. I'm not marrying him. I can't be married to anyone else." My heart skips a beat. Is this too good to be true? What phone is she calling me from?

I need to find out for myself. "I'll be right there," I reply. Adrenaline pumps through my veins and replaces the tired worn out feeling that's haunted me as of late. I bid my friends farewell and tell them they should stay and hang out. Horse is wary, Molly rolls her eyes, and Van tells me a shortcut to get to the address Lainey is at. I head to my bedroom, pull on a ball cap, squirt on some cologne, and rush out the door.

Twenty minutes later I'm standing in front of a huge house that looks as if the gardener quit weeks ago. There's no car in the driveway, but there could be one in the garage. For all intents and purposes this house is vacant. I look down at my phone to make sure I'm at the correct address. When I look up, Lainey opens the front door. She makes sure I see her then disappears back into the house and leaves the door open behind her for me to follow. She doesn't greet me, or show her face.

A bad feeling washes over me. I'm in the business of dishing out bad feeling, so I tend to listen to my gut more frequently than the average Joe. Walking quietly and quickly down the cobblestone walkway, up the front steps and then through the door, I don't take my hand off the concealed gun that lives on my belt strap. Some people can't leave their house without their phone, or their wallet. I can do without anything else except my gun. I need it to feel safe in this new, sharp world. People play Cowboys and Indians in the grocery store these days. I have so many questions and I know there's only one way to get answers.

Pushing through the front door, I look around. The air is stagnant and there's white, dusty sheets draped over furniture. "I'm in here," Lainey yells in a stuffy voice. "I'm trying to fix my face." Like I care what her face looks like. I'm worried about her. Her makeup doesn't matter to me. It never matters, actually. I follow the sound of her voice, stalking around corners and never forgetting to check my back. There's running water in the kitchen. I make my way toward it. Lainey's standing at the marble glazed sink with her back facing me. She's wearing a short silk robe that's emblazoned with the word 'bride' and it makes my stomach flip. Her legs are dirty and her hair is matted and wet. Upon further inspection I notice her whole body trembling.

"Baby?" I ask, swallowing hard. "Come here," I order, softly. She's scared and upset and God knows what she's going through right now. Lainey sobs loudly. She turns around quickly. Her face is caked with dirt and she has dried blood mixing with fresh blood at the corners of her mouth. She's beaten and bloody and her eyes are so red that she doesn't look like herself at all.

"You don't want me," she says, her gaze glazed over and completely out of this world. I don't hear her, though, because I see red. I'm furious and petrified at the same time. I rush across the room and almost make it to her before someone knocks me to the floor with a fucking Taser gun. Can I control my arm enough to get to my gun? Nope. Can I turn my head to see who my attacker is? Not a chance. Can I hear Lainey sobbing? It cuts me like a fucking carving knife.

A voice. *The* voice from the past echoes through the room. "Well done. Well done. For the first time in years you have done something perfectly, Elena."

No. This can't be happening. My worst nightmare is unfolding in front of my eyes. He comes into view and takes Lainey by the shoulders. That makes it his three hundred and sixth offense. Maybe even three hundred and seventh because he's fucking up my revenge plan. The electricity coursing my body is wearing off. My fingers twitch by my sides. I only need a few more seconds and I'll be able to reach my gun and shoot him in the leg. Not the head or the chest, no. That would be too humane for a person so evil.

"Don't even think about it, X," he says, voice low. He pulls the hammer back of his own gun with his thumb and aims it at her head, smiling. That same grin used to haunt me. Funny how things change when it's not my life at stake anymore. It's a life that is of more importance. Lainey shuts her eyes, wincing, and a wail escapes, her lips twisting in a horrified grimace. I let my arms fall back to my sides, wide open like a fucking snow angel. I bet on a lot of things. I won't bet on her life; not for all the tea in China. V speaks. "Disarm yourself. Slide all of your weapons to me and then I'll

285

tell you what to do next." V is using too much force. Lainey will have an imprint of the gun barrel on the side of her temple. I growl.

"Ease up on her!" I yell. He grabs her chin, lifts it up, and kisses the hollow of her neck with his dirty mouth. I clamp my mouth shut so tight my teeth might shatter from the pressure. She can recover from a kiss and a welt on her head. Bruises heal and cuts fade away. To my knowledge he hasn't done anything to irrevocably break her. *Breathe, Cody. Breathe.* I remind myself.

"Is that better?" he asks, sneering, his lips still touching the skin on her throat. Three hundred and eight. This won't end well. Emotions are overtaking the room. There's no distancing myself from this— retreating to that dark corner of my mind. To be strong for myself is one thing, but with Lainey in harm's way I'm liable to do something outright crazy.

I sit up slowly, holding my arms straight out like a T. "Let her go," I say, motioning to the gun on my hip. He nods once, gaze glued to my hand and I slide the loaded gun to his feet. I don't need it. My rage alone is lethal enough to kill him. I hear people chattering in the other room and realize we're not alone. I count footsteps and different tones of voices. I hear three people, but count four sets of footsteps as they enter the kitchen behind me. I don't glance. I don't take my eyes off of Lainey. As V's minions enter, Lainey's face changes. Pain and sorrow are replaced by guilt and embarrassment.

"Don't move. Your best friend will join you momentarily," V says to me. To the people behind me he says, "Cuff them together. Right there on the floor."

"Can I take Cody into one of the bedrooms for an hour or two, first?" Rosy says as she rounds the front of me, with her pointer finger dangling from her mouth. Fucking bitch. "He's so yummy. It would be a shame if I don't get to use him for a bit first." I was so busy trying to get over Lainey that Rosy's lies never registered. I wasn't looking for them.

"Don't be such a little whore, Rosy," V chides. "She took over Elena's job after she fell off the radar. She's not as good as you. Her mind wanders elsewhere too quickly," V says, stroking Lainey's hair. "No, you were my Hope diamond. You deserted me."

"I'm sorry," Lainey squeaks out. Her voice is hoarse and childlike. "Forgive me." I wince. Hearing her submit to him makes my fucking skin crawl. Ignoring Rosy is easy. It's what I've been doing since the first time I saw her. She keeps talking and I formulate a plan to kill them all. A man dressed in all black brings a large man into the room and pushes him down on the floor next to me. He's wearing a black hood and he's obviously drugged or hopped up on electricity because he's not fighting at all. V brings Lainey closer, keeping her pinned with his gun. Rosy hands him my gun and he pockets it. Fuck. That option is out for the time being.

"Let me! Let me!" Rosy squeals as she dances back over to my lumbering companion. She pulls the hood off like a child at Halloween. It's Dax. As if my day couldn't get any worse.

Lainey cries out. His head spins to her voice. "Lainey. Are you okay?" Dax asks, confused and groggy.

V finally lowers the gun. Lainey wipes underneath her eyes with her fingertips, smearing her black mascara. "You did so well getting them here, Elena. Thank you," V says, and then he mutters something to her in Russian.

Lainey laughs, tucks a strand of blonde hair behind her ear, and ties her robe a little tighter. "Both of you deserve whatever comes next. The saying should be bad girls finish first," she says. Like a light switch being thrown in the middle of the night, she's on. Or off. I can't be certain because she's masterful in her element.

"What the fuck, Lainey!" Dax screams. If I'm confused, he's the definition of in the dark. "What's going on here? You called me and wanted me to meet you here. Said you wanted to talk about the wedding and I get fucking knocked out the second I walk through the door." She smiles. It's beautiful and scary. She walks over to him and stoops down. Lainey isn't close enough for me to reach, yet. She knows exactly how far to stay away.

Tilting her head to one side, she says, "Dax. You were always too eager, rushing me into things I didn't want, convincing me of truths that were actually lies. I thought you were a good man." She shakes her head sadly. "Did you trade information with Cody?" How does she know? My mind is reeling. She isn't playing a game, she's pissed. We're about to pay for it, too.

"Not really, no," he says.

Liar, liar, pants on fire. Her smile fades and she presses her mouth into a sharp line. "Fine. Cody," she says, turning her head to me, her gaze piercing me. "You broke up with me because of Dax. Didn't you?" I'm not sure of the best way to go about this. Perhaps Dax had it correct with the lying. She'd know. Of course she'd know the second the lie came out of my mouth. "I was a pawn in your dirty little game of revenge."

"Fast Lane," I plead. She shakes her head. Her eyes close. V cackles from behind Lainey. I don't even look at him. I concentrate on my woman, and the second her soulful eyes open, they flash with anger and disappointment.

I tell her a truth. "He *is* the better man. Dax, I mean. That's not a lie."

"My relationship with Dax was built on lies. Mostly that's my fault, but it doesn't change the end state. Dax," she says, looking back at him. "Our relationship was

289

built on lies." Ouch.

Dax is enraged. I feel his hands shake next to mine. He'd be killing something right now if he weren't restrained. Maybe he'll be on my side when the shit hits the fan. It's not a matter of if, just when. "What the fuck is going on here, Lainey? You need to tell me something right now," Dax growls. I feel for him. He's about to get information overload. He knows who V is, sure, but he has no idea his fiancée has deep ties with him. That she founded her roots in Virginia Beach to spy, gain intelligence, and wedge her way into the SEAL community for monetary gain. She's infiltrated not just our hearts, but the very core of our community in the worst kind of way. It's unforgivable for a man like him. For me? I forgave without blinking. She came clean the very first time I caught a whiff of something that didn't add up. She had too many cell phones, too many email accounts, her meetings were late at night, and her phone conversations were spoken in hushed whispers.

Lainey sits down, folds her legs under her, and tells him a story about a young woman who wanted a better life. She wanted to make money and be around hot men. One particular hot man ended up being the love of her life. She turns around and looks at V when she gets to the part of the story where she cuts ties with him and begins her interior design business. She talks about being engaged to me and how she left everything behind and started fresh, how her espionage roots didn't matter. Both Dax and I are equally as captivated by her tale. She moves her hands when something excites her and she looks legitimately sad when she speaks of the time when I was taken. She tells us she suspected that V was responsible for my disappearance because he sent vague messages through messengers of one sort or another. I find myself leaning forward to find out what happens next, even though I know all of our actions and decisions have led us to this right here. On a kitchen floor tied up together without any chance of a peaceable reconciliation. Lainey tells this story so effectively that there's no way Dax can be upset with her. She has this way of weaving a story and then injecting it with just the right amount of guilt. Is he even aware she's doing it?

Dax takes a deep breath and I feel his back relax against mine. It's not time for that yet, bro. "Jesus, Lainey. Why didn't you tell me this sooner? Why did you let it go this far?" My ankles and hands are numb from the fucking zip ties. I wonder how many zip ties I can fit down V's throat.

She sits back on the floor and pulls her knees up to her chest. "You were my shot at a normal life. That woman I just told you that story about doesn't exist anymore. I'm still an interior designer, Dax. We just have more in common that you knew," Lainey says. V grunts, groans, and tells her to finish chit-chatting. I'm surprised he's humored her this long.

"You realize what you did was against the law? You could go to prison for the rest of your life. I mean, hell, Lainey. I'm a Navy SEAL. My morals were about as loose as I can permit back when I didn't know any of this. Knowing this changes everything. Everything," Dax says, hanging his head. I can't help but feel sorry for the man. I bet his uniform is pressed and her wedding ring is sitting on top of his nightstand.

"Morals? You gave him information about Vadim's whereabouts in exchange for my love. Don't say that's not how it went down, because it was. Phones were tapped and conversations were heard. What would happen if the Navy found that out, oh righteous one?" Lainey says. Her eyebrows rise in question and the rest of her body tenses.

"I fucked up because I wanted you so badly," Dax replies. This is getting unbearable. If I had access to my gun I'd put him out of his misery.

I sigh heavily. "How much more of this fucking shit do I have to listen to?" There's only minutes before the shit show starts. I need to get my head on straight and listening to this love fest is making me nauseous and uneasy. I keep eyes on V and listen for footsteps around us. I may have let them cuff me for Lainey's safety, but I sure as shit am not going to die for it. Not after this.

Lainey ignores me completely. "You have never considered what I wanted, Dax. Therein lies the problem. I tried to tell you so many times and you talked your way around it, trying to convince me otherwise. Going as far as you did to keep me isn't love. It's obsession," Lainey says. She stands, walks backward toward Vadim and holds out her hand. Vadim laughs. It's a maniacal sound that reverberates in the large vacant house. "And now you both must atone." My fucking stomach lurches. *Atone?*

"Got everything off your chest, honey?" V asks Lainey. She nods, swallows, and grabs my gun that he's dangling off his finger in the air in front of her face. Fuck. What the hell is happening right now? "Go ahead and take care of business so we can get on with our night. We need to celebrate your freedom and your return to me," he says, pulling her close under his filthy arm. His mere presence makes me murderous, reminding me of all the things I work hard to forget. The dripping returns, as do the memories of days filled with blackness and pain, hunger and boredom so severe that it handicaps the mind. The years of life he stole from me in the name of revenge are worth more than my own revenge plot against him. Death is easy. Living like he forced me to is agony in comparison.

Lainey weighs the gun in her right hand, balancing it on her palm. She flips it over and checks out the other side, and then makes sure it's loaded and ready to fire. I shake my head. Dax tenses and starts trying to pull away from me. Yep, this is the woman you don't know.

She's a real stunner. Literally. I wish I could see his face, to try to gauge his reaction to this. It's not every day that you find out your fiancée is skilled in espionage and has the means to murder you. It should be a book or something. Lainey would make for one hell of a character. Her huge, blue eyes find mine and hold steady. I stare back, willing her to hear my thoughts. She turns away.

"Which one will you choose, Elena?" V asks. She narrows her eyes at Dax and bites down on her perfect, pillowy bottom lip. These could possibly be my last moments on earth and I'm getting a boner from her fucking mouth. A mouth attached to a woman who has the means and the desire to kill me. My vision takes on a surreal quality, almost like a dream.

She aims the gun at us, huddled on the ground. Dax has stopped scooting and has started pleading with her. It's interspersed with swearing at her, because after being a lying bitch she owes him more than this. He makes solid points. She owes me even more. She knows it.

Her hand shakes as her gaze flits back and forth between our faces. What must we look like? A couple of huge, burly men reduced to a pitiful heap. And all for love. Fucking love. Cities fall because of it and lives are deconstructed in the name of it. If I outlive this night, I'll swear it off for the rest of time.

V chides. "You know the deal, Elena. You have to

294

kill one. That's what I want to earn your trust back. So pick. It should be easy. The man who holds your heart or the one who repaired it after it shattered. It's a dilemma for sure, but one man has clearly already paid his dues." V aims his gun at me and Lainey aims my own goddamned gun at Dax. In a twist so fucked up that not even I saw it coming, I understand that nothing matters anymore. Not revenge, or what I've been through, what Lainey's been through, not what Dax has dealt with. None of it matters because this is the fucking end.

V groans when Dax begins threatening. I don't hear specific words, just the tone of his hysterical voice and the word 'fuck' laced throughout. "You know why nice guys finish last? They're never the ones holding the fucking gun," V says, playing Ghandi. We're always the ones holding the guns. That's why this whole situation is so laughably stupid. I'm not a nice guy. Neither is my cuff mate.

Lainey glances at me. Her eyes fill with unshed tears. She mouths a single word. A word that tells me everything I need to know. *You.* I blink twice and give her an imperceptible nod. This is it.

She takes a step closer and focuses her aim on my head, right between my eyes.

The kitchen sink drips.

CHAPTER TWENTY-FOUR

Lainey

"I need to be alone with them," I say, my voice shaking. It matches the rest of my body that seems to be in the middle of some sort of shuddering panic attack. I'll never get this vision out of my mind. Dax and Cody sitting on the floor of this vacant house, looking horrified because of me. Cody's beautiful face in the crosshairs of his own fucking weapon—all of it is of the wildest caliber of macabre. Handling this situation requires more finesse than I'm capable of. I called them here and told them I needed them.

When V doesn't respond I clear my throat. "Just for a second. To say goodbye. I owe them that," I say, flicking my gaze to Vadim. I smirk, the confident one that lets him know I'm in control and ready to do as I'm asked. He looks nervous, leery, but I'm holding a gun. What choice does he have? I'm on his side, remember?

I return my gaze to my gun, not to what I'm aiming at. If you aim a gun, you should be prepared to fire it. It's the number one rule of gun ownership. Uneasiness mixes with my nerves and it's about as unpleasant as a UTI and a yeast infection at the same time. The black gun blurs in my vision. I can't fucking pass out now. *Don't you dare pass out, bitch,* I tell myself.

"Do it quickly. The mark of a good agent is the speed in which you make life or death decisions," he says, eyeing me up and down. He has so many of his goons in this house that I'm not sure exactly how I'll get out, or how we'll manage, but I've stalled as long as I can. He's right. We're alone on this side of the house, so my only hope is that I can be quick enough to do what needs to be done. Sucking in a deep breath, I try to calm my nerves. It's been a while, but I can do this. I don't—can't—make eye contact with Cody or Dax again. I feel too much when I do. They make it worse. V begins his exit.

Sweeping the gun right, with my finger on the trigger, I stop when I have Vadim in my sights. His back is to me. It's a low blow move, but too much is at stake right now. Way more than I anticipated. With my hand steady, my aim perfect, I pull the trigger and watch as the bullet flies and enters V's back. He slumps first to his knees and then onto his stomach. I have seconds. Maybe even less. This is it.

I still don't look at the men in the face. I stoop down,

pull a kitchen knife out of the back of my pajama pants, and cut off the zip ties on their ankles and then their hands. From shooting Vadim to cutting them free it takes less than ten seconds. I catch a quick glimpse of Dax in my peripheral and notice he's staring at my face, like truly staring, wondering who the fuck I am. Cody isn't wasting any time wondering who I am. He knows. He's pulling another gun out of his leg holster and preparing to pepper whoever comes blasting into this room next. Dax backs away, looking down at V. He's moaning, not dead yet, but it's a grave injury. I made sure of it. No words are exchanged, but we're all on the same page. Cody drags Vadim behind a kitchen island, leaving a trail of blood as he goes. I imagine he wants to mutilate him with a dull spoon and a hot pan, but currently there's no time. There will never be enough hours in the day for him to inflict the type of pain he deserves. I swallow down the guilt and try to remember to breathe. It's unfortunate and fortunate at the same time.

"You got any more fucking guns on you?" Dax asks, an unwitting, sarcastic smile playing on his lips. "I would have brought my kit if I knew I'd be working tonight." It's a joke, a really bad one at the moment. Cody responds in the negative, so I toss him my vegetable knife and Dax hurries to grab Vadim's weapon from the floor. "I should have known better. It's always a battle if Lainey has anything to do with it,"

Dax mutters. His words are dry, emotionless, and I know that our relationship is damaged beyond repair. Funny how it takes a gun fight with mobsters to make him understand. Or it could be the fact that I shot a man in the back when he was in the same room. Either option doesn't make for good wife material.

That's when gun shots echo in the air. Hard pops sound and grow closer. We slink behind the island. While texting with one hand, Cody takes a towel he pulled from a cabinet and shoves it in V's loud ass mouth. He's getting blood everywhere. The smell makes me want to vomit up all the bourbon I spent all night drinking.

"I'm so sorry, Dax," I whisper. He looks at me pitifully, shakes his head, and holds up his knife in a salute. "I'll make sure your name stays out of this," I vow. I can make good on this one.

"My men are here," Cody says, putting his phone away. "They're cleaning house up front. You can put away your tomato slicer, bro. The big boys are here now."

"Fuck you," Dax spits. "Fuck all of you and the nightmare this day has been!"

V wails beside us. Cody punches him in the face so hard that I have to look away. He's silent after that.

"Why is RC here? How did you tell them?" Dax asks. A few more gunshots pop in the front room and then silence.

299

"Lainey called and asked me to come to a weird house in the middle of the night twelve hours before her marriage to you. I figured something was up. It was either going one of two ways. In case it was going to swing badly, I told them to come here if they didn't hear from me in twenty minutes. They're here now. For what it's worth, I'm sorry you got caught up in all this bullshit as well," Cody explains. Dax puts his head down between his knees and groans. My stomach ties in knots at the sight. I'm the cause of his pain.

I'm still shaking because of the shock and adrenaline pumping through my system. I want to take him in my arms and hold him so tightly that nothing can touch him unless it goes through me, but I'm afraid we're past that now. This entire mess is because of me. I look at Cody. "I can't even apologize for what I've caused you. I'd never forgive me if I were you," I tell him.

It's not the time, nor the place to have serious conversations. With our enemy bleeding out beside us and my fiancé wondering what the hell is happening. Cody's men are mowing down villains in the next room, but all I want to do is talk to him. I want to tell him that he can be free now. Free from V's heavy-handed thumb. Free from looking over this shoulder. Free from me dragging him down at every corner. Even with Vadim's cold heart still, I can't be the woman he wants me to be. I'm a killer. I'm a person I don't recognize. The woman

I left in the past is back and she's a nasty, scary bitch.

Cody's huge, hulking killer comes in the kitchen. I know it's him because of the sound his huge boots make against the floor. "Cody!" he yells.

Cody stands from behind the island, leaving Dax and I beneath him. "Horse, we're over here. Everyone is okay." Horse approaches, followed by one of his other men and a few others. When Horse sees V his eyes widen and his lips curl. V is moments away from death. His breaths are shallow and irregular. Watching him brings me pain and suffering. The horrendous scenarios from my past are in the forefront of my mind. They're leaving me, very slowly one by one. It must feel the same for Cody, who is also glancing at V's body with an unfamiliar look. Swallowing down a mouthful of spit, I take a huge, deep breath.

"I didn't even get to do it," Cody says. Horse looks confused, so Cody nods down at me on the floor. A sight I must be with my arms wrapped around my dirty legs. They both look at me with wide questioning eyes. *What exactly did I go through tonight?* Would be my best guess. They tell Cody they've cleared the house and have taken care of V's men. I sit and listen, overhearing everything. Cody dials Molly and tells her he needs a serious cleanup. And they also need one hell of a cover-up. Probably one so amazing the world has never seen the likes of it. Cody speaks about Dax's involvement, wanting to make sure it's known he had no part in tonight's mess. I appreciate this more than he'll ever know. He doesn't have to care about Dax. He does. It makes my heart thud for a reason other than fear. The last thing I want is him getting discharged because he got messed up in our catastrophe. Cody talks to his men about how it all shook down. Van, another of his main men, tells him he knew right away when he saw the house and radioed for backup. It was a job well done. Thank God his men came tonight. It wouldn't have turned out in our favor otherwise. One glance at Vadim confirms that all evil has fled the room. He's dead.

"Boss, we found this one hiding upstairs. What should we do with her?" one of the men asks Cody. This makes me stand up, turn around, and come face to face with Rosy. Fucking Rosy, the snake in the grass.

She smiles at me, then fixes Cody with her gaze. "For what it's worth, I really did want to fuck you. Too bad you're still hung up on that one," Rosy says, glancing back at me. I suck in a deep breath to control the rage. I'm so jealous that I'm sure it's oozing from my pores.

"Don't make false statements. You say that like I would ever fuck you in the first place. Kill her," Cody says, shrugging, and then turns back to Van. I snicker and can't help but smile. Cody sees and he's thoroughly amused by me. Bringing humor to inappropriate situations since 1986. What can I say?

"You did kidnap me, ring around the Rosy," I say, making sure it's loud enough for everyone to hear. "You can't expect to get away scot-free, can you? I think Cody has a brilliant idea." I glide across the room to stand in front of her.

"No! I'll do anything. Please. Please, Cody! Don't do this," Rosy wails. Ah, so she does have a soul. A black one, but something nonetheless. I rub my wrists where she cuffed me too tightly.

"Anything? You'll do anything? Molly said you would have made a worthless employee, so you're basically useless to me. And you know too much," Cody says, keeping his back facing away from her so she can't see his huge smile. I'd like to kill her, but with V gone I'm feeling quite satisfied with my killing quota for the day. I won't go completely savage on anyone else. Not yet.

Rosy says, "I won't talk. I swear I won't talk. I'll sign my name in blood if that's what it takes." She does think he'll kill her. It's comforting to know she feels fear. For a brief period I wonder how Rosy got mixed up in this and then I remember my early start in espionage. It happened for her just as easily. Nothing is ever as it truly seems. Beautiful women are spies and men hunt others for sport. I fell into it effortlessly. Most of the time it didn't even seem like work. I got a paycheck for hitting up the bars and talking to beautiful men. Navy SEALs. They would tell me details about their training, or their start times. Sometimes if they were really drunk they'd tell me names or neighborhoods where their friends live. Basically by having drinks bought for me and the occasional lunch with SEAL wives I was able to afford a lavish lifestyle. Even knowing this I can't feel bad for Rosy. She's a bitch.

Cody dials Molly again and tells her to deal with Rosy because she was her project that failed miserably. Her mistake. Her problem to deal with. She agrees without much fuss and Cody sends Rosy to her. While he handles that mess, I'm on Dax's cell phone, pleading with my mother to help me clean up the wedding fiasco. I tell her that it was a mistake and that Dax and I make better friends. She doesn't buy it, but she also doesn't make waves. She knows how upset I've been and is trying her best to coral my friends and family without inciting a riot.

"The champagne for the reception is in my wine cellar in big black boxes. Bring it upstairs and explain the situation to them," I tell her, begging. "I'll cater a huge lunch for everyone. Hell, I may even be able to show up with Dax and apologize in person." She asks what happened to me last night. I tell her I went somewhere to think and ended up meeting Dax and deciding to end our engagement. She clicks her tongue.

"I'm happy you had the courage, Lainey. I just wish it didn't come in true Lainey fashion at the very last minute," Mom explains. She's right. I can't even argue with that logic.

"I'm sorry, Mom. I love you. I'll see you soon." I need to clean myself up before I show myself in public. Dax listens intently, shaking his head as I speak to her. He knows exactly what I'm dealing with. It's kind of an unspoken fact that we're splitting up for good this time. I watch as he heads toward Cody.

****

Cody

It shouldn't surprise me, but a little part of me thought she'd want the normal life with him after all. I heard her calling off the wedding. As for me, this is it. I'm handing the company over to my men. I'll sit on board and fund them to continue the important work they do, but I don't want to be on any jobs. My coding makes enough money to fund a small country and that's where my time is best spent. This could be the start of my normalcy. Will I miss the rush of adrenaline and the pump of my heart as I track bad guys and hunt down evil? Perhaps. Some risks are worth the reward.

Dax walks toward me and I'm not sure if I'm ready for this conversation. "Listen. Fuck you for being alive, but fuck me for being an asshole. Had I known all this before, man. Well, things would have been different. I love her. Part of me believes I always will, but this is

305

officially my cue to exit stage left and never look back. I'll take responsibility for my actions, of course. Right now I have a suitcase full of wounded pride with a carry-on of how the fuck didn't I know any of this? Once I unload those, maybe we can be friends." He smiles, but it's weak and tired. We'll never be friends in the true sense of the word because our bridge has fucking burned into ashes. Perhaps we can breathe the same oxygen standing next to each other without choking one day. That must be what he means. I've also gathered he will not be having Lainey after this debacle. Not just as his wife, but as a whole.

I take his offered hand and shake it. "Normal girls are no fun," I joke. "Here's to unloaded baggage and moving on. Nothing about this mess will mix with your name. You have my word. The Feds will be happy to have Vadim out of the picture. It's a drug bust gone wrong, obviously. Check your bags and enjoy life, bro. It's too short," I say. I watch as a few men take V from the room. That's all my baggage in one human corpse. The breath that comes next is the freshest breath I've taken in years. This is messier than what we had planned and the cover-up will be extensive, but it was worth it because it has the same end result. Dax returns to Lainey and they speak in hushed whispers. She looks sad and utterly exhausted, but still talking with her hands. She walks him to the front door and returns to me. My men are shuttling us home.

Her arms by her sides, and her glassy eyes studying my face, she says, "Sometimes there aren't words to express gratitude. Most of the time there aren't words to convey love, either. I'm thankful to you, but I can't say I love you. Not right now. I'm not sure who I am in this moment of time. I need to fall back in love with myself before I can process everything that has taken place. If I think about it now, it won't make sense. I'll hate myself for an eternity. I'll offer my gratitude for everything you've done for me, as meager as it sounds. Vadim ruined your life because of me. There's no way to sugarcoat that. I deserve this—the pieces of my life strewn about in such a haphazard manner. You can't witness this, Cody. I won't ask you to, and...I don't want you," Lainey says. She hasn't blinked once since she began speaking. Her words sear my heart and force me to come to the realization that all of this hasn't changed anything. She's not mine. She won't be mine again. You know in the movies—because our life really is like a movie—when the heroine comes running into the hero's arms after they face certain death? That shit is fiction. Real life is much more complicated than that. Hearts are wounded, spirits are broken and desolate, lives are demolished so completely, that a relationship would only add to the confusion.

"Fast Lane," I whisper, taking the side of her face into my hand. Her skin is cold, clammy. "Your life is fully intact. He's gone and he's not coming back. Sure,

307

you pissed off some people with your runaway bride stunt, but come on...you know they expected that anyway. A plus for giving the audience what they wanted. They'll be talking about how flaky you are for months," I say, smiling wide. She sniffles, because she finally breaks down and lets her tears fall, but smiles that radiant smile. I continue, "You don't want me. I may not agree with that, but I get it. By all means, love yourself. If you need someone by your side while you figure out how amazing you are, I'll be here for you. Always. It takes a special kind of person to do what you did today." She even had me fooled. I won't admit that to her quite yet. Hesitantly I grab her other shoulder. "You are amazing and brave. You saved lives and you took the one who stole pieces of mine. I should be the one thanking you," I say. The need to kiss her overcomes me and I lean forward a touch, but stop myself.

"Don't thank me, Cody. If you want me to be happy, then live your life." She pulls my hand from her face and looks at the side. Her profile is so perfect, even marred by tears and streaked by makeup. Her skin is flawless underneath. Her nose is small and button like, her lips push out, so damn wet and kissable. Lainey will always be my perfect. She's lost in thought, daydreaming or having waking nightmares about our night. "I have to go. I have so much damage control to deal with today that I'd make Martha Stewart have a heart attack. I'll be in touch." She won't. That's okay. I've done everything I can. "And Cody?" she says, turning as she goes.

"Yeah?" I ask.

She pauses. "I'm glad you're okay."

I smile. "Me too."

"And Cody?"

"Yeah?"

"The café is still mine." Her smile is sad.

"I'd never dream of stealing your lettuce. Of course," I reply.

I watch her walk away, her 'bride' emblazoned back marking the obscene irony of this situation. She leaves the bloody kitchen and strolls out of the front door as if she's heading somewhere important. Her head held high, shoulders back. She killed a man today and now she's dealing with it in her own way. Patience is something I recently learned—the one thing V taught me, unwittingly. I have all the time in the world to wait for Lainey.

The world is a giant triangle. We are the points, connected to each other whether we know it or not. At times like these, it's obvious to see who is attached. For others it's more vague, like an echo. An echo is air missing noise. What it boils down to is I'm just space waiting for my time.

I know it will come. Eventually.

CHAPTER TWENTY-FIVE

Cody

Six months later

I have no clue what Lainey has been up to. Of course it's a task to keep my mind from wandering to her from time to time. They say distance makes the heart grow fonder. That is so fucking true. But it also forces you to realize you can function, happily, without being in the same proximity of that person. Do I miss her? Every heartbeat. Knowing she's safe and living life on her terms helps me cope. I can breathe freely for the first time in my life. Each day is a gift. After spending three and a half years locked away dreaming about my old life, I get another chance. He's gone and my freedom is assured, always. The cover-up went about as good as a cover-up can go. No one got in trouble because it was official RC business and V and his men shot first. The

Feds were more than happy to have several of those men off their kill lists and turned a blind eye to some of the hinky details that came to light. Molly and our attorney handled everything effortlessly. Molly got several bonuses during that trying time. I'm pretty sure I've funded her kids that she doesn't have yet and her future grandkids by this point. Good help is hard to come by. Help that is more like family is even rarer.

Although I keep my house in Virginia Beach, I live most of my days in my high-rise in NYC. There's less temptation to knock on Lainey's door and ask if she's done enough soul-searching yet. I get small, regular Lainey updates because I have my ways. Dax is still a SEAL in Virginia Beach and has avoided any backlash that my feud with V caused. After the wedding went belly-up he decided to stay single, or so Steve and Maverick tell me.

Work does take up a lot of my time these days. I break it up by hanging out with my friends and checking on things at RC. I'm proud of the company I founded and I'm happy that everyone there is making money, cleaning the world, and having a good time. Along with coding, I've been developing software and programming. I made another large sale to a biotech company and set myself up nicely. I set everyone up nicely is closer to the truth. To combat the hours on the computer I do a lot of running for cardio. It clears my mind, gets me amongst people, and helps deepen my V.

That kind of V, I'm okay with. I work hard for it.

Today Maverick is running with me because he made a spur of the moment trip to the city to buy Windsor an anniversary present. I don't think it's a wedding anniversary they're celebrating, but maybe a dating anniversary? All I know is that the diamonds weren't big enough in Virginia Beach. Manhattan has exactly what he wants. He popped the rock into his shorts pocket when he bought it mid-run. The pace we're keeping is fast and I'm just waiting for the box to roll out of his pocket and down into the sewer.

"I'm getting hungry," Maverick pants. "Let's stop and eat something." We're back in my neighborhood, just around the corner from my house. I smile when I see which café we're approaching.

"You want a good salad?" I ask, slowing to a walk. He grunts next to me, catching his breath.

Maverick dodges someone on the street, or I should say someone dodges him. "We did just exercise. I guess a salad would be the most rational thing to eat." My eyes scan the restaurant as we enter, searching for her. Of course she's not here, but being in here is enough to make me miss her more than usual.

"I wonder what Lainey's up to," I say casually as we wait in line to order our food. We're both sweating and sticky, which causes business men in suits to stare. That or the ripped muscles and dark tattoos. It could be either.

Maverick huffs. "I can't ask Windsor to do any more reconnaissance this month. It's too obvious. You know she's not dating and she's working a lot. What more could you possibly need to know?" He smiles as he fumbles with the box in his pocket. "If you want to know what she's up to, you should call her. Go see her. I don't know, let her know you're thinking of her. It's been like a year!"

I shake my head. "No, only six months. I'm trying to respect what she wants. It would almost be easier if she were seeing someone else. I'd know that she's moved on and happy. I'd be pissed as fuck, but it would be something factual. It's like she's in limbo."

An employee interrupts our conversation. "Can I take your order?"

We order our food from the nice lady with kind eyes. She checks us out more than once. Maverick smiles at her in that way only he knows how and she practically falls over. As we move away to our seats, I ask, "Why do you do that?"

"Do what?" he asks, looking sincerely confused.

I quirk a brow. "You do this smile thing and I'm certain it's not flirting because you're the most taken man I've ever met, so I'm just wondering why you do it," I say.

Maverick runs a hand through his hair. "Must be my smile. Don't know what to tell you," he says, smiling again. I shake my head at him. "You never said why

313

you won't call her," he prompts.

I sigh. "I'll call her. Buy some more furniture or something."

He laughs. The waitress comes and brings the food we ordered. She sets it down in front of us without taking her gaze off of Maverick's laughing face. I tell her we'll let her know if we need anything and she disappears to the back to tell her coworkers about *the smile.*

Maverick takes a bite of his salad that has everything on it. I'm pretty sure it doesn't count as a salad. "Not furniture. Tell her you want to fuck her brains out and love her until death do you part. That should mean something because death already did you part once," he says, his mouth full of food. He has jokes. Jokes that make sense, at least. He pulls out his cell phone from his pocket and the ring box from the other. He texts Windsor a photo of the box.

I nod. "That will go over well. She's liable to slap me or shoot me," I say, but Mav interrupts.

"Or fuck you," he says matter-of-factly, snapping a photo of the box from a different angle. He texts some more and then resumes eating.

"Yeah, I guess that is in the realm of possibility if she's as celibate as you tell me she is." I take a bite of my own food and ponder what he's said. I want to get laid so bad. I need it. Regular sex is something that far too many people take for granted. Being able to roll over in the middle of the night and fuck their wife or girlfriend. God, what a luxury. I get to roll over and fuck my hand. Not something to be proud of.

He nods. "Go ahead. Call her now. I'll know you followed through," he replies.

"Fuck you, dude! I'm not calling her now in this loud ass restaurant and especially not in front of you," I say. "I'll call her when we get home."

Maverick shakes his head furiously. "Now. Or I make a scene."

"You make a scene wherever you go whether you want to or not," I deadpan. I humor him, assuming she won't pick up anyways. I have a new phone with a new phone number. It will pop up on her screen as 'unknown'. She'll wrinkle her fucking cute nose and then hit decline. I know it.

I dial the number I know by heart, hit send, and stare Maverick straight in the goddamned eyes. She answers on the first ring, "Hello." Her voice. That voice. It sends chills down my spine and my cock comes out of hibernation. Shit. I wasn't prepared for her to answer and I choke on my own breath. Maverick chuckles under his breath.

"Hey, it's me. I, uh, wanted to talk to you about…decorating," I say, my words spilling out awkwardly. Lainey will see right through me.

"Cody, is that you?" she asks. I must really sound like a real asshole if she can't recognize my voice.

315

"Yeah, hey, Fast Lane, what are you up to?" I try a new approach. A didn't work, let's go with B.

I hear noise in the background and horns blaring. "I'm actually in the city this weekend for a décor show. It's been a while, Cody," she says.

I swallow down the heaps of emotion I feel because of what I hear in her voice. "It has. That's why I'm calling," I say, looking at Maverick and shaking my head. Here goes nothing. "Want to get together while you're in town? I understand if you don't. I figured you're probably still doing your own thing, living life, decorating lives, but I miss you and wanted you to know that."

She's breathing deeply on her end of the phone. "That's nice," she says.

I raise my brows. What the fuck is this? "It is nice, isn't it?"

The café door chimes, signaling someone has entered. "Yeah, it's nice that you miss me, yet you can't keep promises about keeping away from my fucking lettuce," she says. I turn around in my chair and lo and behold, the most beautiful sight in the entire universe.

I say her name out loud even though she's too far to hear me and it's only really for my benefit. She's smiling widely, and her bright white blonde hair is chopped in a blunt cut that barely touches her shoulders. Her eyes, that gaze, is all fucking mine. Tossing her phone in her purse, she puts her hands on her small hips.

Like a moth drawn to flame, I rise from my seat and cover the distance between us in seconds.

"Maverick is playing matchmaker again," she says, explaining her presence. Lainey doesn't have to explain anything. I'm satisfied gazing upon her until my eyes fall out. I've missed her so much that everything about her looks brand new. How can I possibly be mad at Maverick for bringing me this?

"How are you? I mean, you look like this, so I'm guessing you're better than ever, but I have to ask," I say, tripping over my fucking words. She laughs, and the lines around her eyes crease, making her look even more stunning.

Her face softens as her blue laser gaze meets mine. "I'm good. Much better now," she says. "It's been hard to stay away, you know? It's better, though. I'm better now." Can it be true? Has my patience paid off? Will I finally be rewarded with life's greatest gift? "Don't think I didn't want to contact you. I think I composed one hundred emails and then sent them to trash instead of sending them. It was therapeutic for me. I guess they never really helped you any, though. Enough about me. How are you?" she asks, her eyes sparkling. She crosses one foot over the other and tucks her arm around her bag.

"Want to get out of here? Go talk? Catch up?" And have sex until we're sore for days. That's my dick talking. Right now I'll settle for merely talking to her, being in her proximity again. She looks hesitant, her gaze flicking behind her to the door.

"Just talk," I repeat.

"Oh, it's not that. I need to be somewhere, but I can cancel, I guess. There really was a décor show here. Maverick lured me here and promised me food," Lainey replies, smiling over my shoulder at Maverick.

I hold up one finger and rush back to the table. Grabbing my sandwich, I bring it back to her. "It's not lettuce, but I think you'll like it." I extend the plate to her.

She looks at it and then back up at me. "Get it to go and you have a deal." Maverick hoovered his lunch and is finished. Sneaking up behind me, he slips the jewelry box in my pocket and leans over to whisper, "It was never Windsor's," and then he greets Lainey briefly and leaves out of the door. It chimes as he exits. What the fuck does that mean? I didn't see what he bought in the jewelry store. I was eyeing a new TAG Heuer watch while he made his selection. It weighs a ton in my pocket and there's no way I can open it and find out what the hell is in here now. We get my sandwich to go and head out into the street.

"I'm staying at the Ritz tonight," she says. "We could go talk there if you wanted? They do a killer dinner." Somehow dinner is the last thing on my mind.

I motion down at my sweaty gym clothes as we walk. "How about we head to my place first? I'll shower, you can eat lunch, and then we can go anywhere you want," I offer. "I'm sure the eau of man is appetizing with all the pheromones I'm giving off, but the Ritz won't let me in their dining hall like this." I catch her smile out of the corner of my eye.

"Okay," she says, looking up at me without turning her head. "You wouldn't be trying to take advantage of me, now, would you?"

I chuckle. "Me? No way. I want to talk to you."

"But you also want to fuck me," Lainey says. A mother walking with her child leans over and covers her kid's ears and scowls at us. I laugh. Lainey looks behind us, trying to pass the blame onto the people trailing us on the busy street.

"I see your language is still as colorful as ever. What changed? It's been six long months."

She narrows her eyes at me. "You're not answering my question."

We get to my apartment building and enter the elevator. It's not empty. "Yes. To answer your question. Of course," I say, mumbling quietly but loud enough that she can understand. She leans against the back of the elevator car, smiling like the cat that got the mouse. There's a few people between us, but I can see her over their heads. Her new haircut accentuates the angles of her face. Her long hair was a huge turn on, and right now I'm second-guessing myself because she looks smoking hot. We exit on my floor and I let her lead the way to my place. Leaning over her, I unlock the door, push it open, and give her the 'after you' wave.

She glances around, checking everything out like any woman or interior decorator would do. "Is Maverick coming back for his things?" she asks. Sometimes I forget about her past, how she's just as observant, if not more so than I am. I notice a leather duffel in the corner and a shirt lying on top.

"He must be, yeah. Unless he's leaving it here until next time."

I hike my thumb down the hall to my bathroom. "I'm going to shower. You can help yourself to anything in the kitchen. Sparkling water is in the fridge and plates are in the cabinet next to the sink if you don't want to eat out of foam."

She reminds me that she's been here and knows exactly where everything is and I retreat to the shower. I'm antsy, wound up, too excited to think straight. This is the moment I've waited for and I don't have a game plan. First, I start the shower to heat up the water and then I slip the box out of my pocket and crack the lid. It's not a bauble of the highest caliber, it's a wedding band. Lainey's wedding band that I had made especially for her. *How did he do this?* It has diamonds wrapping the entire band and an inscription that reads. *We're better together.* How fucking intuitive was I, back then? What does Maverick think I'm going to do with this now? I take a deep breath because it's been almost a minute and I haven't breathed. This takes me back. What if we'll never be there again? Who knows what she's thinking? I'm a part of a past she wants to forget. I'm holding the ring, wide-eyed, shirtless, when Lainey knocks on the door.

"Can I come in? I'll sit on the toilet and talk while you shower. I know how lonely you get when you have to wash yourself."

I slip the ring into a drawer, throw off my shorts, and jump into the shower. "Come in," I yell. The steam has clouded the glass shower, so she can't see me. I'm sweating bullets and contemplating huge decisions. My face is probably contorted beyond recognition.

I hear the door click open and nothing else. She must be barefoot. "Thanks for the sandwich. It was so good I ate it quicker than it takes you to jack off. That's what you're doing in there, right?"

I see her outlined in the bathroom. She's standing, not sitting like she said she would. "No, I'm actually planning my attack," I say, shampooing my hair and then washing my face with the run off. "Tell me about the new you. Then maybe I'll be able to come up with something."

"I'm not something you should attack, Cody," she replies, laughing. "I'm the same person, just new and improved. You know those women who go from relationship to relationship in short time frames? Like a serial dater except it's more than dating. Well, I feel like those women never truly find themselves. They only know who they are with another person. Sure, I bet they change a little with each new man, that's necessary, but who are they really? Do they like watching Discovery TV on Friday nights or is it just because their significant other does? I bet they'd rather be playing strip poker instead. What I'm trying and failing at saying is that I found more of myself when I was alone. I wasn't lying to Dax about my past or trying to fix some horrendous mistakes with you. I just was." I'm intrigued. It makes sense, but it also is worrisome.

I clear my throat. Soap got in my nose. "Are you happier single? Without me? Without anyone else? Is that what you want now?"

"No! God, no. I like dick too much. You know that. It's been torture not having someone to hold me and love me and well, you know. I learned a lot, though. I can cook for one person. I can successfully babysit multiple kids for entire weekends, I like the farmers' market, and most importantly, I love you."

My heart skips a beat. And then another. I see her approach the glass. She puts both of her hands up. I put one of my hands up to meet hers. "So the question isn't am I happy single. It's are you happy single? And do you want to try this the old-fashioned way? From the beginning?"

I sigh. I'm clean, so I push open the door. Smiling,

I say, "It's not really old-fashioned for you to see me naked, Fast Lane. No, I'm not happy without you. I'm okay without you, because you forced me to be, but I'm not happy. The second Vadim died the only thing I've wanted is you. You're the last piece to the puzzle, the last thing he stole from me that was obtainable. I lost those years and so much more. But you're here and perfect and by some act of God, willing to give me a chance. I thought I fucked it up," I say, keeping my gaze locked on hers even though her gaze is slipping down, around and all over my body. "I missed you, Lainey. I love you, always," I say. I've proclaimed my love for her standing stark naked and wet. That counts for something. It has to. The time apart has changed me, like every experience in my life or in anyone's life, really. You are everything that has happened to you. The good and the bad. The experiences sink into your soul and stain you. No one knows, of course. They can't hear the screams or see the smiles, but they belong to you forever. Take them, before they take you. As for the opportunity standing in front of me, I'm taking it and running.

She smiles as a tear runs down her face. "I know we're taking it from the beginning, but you're the only one naked, and I really want to kiss you right now," Lainey says, tilting her head to the side with that look in her eyes that drives me wild.

"Kiss me then," I say, raising my chin. Softly she

takes a large step toward me and falls into my arms, mouth first. I catch her with my lips pressed against hers, the scent of her perfume filling my senses.

I inhale deeply. "New perfume?" I ask without taking my mouth off of hers.

She smiles against my mouth. "You like it?" she asks, replacing her words in my mouth with her tongue. I'm not giving up her tongue, so I merely nod, pull her clothed body closer, and relish this moment.

Lainey moans and my cock strains against her and every hair on my body stands on end. How easy it would be to tear off her fucking clothes and sink inside of her. I'd bang her against the glass wall so hard I'd worry about shattering it. The hard way is what needs to happen.

I pull away, panting. "If we're taking it slow, then I need to turn the water on cold and truly jack off this time. Just quickly."

"Tell you what. You jack off and I'll masturbate at the same time. That's totally old-fashioned, right?" Lainey asks, a glint of mischief in her eye. If she gets naked, I'm liable to slip and fall inside her. She knows it. This might as well be my invitation. Have we made any headway about our future? About our past? Does it matter right now?

"To be honest, when I told you I needed to come home and shower I really did intend to shower by myself and then do whatever you wanted. I didn't expect—"

She cuts me off by holding up one finger and then removing her skirt and blouse.

She tosses them on the floor by my running shorts. "Sometimes what you expect and what you get are different. Other times what you want and what you get are the same," she says, voice breathy. Sliding off her black string panties, she's bare to me. "You also didn't expect me to be so fucking horny I could cut glass with my nipples and water a third world country with my pussy. I need to get off. Do you want to watch me get off?"

There's my girl. My crude, wildly beautiful, uninhibited woman. I nod to the other side of the shower, where there is a stone seat. She sidles past me, brushing her pink nipples on my stomach as she passes. I close the door of the shower, turn on the hot water to steam it back up a bit, and grab my dick. Lainey sits on the seat, tucks her heels beside her, and lets her knees fall open. She is deliciously wet and pink. I haven't seen pussy, her pussy, in way too long. I want to kiss it, lick it, slide my thick dick inside it. I start stroking my cock, long deep thrusts as I think about fucking her. Leaning her head back against the glass, she pinches her nipples and then slides her hand down her flat stomach to her small clit and starts rubbing it. I wish my dick was rubbing it. I groan. "You like when I rub it like this?" she asks.

"I want to be the one rubbing it," I growl. "You're so fucking beautiful, Lainey. So beautiful. Finger yourself. I want to watch," I say.

She does. She dips her middle finger into herself and lets it sink in slowly. Watching her finger disappear into her hot tightness, I let myself imagine my dick in its place. "I'm so tight, Cody," she whispers. It's steamy now and wisps of it wave in between us, causing condensation on the four walls of glass.

My dick is throbbing, and pre-cum is seeping onto my fist as I beat it. "How tight?" I ask, squinting through the steam to see her pussy eating her finger. She's working her clit with her other hand, using small quick strokes. It's just how she likes it. She'll come fast and fucking hard if she keeps it up.

Her blue-eyed gaze meets mine. "Want to find out just how tight?" Yes. Yes. I'd give my life savings.

"Yes," I say. "Please." Manners go a long way, especially when a nice woman is about to let you feel how tight she is.

"Fingers first," she orders. First? That means I get a second, too. And I almost come realizing it. I stop stroking my shaft immediately at the turn of events. I'm on my knees in front of her with my finger replacing hers quicker than you can say 'home run'. She is so fucking tight.

"Your pussy is tight around my finger, Lainey. Can I try two?"

326

She nods, bites her lip, and spreads her legs farther. I flip my hand over and slide my pointer and middle finger in. It's difficult. "You haven't been properly fucked for a while," I say.

"Not since you," she replies, her eyes closed in pure bliss. I lean down because there's no way I can avoid it and lick her clit. She cries out and holds my face to her pussy while I finger her and eat her out. She comes the second I begin applying pressure with my tongue. I feel her muscles tightening around my fingers as I stroke her G-spot.

"Fuck, that feels so good. I missed you," she says, raising her hips up in an attempt to keep my fingers inside her. I kiss up her stomach, lick each nipple, and then tongue her neck up to her mouth. She kisses me greedily, sucking her wetness from my lips and tongue. Slowly I remove my fingers from her pussy. "You sit," she says, pointing to her seat. She trades me places, looks me in the eyes, and straddles my lap, placing the head of my cock at the entrance of her sopping wet pussy.

Lainey bites her lip, tells me she loves me, and sits down on my dick.

CHAPTER TWENTY-SIX

Lainey

He's so big and it's been so long since I've had something this massive inside me. The paltry dildo I play with at home has nothing on Cody Ridge. It's basically an orgasm meat stick. Lowering myself down onto him isn't easy. I have to pause, wait for it to stretch out a little, and then drop down a little lower. Cody's eyes are rolled back and his hands are planted firmly on my hips. He wants to pull me down, but he won't—he'll let me take my time.

"Your dick feels so good inside me," I say, licking his neck and edging my way lower. I'm filled completely and he's not all the way inside. I just sit down and relish the feeling of being consumed by him. By Cody Ridge. The first and only man I'll ever love the way I'm supposed to. He leans over and places a tender kiss on my shoulder, just letting me be connected to him without moving. His dick throbs inside me, telling me what he truly wants.

I rise up and down again. He hisses in delight, a satiated smile transforming his face. "Yes. More of that," he says. I give him more now that I've acclimated to his girth. I ride his glorious cock while admiring his muscles painted with tattoos and his fucking hot face, all the while bringing myself closer to an orgasm. Cody uses my hips now. He brings me up and down, using only his biceps at a pace that drives me wild. Too slow, yet not fast enough to send me over the edge. The steam from the shower causes the perfect amount of friction between our bodies. A little bit slippery, but not too wet.

"I'm going to come," he says.

"Where do you want to come?" I ask, licking his neck.

"In your fucking mouth. I'm going to come in your mouth." I ride his dick, rocking my hips several more strokes until Cody pulls me up and off him. I replace my pussy with my mouth. He grabs a fistful of my hair and pushes my head down over his cock until it's down my throat. He comes in hot waves as he groans and growls, jutting his hips up with each hot burst of semen.

"You were always good at swallowing my dick," he says, out of breath. "But never that good."

I raise myself up, wipe my bottom lip with my thumb and pointer finger, and look him square in the eyes. "I need more. I was about to come," I admit. He smiles, grabs me by the waist, turns me around so I'm facing away from him, and fucks me doggy style so hard that I'm sure the neighbors heard my orgasm. Cody comes again, deep inside me, saying my name like a prayer.

****

"So much for old-fashioned," I murmur. We're wrapped up in his sheets in his large bed.

"Doggy style is so old-fashioned, Lane. I mean, animals do it like that. I bet the first humans that had sex fucked doggy style. There's your old-fashioned."

I stroke his muscles, tracing his tattoos, my head against his chest. "It's hard to go slow with you. We paused for over three years. That was our slow period. Don't you feel like we should be making up for lost time? Even though I'm the one who did most of the wasting of time. You're right about doggy style, though. Very old-fashioned." He laughs and with my ear pressed against his skin I feel the rumble of his laughter all the way to my toes.

His chest has stilled and his breathing has evened. Content is how I feel in this moment, at ease with my choices and full of forgiveness and willingness to grant second and third chances. Not just because no one else can rock my world like Cody, but because I know this feeling inside of me is only sparked by him. I lied to myself with Dax. Our love was real, but it was different. It was tame and safe. The work it took to come to this realization should have been my first tip off that something wasn't quite right. Love with Cody isn't work. It took me six long months to develop the right mindset to be okay with that. It's okay to be stupidly in love with someone, to want to sacrifice everything else because of said love. Maybe it's not like that for some people, but it's like that for us and I'm okay with it. Volatile, passionate love that shakes us to our core only comes along once in a lifetime. During my time away, I soul-searched. Is this what I want? Will I ever truly be what he wants? Can he see past our rocky, and frankly, murderous decisions from days past? I'll always be that woman, but now I'm more, I'm the woman free from my chains. No one will control me again nor use my love to destroy me. I'll never wait with trepidation wondering when the other shoe will drop. I'll never wait. Cody waited for me. More than just the six months, I realize. He's waited for me for years.

"I never told you, but thank you for always waiting for me, Cody," I whisper.

He strokes my hair. "It wasn't too hard, Fast Lane. Especially because I was waiting for my forever." I swallow down the lump of emotion in my throat, and perhaps a touch of guilt for the time I spent figuring this out. He drags his thumb across my bottom lip. "I hoped it would turn out like this. I wasn't sure. After everything I've been through, waiting for you was the easiest decision I've ever made. No more pause button or lost time. This is it. I'm calling it. No referee needed."

"Calling what?" I ask, as a tear sneaks out of the corner of my eye and falls onto his tanned, warm skin.

I glance up and his gaze flicks down to meet mine. "I'm calling this our time and space. Right here. Right now."

"It is, you're right. Guess it took a little while to get it right," I say, laughing and crying at the same time. He sits up in the bed, bringing me with him.

He clears his throat and says, "And because I'm not wasting another second, I have something I want to give you." My hand on his chest senses his heart hammering away, pumping overtime. Cody's eyes are wide and questioning when I look at him. "It's our time, Lane," he says again. The emotion pouring from his gaze is enough to kill a woman not as strong as me. Still, it renders me speechless. I can only nod my head, like a small child.

He hops out of bed, buck naked, with his dick still semi-hard, I might add, and bounds into the bathroom. When he comes back he has something clasped in the palm of his hand. Tucking the sheet around me, I move from the bed to stand in front of it. "A present for me?" I ask, innocently, batting my eyes and cocking my head to the side coquettishly.

"I thought he was fucking crazy. He romanticizes love to the point of fictionalization, but he's right, God damn it. He's right about this," Cody says, making no sense.

I quirk one brow. "Who?"

"It doesn't matter." He hits one knee, still naked, and says, "This was supposed to be your wedding band. I designed it myself. I won't ask you to marry me because that time for us has passed. Keeping in tune of our time and space, I'm just asking you outright to be my wife. Right now." He extends a small, diamond encrusted band to me. I swallow, wipe away a tear, and walk toward him.

"Am I wife material?" I ask, smiling.

"It doesn't matter to anyone except me and you're the only woman I've ever wanted to be my wife. There will never, not even in my wildest dreams, be another woman I want to be linked to for all of eternity. I stake my life on this claim."

"Then yes. I am your wife," I say, extending my left hand to him so he can slip the band on my finger. The morning light hits it just so, and it sparkles brilliantly, like a million rainbows finally showing their faces upon people who desperately need happiness. "That was the best non-proposal ever. It was hard to keep my eyes off your dick, though. I might like that better than bling," I say, kneeling in front of him and wrapping my hands around his neck.

333

"I love you so much, Cody. I'll be the best woman for you I can possibly be." I press my lips against his.

He shakes his head. "All I want is you. Be you, Lainey, and I'll be the happiest man on the planet." Flaws and all, this man loves me without reservation. Cody deepens the kiss, using his tongue and tilting my head back with his hands.

"Get dressed, Cody. We need to finish this deal as soon as possible and if you don't put on pants I'm liable to glue your dick inside my pussy and keep it there for sixty-two hours straight," I reply.

He shakes his head. "How did I get so lucky? I found the only woman on the planet who talks about gluing my manhood inside of herself and it doesn't turn me off, it gives me wood so hard I could cut steel."

I chuckle. "I'll be here all day, but seriously. We should go. I've lost you once and I'm not doing it again. Time is of the essence." I pull on my outfit from yesterday and throw him a pair of jeans that I find hanging over a chair in his room. The huge plate glass window is a one-sided mirror. We can look over the crazy beautiful city, but no one can see in. It's an ideal feature when your ass is pressed against the glass while you're being screwed to perfection, if you ask me. I scroll on my cell phone, looking for the information I need, and quickly find it. "Good. They're open."

Cody pulls on his pants and leaves them unbuttoned in that fantastic way that super buff guys do. So nonchalant and effortless, but it drives women batshit crazy. He ruffles his hands through his hair. "If I'm not even showering, you'll have to humor me and tell me where we're going." He's right. I need to at least wash my face. I rush into the bathroom and tell him it's a secret. He walks up behind me while my eyes are closed and my face covered in soap that smells like him. "I have one more thing for you," Cody says, twining his hands around my waist and pulling me back against him.

"This is hardly fair. I'm blind right now," I exclaim, trying and failing to rinse my face without splashing water all over the exquisite countertop.

"Finish here. I'll go get it."

I look in the huge mirror above his sink and find myself barefaced and…happy. So happy, that I want to scream it to the world. This is how I'm supposed to feel. In Cody's world, wrapped in his sheets and arms for the rest of time.

When I exit the bathroom Cody's entering the bedroom with something behind his back. He's dressed, his blond hair is coifed with water, and he tells me to close my damn eyes again. "Hurry, hurry!" I say, closing my eyes and stomping one heeled foot. "We need to go!"

He says, "Open them."

I do and I come face to face with the dog. The same one he gave me on our first Valentine's Day together.

335

The same one I soaked with tears when he died. The very same one I buried in his coffin when they couldn't find his body. It's a trivial, cheap, black dog that he picked up from a toy store on his way home from work that cold night in February. I, of course, loved it because even as an adult, getting a soft fuzzy animal lights you from the inside. "Dog," I say, taking the mangy thing from his hands. His moniker is very original. I look up at Cody's face. "Where did you get him?" I ask.

"They gave me my things back that were in my coffin. It was like the time capsules we buried in elementary school. When I saw Dog I knew I should keep him. I can't believe you put him in there. How did he breathe?" Cody asks, chuckling. "The whole business of dying but not really is exhausting."

How odd must that have been for him. To be able to look at the things given to a dead man. "I loved that dog. It was the one thing tangible that reminded me of you most. I figured if I couldn't bury your body, this would have to do. Lame, I know." Saying it out loud is embarrassing. I love you and I'm burying a stuffed animal in your place. Jesus save my horrid soul.

He cradles my face in his hand and brushes my hair behind both of my ears. Tilting my face up to his, he says, "It's not lame at all. The memory stick of code you threw in there? Bought Dances like the Wind," he says, ushering me out of the apartment and down the

336

hall to the elevator. I never thought much about putting that in there. It was his. What would I do with it? I don't even know how to read code. Or open the encrypted data. To me it was just another memento that represented a facet of his personality.

"No shit?" I ask when we get on the elevator. "So basically my lack of knowledge about what was on that stick afforded the mansion in the Hamptons?" Cody nods, laughs at my expression, and tucks me to his side. I do a little dance in the lobby as we head out the door and into the cool morning. I know exactly where we need to go, so I hail a cab, raising one hand in the air.

Cody just smiles when he hears me give the cabbie the address. Shaking his head, he says, "You really couldn't have told me before we left the house?" He motions down to his jeans and long-sleeved tee.

"What? You're hot. No way. It's better this way. They open at nine a.m. and we need to be there before it gets too busy."

The yellow cab pulls in front of the huge, columned building and lets us out at the steps. "The courthouse. You want the husband and wife to be official. Right now? You're ready for that?" I haven't been more ready for anything in my life.

I hold out my hands, palms up. "I'm not shaking, my palms aren't sweaty. Go ahead, touch them," I say. He smirks, but humors me. "I'm already wearing your wedding band. Let's do this, Cody. Finish what we started before life got in the way."

Holding my hands on the steps of the beautiful, old courthouse, to a passerby it looks like we're saying our vows. "It's our time, right?" I ask.

Cody kisses me as a response. Wrapping his arms around my body, he pulls me to him and then up off the ground. His lips are warm against mine and they're curled in a smile. "This is the best decision you've ever made."

"Better than all the furniture I picked out? I'm mollified, Cody Ridge."

"Let's do this, Fast Lane. I love you."

So we do. We fill out paperwork until we're blue in the face and also a waiver, because you can't get married in NYC the same day as the marriage license is granted without one, and we get married. It's held in a small room with tacky plastic flowers hanging on the walls and carpet that looks like it has seen a billion pairs of feet. The woman marrying us is a twin. Her sister is our witness, and she smiles as we seal our lives together for the rest of time. Cody kisses me chastely when she pronounces us husband and wife and they both clap overzealously. It makes us laugh, kiss again, and clutch each other tightly. Cody picks me up around my bottom and spins me around in a circle. Everything else fades away.

"You're my wife," he says, his grip tight, sure.

"And you're my husband," I reply, feeling

adrenaline swirl around my body. Sheer happiness is the best rush. The look in his eyes, now that I'm officially his, is one of pure rapture.

He lowers me down until we're eye to eye, nose to nose. "Forever," he whispers, before his lips find mine.

The twins clap some more, and I get lost in his kiss, his love for me, knowing that when he says forever, he means it.

CHAPTER TWENTY-SEVEN

Cody

Two years later

The things that happen when you're busy making plans are what form your life. If you wait for the next weekend, or a time when you're less busy, or perhaps 'next time', you're squirreling away precious moments that could be better spent by just saying 'yes'. Because of our sordid, nefarious past, I try to always say yes to Lainey. It makes the positivity rain. And when it rains positivity I'm likely to get whatever I want as well. We live in Dances like the Wind, because she loves the house and I can't deny her anything she loves. Our two years of marriage have been bliss. For me, this time with her has been better than any expectations I had for marriage. She tells me she feels the same way. It's easy to love a person when you've lost them before. You appreciate them more, you embrace and cherish every millisecond you get. Lainey Ridge is my biggest blessing that started off as my biggest curse.

Our past rarely comes up. Her spy work comes up only if there's a funny anecdote she wants to tell, or if I ask her specific questions. She's an open book. Lainey wanted to talk about my time in captivity. It was a conversation we had only once. I spoke for over an hour about my life and several things that happened to me while I was there, and it ended with her clinging to me like a koala and soaking my shirt with guilty tears. Believe it or not, I don't blame her for my kidnapping. Sure, Vadim's reason for taking me was to spite Lainey, but I'm a fucking Navy SEAL. It's my fault they took me. My unpreparedness caused it. She doesn't blame herself like she used to. I think that's the main reason she stayed away from me for those limbo inducing six months. She was giving herself permission to forgive, forget, and move on.

Since our wedding we've discovered things about each other. Every day, and every year, it's something new. Sometimes it's good, like the fact that Lainey knows how to plunge a toilet in the middle of the night better than me, and sometimes it's bad news, like when the doctor told us that I'm unable to have children. Vadim stole something else from me with the endless hours of torture. I was mad at first, because it was something Lainey wanted and I couldn't give it to her.

341

When I got my head out of my ass and actually started listening to her, and the word 'adoption' that she kept saying, I realized not all hope was lost.

It's been a long, drawn-out process to come to this day—the day when we'll be able to call this little boy, Evan, our real son. He will belong to us legally as much as he's already captured our hearts. Evan is one of the children I rescued from the dingy room in Mexico. His huge sad eyes that were too big for his face and held more sadness than a child had any right to have, stayed with me. When we decided to adopt, I knew who I wanted, and it just so happened that he wanted me, too. Molly was able to dig up the information we needed, and so it started. We entered the system as his foster parents. For a tiny child of barely three, his eyes told a different story. A couple of years later, and he's just like any other child, maybe even a little too doted on.

"Do you think we have enough balloons and cake? Evan loves cake. Maybe he would like to have two? Can you move that stack of presents into the other room before he comes down for breakfast, honey?" Lainey asks. I sigh and do her bidding, returning just in time to see Evan at the top of the stairs about to descend the banister on his arse.

"Your mommy will have a fit if she sees you. You could get hurt," I explain. Evan's eyes light up when he sees me. Cuppie, his gray raggy blanket, goes down the banister and he bounds down the stairs into my arms.

The gray rag is a steadfast in our world, but he needs it less and less. He leaves it at the bottom of the stairs. I carry him into the kitchen, his warm body, fresh from his covers, pressed against my chest. It's the second best feeling in the world. He hops down and crosses the kitchen in several small bounds when he sees Lainey, and I have to smile because this boy is so enamored with her that he could be her biological child.

"Sweet boy!" she exclaims as he runs into her arms. She picks him up even though he's getting too big for that and peppers his face with kisses. "How did you sleep?"

Evan hops down and climbs up a stool to sit at the breakfast bar. "I slept good, Mommy. I get to have the party today?" he asks.

Sitting next to him, I ruffle his hair. He leans against me. "Yep. All for you, buddy. You're stuck with us forever now," I say. Lainey squeals in excitement.

"I'm so excited, Evan. Everyone will be here any moment. The adult paperwork was finalized last night. You are Evan Ridge, most awesome kid to ever grace the planet," Lainey quips. She's sworn off swearing. Mostly when he's not around she'll drop an F bomb here and there. It's a novelty now. I tease her for it.

"He's going to let it go to his head, Fast Lane. Give the boy some breakfast and let us do man stuff. I'm sure you're going to make us wear those leg cages again."

She scowls at me as she places a plate of eggs and

343

fruit in front of Evan. "They are skinny jeans," Lainey says, correcting my terminology.

"You know my thighs don't fit in skinny jeans. They are cages for my thighs. And Evan can't jump on the trampoline well with his on. Right, buddy?"

Evan swallows a bite of food. "He's right, Mommy. Can we wear gym shorts?"

Oh, yes. Allied forces unite. Lainey looks like she's honestly considering letting him wear gym shorts, but her fashion sense wins out in the end. She tells him that his corduroys will do instead. Me? I get to wear whatever jeans I want. I celebrate with a fist pump and kiss my woman so thoroughly that I dip her backward. Her blonde hair falls in a cascade toward the floor. It's long again. The caveman in me approves.

The caterers arrive and the guests trickle in. Evan is celebrated properly. Maverick, Windsor, and their brood arrive fashionably late. Evan is excited to show the kids his new toys and they hurry off to play somewhere less adult.

Maverick slaps me on the back. "What a happy day, man. You guys are so lucky. He is a great kid. Really something special," he says. Windsor leaves his side to bring a bottle of champagne and a wrapped gift to a table in the far corner. Maverick watches her walk away, shaking his head, like he can't wait for her to come back. And then promptly have her for lunch.

"Nothing ever happens how you think it should,

does it? Evan came to us by unconventional means after our unconventional relationship. He's the biggest joy in my life," I say, pressing my lips into a thin line. "Thanks for everything, Mav. Nothing probably would have happened otherwise. I'd still be sitting alone in my apartment, waiting for her to call. You and your dick moves that end up being awesome. You're the king of that, aren't you?"

He smiles. "Let's put it this way. I know a thing or two about second chances. Rarely does waiting benefit them. I'm glad I could be of service, brother," Mav says. I owe him, but he'd never let me pay him back. Real friends never expect payment. They're happy to make you happy. Windsor comes back, kisses his cheek, and smiles sweetly at him. She congratulates me on the official adoption with a small hug. She has tears in her eyes. Today has been far more emotional than I imagined it would. He's been ours for a while now. Just because it's official shouldn't make me feel any less different, love him any more, but I think I might. Molly, Horse, and Van stop by and Evan is excited to see them. They're like his aunt and uncles. The fun ones who bring horrible gifts like Play-Doh and goopy games you only play once because of the mess they make. Today is no different, and Evan is excited to try out his new science kit in the kitchen. Lainey's eyes widen when she sees him trying to climb the counter to the stove. I laugh.

Ridge Contracting functions without me. They are more than capable of running things themselves. No one ever talks about Vadim or the largest cover-up in RC's history. Maybe that's part of the cover-up. Not talking about it. I owe them, too. I check in every once in a while because it bears my name, but I've given up the fast lane completely. Aside from hitting our home gym daily, nothing else is at the receiving end of my fury. It's nice. It's odd. It's what I want. Lainey still has her interior design business, but has slowed down to be around for Evan. We could easily afford nannies and babysitters, but she will have none of that. *He's hers.* She reminds me of that all the time. To which I promptly respond, he's mine, too. She relents then. It usually earns me a blow job, or the equivalent of an extreme orgasm.

I slip away from the party and head up to my office. It's huge and light, at Lainey's insistence. I want to give Evan something today, and I need to find Dog. I know he'll love it. It's old and torn up just like Cuppie. He'll love it just as much as Lainey does. I unlock a wooden cabinet that's in the bookshelf and pull out Dog. The rest of the things that Lainey put in my coffin are nestled safely inside here. There's a picture of us when we dated all those years ago. We look like children, but I know why she picked this photo. We're looking at each other and smiling like mad. It was taken by a passerby during the same trip when I proposed to her. Behind that is a sealed envelope I've never been able to open. It's a letter from Lainey to me composed after I was pronounced dead. I only know this because she told me when I asked. A more curious man would have opened it sooner, but maybe I wanted to have everything first, to combat the nothingness she felt when she wrote this. Today, I have everything, so I open it and find her neat handwriting filling the page.

Cody Ridge,

You were supposed to give me everything. I put all of my eggs in your proverbial basket. All of the love in my heart belongs to you. I find myself crying for no reason and then realize it's because I don't know how to like anything if I can't love you. You're gone. They couldn't recover your body and I don't know what to put inside the box that's supposed to hold you. You always loved my words. You would always watch my lips as I spoke, like you couldn't wait to hear what I would say next. Remember how you'd lean over my shoulder and watch me type mundane words to clients? I thought it was just so you could be close to me, but that wasn't it, was it? Words. My words. Even my boring ones you wanted.

I would have loved to give you a million words in this letter, but all of the words that currently come to mind are about pain and suffering and heartbreak so strong that I feel like I may die myself. Even dead, I wouldn't want to read that. So instead, I'll write to you as if you're still living. I'll give you happy words that tell you where I wanted to end up with you. Because that's what life is about, right? Where you end up? I'll be okay as long as I eventually end up next to you. Wherever that may be. I better stop swearing, huh?

For Cody:

In the summer, in the sand, in the hot, hot sun

You kissed me under swaying trees and I came undone

Oh, you're the one

Oh, you're the one

In the fall under the moon in the bright, night sky

You promised me forever and I thought I might die

Oh, you're the one

Oh, you're the one

In the winter in the snow looking at the big, lit tree

As tears trickled down, you asked to marry me

Oh, you're the one

Oh, you're the one

Now old and gray and seasoned in life

I'll love you forever, me and you, man and wife

Oh, you're the one

You're always the one

In my heart always,

Lainey

Her words stare at me from the page like a dream. It's like going back in time. A dark time. I now know it was a time when she could have written anything to me, instead I get this. I swallow down the emotion and try to check my pulse. It's hammering so hard I can hear it in my ears. This, this letter is more difficult to read than a hundred beatings from V. I lock the letter away and bring the dog downstairs. She catches me on the stairs and smiles when she sees the stuffed toy in my hands.

"He's going to love Dog. Help me in the kitchen, please?" Lainey asks, breaking me from my daydream.

Wrapping my arm around her waist, I let her lead me away. I'll let her lead me away anytime, and anywhere. She's my one. I kiss the side of her head, trying to shake the image of her writing that letter away. "Time for cake?" I ask when I see Evan drooling over the chocolate confection. I truly do have everything. I lost everything to gain more. You'll hear no complaints from me.

"It is. I thought we could sing a little song for him with some candles on top. It's like his adoption birthday. Just us three, though. What do you say, Evan?"

Evan's eyes light up and I'm rewarded with the biggest smile. It's there. The fullness of his heart shining through eyes that were once vacant. Pride beams through me at full strength. This moment isn't for me or for Lainey, this moment is for the two-year-old who didn't have clothing or shoes, who was being held in a cellar without food and sold like an animal to do ungodly things. This moment is for him. Because that boy is gone and will stay that way as long as I'm living. "I love you, Mommy and Daddy," he whispers. Lainey breaks down and I hug my son, feeling his heartbeat against my own.

In a low tone I sing 'happy birthday' and slip in words about love and family. We're all crying when I finish the song, folded into each other as a group—my girl, the boy who got a second chance at life, and the man who did, too.

We've painted our unconventional masterpiece and we don't get to just admire it, we get to live it.

Our time and space is perfect.

Acknowledgements

To all that made this book possible: I love you. Thank you from the bottom of my angst-craving heart. Cody flexes at you. Lainey smizes in your direction. I merely bow graciously for everything you've done.

Readers: thank you for going on this ride with me. Cody and Lainey's story was (very loosely) based off of a story someone told me about a real life situation. The man came back after being declared dead. A decade had passed. The love of his life had remarried, made children, and was living a new happily ever after when he finally returned. The man didn't remarry, and his story didn't leave much room for second chances. Because I write fiction I get to play matchmaker and fix shit. I mean, how sad is real life?

Time and Space is a second chance story for anyone who needs one. It's for the person who took the leap of faith and dove into unknown territory. It's for the person who went against the grain and called off a wedding last minute. Perhaps it's also for the woman who married the wrong man and wishes she'd chosen differently. This story is for the man who can't let go, the woman who can't make up her mind, and it's for those who follow their hearts against their better judgment. I suppose I also wrote it for those that can only imagine what it must be like to love two men at the same time.

May the love you have be so strong that no word can define it.

-Rachel

OTHER TITLES BY INTERNATIONAL BESTSELLING AUTHOR, RACHEL ROBINSON

Contemporary Romance

CRAZY GOOD

SET IN STONE

Paranormal Romance

Publisher: Eternal Press

Escaped: A Samantha Scott Novel

Embraced: A Samantha Scott Novel

Six

Visit Rachel Robinson online

http://www.racheljrobinson.com

https://www.facebook.com/racheljeanrobinson